# THE IMPOSTOR

First edition published by 82 Mercer Publishing, 1160 North Coast Hiway 101, Encinitas, CA 92024

Cover design by Rafael Andres

Interior design by Jack Poppy

Editing by Barbara Ann Temple, Ph.D.

Connect: DavidTempleBooks.com

ISBN 978-1-7370048-0-6 (paperback)

Manufactured in the United States of America.

*For Tammy—your love lights my path*

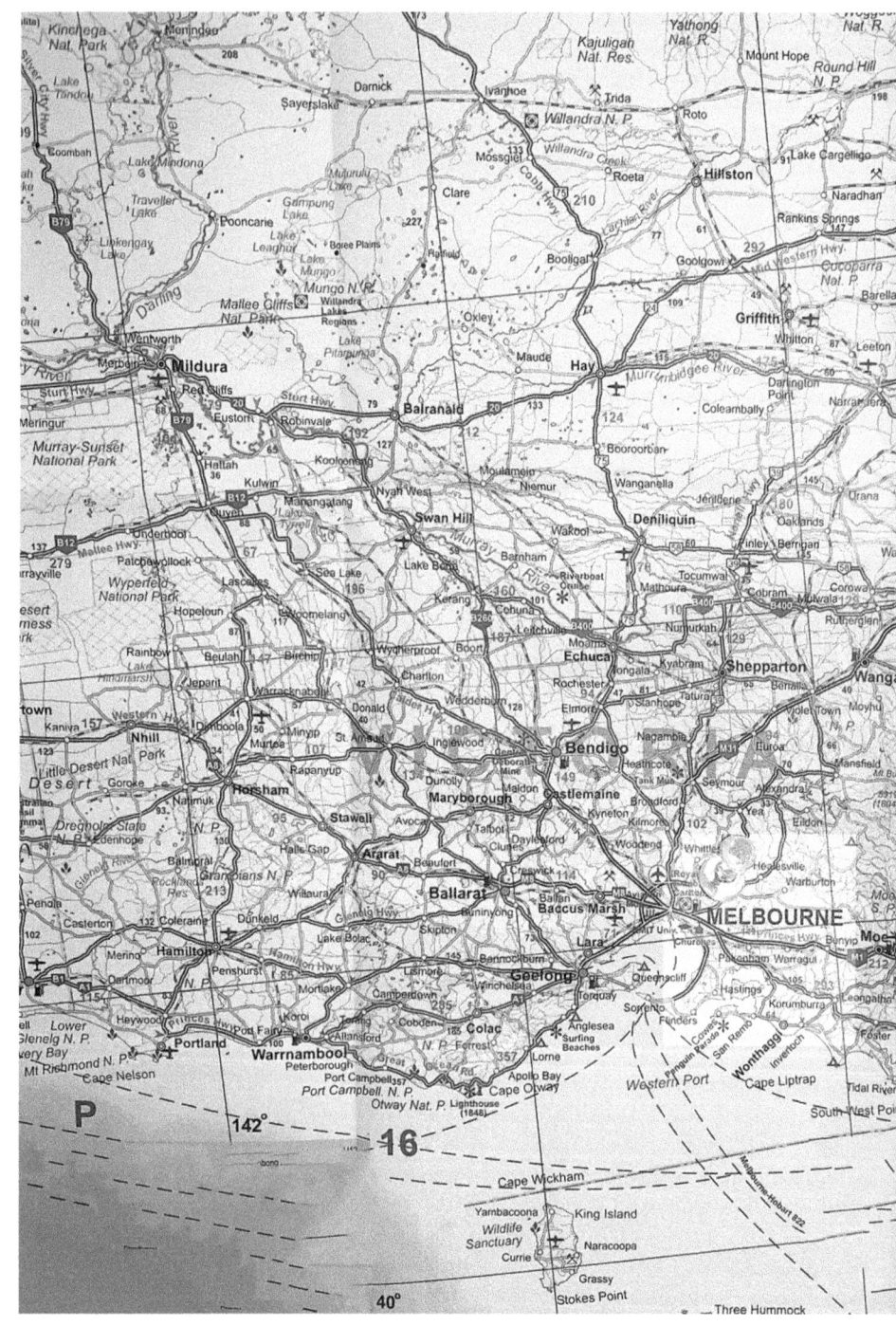

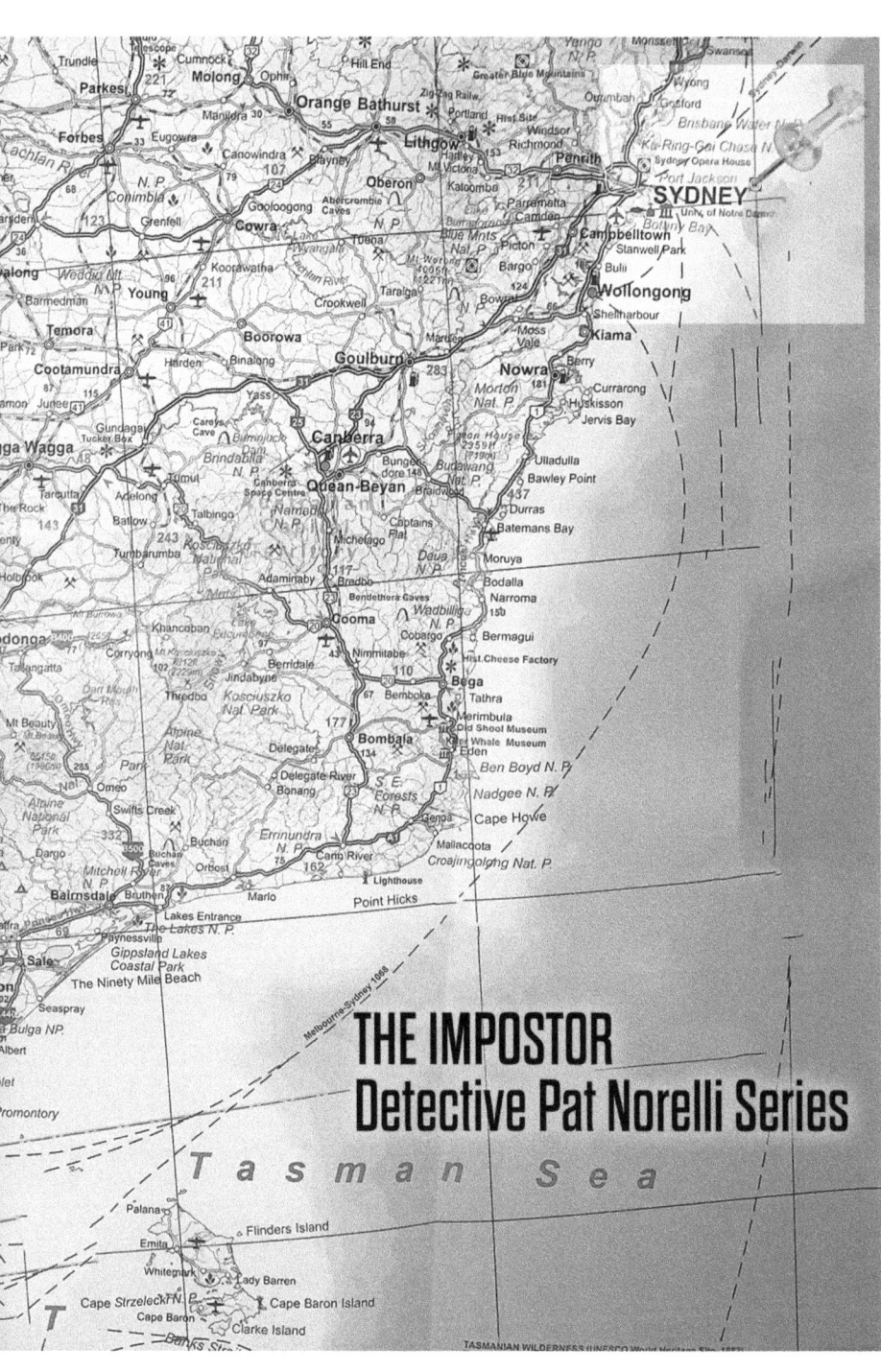

# THE IMPOSTOR
## Detective Pat Norelli Series

Unexpressed emotions will never die. Buried alive, they will come forth later in uglier ways.

— SIGMUND FREUD

# CHAPTER ONE

Norelli's eyes flicker back and forth beneath closed lids. Pinched in a permanent frown, her forehead is dotted with beads of sweat. Erratic breathing and twitches punctuate her tanned face. Struggling to get free, she twists in one direction, then the other.

Her mind pushes aside a myriad of haunting images when her eyes suddenly snap open.

The only light in the dark room comes from a bluish glow illuminating a familiar face.

*What?*

"More bad dreams, Patricia?"

She remains motionless, wondering if she is lost in a nightmare or awaking to another one.

Still disoriented, she is blinded momentarily by a sudden flash.

"Nice," the low voice whispers. "Another trophy for my collection."

She slowly reaches under her pillow.

*Shit.*

Struggling to gain her bearings, she works at slowing her breath, then stretches toward the bedside lamp. Her finger finds the switch. With a turn, she lights the room.

"Morning, love," Darius smiles, squinting at the light.

Dressed in black from head to toe, he looks calm and resembles a burglar—but he is neither. His nervous eyes belie his steady demeanor.

Looking down at her feet, she sees familiar strips of silk cloth binding her ankles to the footboard. Her sweat-covered naked body lures him to sneak glimpses.

"Dreams still tormenting you?"

"What are you doing here?" She asks, scanning the room.

His eyes follow.

"Just tying up loose ends," he says, tightening his grip on her ankles with his left hand while sliding the smartphone into his back pocket with his right hand.

She writhes to get loose, but his grip is a vise.

Her eyes widen as he removes a syringe from his jacket pocket—a shock wave of fear shoots through her body.

Removing a plastic cap from the end of the needle with his teeth, he spits it on the floor. "One could say I'm putting a period at the end of a long sentence."

"You're insane, Darius!"

"Perhaps."

"And why in the hell risk your freedom for—"

"Hah," he blurts. "What freedom? You'll likely never stop chasing me."

She is losing circulation and patience. "Not likely," she says, glaring at him. "Certain."

"*Riiiiiight*," he says, pointing the syringe between her first and second toes. "When they find you, they'll assume you had a heart attack. That will be correct because your heart will suffer enough drugs to drop a charging bull—or a raging *Bobby*," he cackles.

With each passing moment, her fear increases.

His staring eyes are glowing. "You wouldn't believe how much I shot into that neanderthal. But then again, you saw the results, didn't you?"

As she tries to sit up, he yanks at her bonds. "Stop! You should know by now fighting me will only make it worse."

Frozen in place, Norelli hears her pounding heartbeat.

"Play along," he growls, "and in moments you'll return to your fitful slumber."

Stuck between terror and bravery, she doesn't see a way out.

"Darius, please, I won't follow you," she whimpers. "I promise. And I can forget you— like it never happened. Seriously."

Sympathy dissolves from his face as he tightens his grip and inserts the needle. When the plunger reaches the bottom, a wave of nauseous heat instantly courses through her legs, racing upwards toward her torso, igniting every vein in her body.

As the drug hits her beating heart, it explodes.

# CHAPTER TWO

*PALM DESERT, CALIFORNIA—*

IN THE NEXT SECOND, I spring up in bed, gasping for breath, trying to gain my bearings.

*What the hell?*

A slice of sunshine between blackout curtains splits the darkness. Reaching for the nightstand lamp, I light up the room and see the covers twisted around my ankles at the foot of the bed. My sheets are soaked with sweat.

*It's gotta be a hundred degrees.*

I look up.

*Why isn't the fan on?*

With my eyes trying to adjust, I look to the curtains; they're still.

*AC's off.*

Catching my breath, I try to quiet my monkey mind.

*I'm losing it.*

Suddenly, a noise down the hall breaks the silence. Kicking off the covers, I reach under the pillow, remove my service weapon, slip on a nightie, and approach the door.

Easing it open, I listen. Nothing.

*Why isn't the pool fountain running?*

Even though the sun has yet to crack the horizon, there is enough light to see down the hall.

Approaching my parent's room, I stop to listen.

*Heavy breathing.*

Padding down the marble corridor, I scan the rooms along the way. Peering out to the pool, I see nothing out of the ordinary.

Suddenly, I hear metal hit something. I freeze, quietly chamber a round, and slowly approach the mudroom that separates the kitchen from the garage entrance. Approaching the garage, I lean close to the door and squint a listen.

*Nothing.*

Taking a deep breath, I point my gun at eye level and count: *Three, two, one.*

Kicking the door open, I crouch low. "Police! Hold it right there!"

The figure drops a flashlight and crashes into a stack of boxes with a thud and a grunt.

"Don't move!"

I reach for the flashlight and shine it in the stranger's face.

"Dad?"

# CHAPTER THREE

I've always enjoyed the sense of solace sitting in my parents' home. Call it a lack of responsibility, a feeling everything will be okay, or perhaps it's just the carefree peacefulness an early morning in the desert provides. Even if—only moments ago—I was within inches of unloading a round of .45 hollow points into my father's handsome face.

*What a difference a dropped flashlight makes.*

One moment I'm sleeping—albeit not peacefully; the next, I'm considering taking a deep gulp of my father's 20-year-old Scotch to tame my tattered nerves.

My mother slices avocados, tomatoes, and fresh mozzarella for breakfast as I stare into my coffee cup, trying to make sense of the last 30 minutes.

Daphne says, "I feel bad for you. Here you come out to escape all the craziness and even try to..."

Mom keeps talking, but I stop listening.

Burying my hands in my lap, I stare out the window to watch the morning sun lighten the tips of the cacti dotting the perimeter of my parents' manicured back lawn. Sleek lounge chairs line the pool, and while it looks inviting, the heat is expected to hover in the low 100's. Between that and the rising heat inside the house, I doubt I'll find much relief. My weekend respite is instead riddled with sweat-crazed terror.

*So much for escapism therapy.*

"…and like I've said before, maybe it's time for something entirely different, you know?"

"You're right, Mother."

My father Samuel enters the room, wiping his filthy hands on a pair of light-colored pants. He stares intently at the amount of grime accumulated before looking up to find us staring.

"First it was the breaker box, then the backup generator…" he squints, then walks to the sink, mumbling, "Never mind."

"Honey, your daughter and I were just having a chat."

"That's nice."

"Saying how it's time for her to take some time off."

"But she is, right? I mean—"

"Samuel, this is different. And after today's near death moment, I think she more than needs it."

Dad looks over one shoulder at her, then rolls his eyes at me. "How's that, Daphne?"

"Your daughter pulled a gun on you in your own home!"

"Mom! I thought someone was breaking in!"

She whips her head at me and glares. "Hon, we live in one of the nicest gated communities in the country. No one is breaking in here."

I hold up both hands in surrender.

"Daphne, she's a cop for *chrissake*. She was alarmed *and* caught off guard. It can happen to anyone."

Mom makes a point to pout, returning to her chopping duties—albeit more aggressive now. She mumbles, tossing a thumb at me, "You can see our daughter is at her wits' end. This has been happening for entirely too long."

"Mom, you know I'm sitting here, right?"

Dad stops to dry his hands, leans against the counter, and eyeballs both of us. "Okay. Let's discuss this like a rational family."

I burp a chuckle as mom cracks a grin. "No, honey, I'm just concerned for our little girl *and* trying to help her find her way."

"And what did you come up with?" He pours a coffee and joins us at the table.

My melodramatic exhale pulls their faces toward me.

"I'm fine. It's only a rough patch. And just maybe…" I pinch my thumb and finger, " a wee bit of self-introspection. Just remember that it was you two who agreed with Captain Nelson when he suggested I see a shrink."

Dad looks into his coffee cup. Mom glances out the window.

"Doesn't help that I don't get any help from the ex."

"Darcy, that's been nearly—"

"I know, you'd think I'd have moved on. And I have. Mostly."

I stare at Mom's bouncing fingertips. "Healing from divorce takes time."

"Mom."

She closes an imaginary zipper across her lips, then mumbles, "It would help if you could sleep."

I shake my head.

"Are you still sleeping with your gun under your pillow?"

I nod.

"Patricia, this isn't going to disappear in a day," Dad says. "You got the Johansen murder case a year ago because you asked for it. Okay, so you solved the case but didn't catch the bad guy. Sometimes they get away."

I force a smile.

"Bottom line? You knew you could solve it. Why? Because you're good at what you do. You work hard, listen well, observe superbly, and put in the time. Sure, maybe along the way your brother and I had some influence on you."

"Of course, Daddy. Without you two—well, more you than Pete—I don't know how far I'd have gotten."

"All I'm saying—which echoes your Mother's thinking—is you should get away. Hell, you haven't taken a day off in forever, and my best suggestion is for you to have a break long enough to make an impact on your mental health."

I frown.

"Now, hold on. You've been riding the rivet—as you like to say—since the minute you moved to first shift. The only time you've taken off in the last 3 or 4 years has been this past month. But coming to see your Mother and me is not what I'm talking about. You need a reset. Or," he says, taking my hand, "I'm afraid you'll burn out. And with such a long career still ahead."

I pat his hand and smile.

"Darius Tercel's just *one* bad guy. There are *plenty* more out there for you to catch. Trust me."

"You're right."

"Good," Daphne says with a clap. "Now, I'm thinking you go see your daughter. Just think how…"

Dad looks at me; our expressions match.

"What?" Mom frowns.

"*I think* she should see her brother."

Pete and I haven't spoken in a long time. It's not my fault he doesn't have time to teach his little sister about climbing the ranks.

I sit up straight. "Okay, enough therapy for one morning."

"Just remember what I always say—distance gives perspective."

Standing, I lean over to kiss his forehead. "You're so smart, Daddy. And since you can't fix the air-conditioning…" I say, heading down the hall.

"Hey, the circuit blew!"

Waving over my shoulder, I shout, "At least my car's got AC."

In minutes, I'm in the shower washing away the troubles of the day —and the terrors of the night.

# CHAPTER FOUR

PULLING OUT OF MY PARENT'S DRIVEWAY WITH A WAVE, I WEAVE through the manicured neighborhood of The Vintage Club, facing a two-hour journey back to Los Angeles. Left on Wren, right onto Vintage, through entrance gates and onto Portola—I'm in the middle of downtown within minutes.

Palm Desert, much like its not-too-distant cousin Palm Springs—only 20 minutes to the northwest—is unbearably hot in the summer and blissfully hot in the winter. Thus, the reason so many wealthy retirees have their first and/or third homes here.

Pulling into the Tower Market Gas Station, I get out and start the pump, standing back and admiring my brand new and very red Z-51 Corvette Stingray. She has full-length dual racing stripes in black carbon and is dolled up with both a performance suspension and exhaust. To say she's a head-turner is an understatement. At nearly 500 horsepower, the 6.2 liter V8 gets me from zero to 60 in less than three seconds.

Necessary? Not really. Sexy as hell? Absolutely.

Guys I know call it a *gear-head's wet dream.*

After snagging a couple of bottled waters and a pack of Big Red gum, I head back outside. Crossing the parking lot, I scan the perimeter of the Palms-to-Pines Shopping Center and see nothing lurking in the short shadows. There are several storefronts: a Bikram yoga studio, a wine bar, a ramen noodle shop, a golf & tennis store, and a quaint bookstore called Deserted Books.

A quote in the bookstore window catches my eye: *There is no greater distance than the one you put between your head and your heart.*

PING goes the pump and a chill scatters down my spine.

*That's delightfully coincidental.*

Returning the hose, snagging the receipt, and driving across the parking lot to investigate further, I decide an audiobook will make a nice travel companion—or distraction. I find a spot under the speckled shade of a tree and head inside.

DING goes a bell dangling from the door and another vibration shoots through me.

Entering, I'm met with stacks of books from floor to ceiling. The place smells of old books and new incense. Esoteric music plays overhead, sounding more like a spa than a bookstore.

A woman pops her head from behind a tall bookcase.

"Welcome in. May I help you?"

Dressed in a tie-dyed blouse and a pair of form-fitting jeans showing off a fit figure, the woman in her early sixties lays aside a clipboard and pierces a bun of silver hair with a pencil. As she approaches, I'm instantly transfixed by her piercing aquamarine eyes and glowing complexion.

"Hi! I was just next door..." I say, pointing toward the front, "when I noticed that quote on the front window."

As I turn back around, she's a step closer. There is something oddly familiar about her.

"Yes, it's by Lao Tse. Are you familiar with the Tao Te Ching?"

Self aware, I say, "Tow tay who?"

"Close," she smiles. "Let me show you. You'll enjoy it," she says, going to the window for a copy.

Glancing at a nearby bookshelf, I spot two books; one makes me chuckle.

Returning, she says, "I know that expression. Something familiar?"

"Sort of," I continue smiling. I take the book from the shelf. "A friend—better yet, an acquaintance—gave me this as a gift."

"Ah yes. *Men Are From Mars, Women Are From Venus.* A classic. Not nearly as influential as this," she says, tapping the book in her hand, "but a seminal work. He must have been sending you a message," she winks.

"Kinda." I return the book and tap the spine of the other. "And this one, I've seen but never read."

"Now, there's a true piece of work. *Many Lives, Many Masters*. It's an eye-opening tome on spirituality. And a true story of a psychiatrist, his patient, and past-life therapy that changed their lives. And opened the eyes of many more."

"Interesting," is all I can manage, suddenly wondering why I'm in this bookstore and not on the road yet.

"But this book—while perhaps not as entertaining—is chock full of ancient wisdom," she smiles, handing me the book. "Lao Tzu was an ancient philosopher and the founder of philosophical Taoism. The title means 'the way of virtue.' Millions around the world have read it. Very insightful. One other thing," she begins, reaching to open the book. "May I?"

I hold it as she turns to a section.

"There's a second piece to the quote that caught your spirit, I mean, your eye: *Between what your mind insists you believe and what your heart is asking you*."

DING goes the bell above the front door as someone enters.

Turning, she says, "Welcome in. I'll be right with you."

A man waves and disappears toward a stack of books.

Her eyes sparkle as she turns back to me.

"That's a beautiful quote," I say, handing back the book.

She puts up a hand. "Nope, you keep it. Consider it my gift to you. And take your time with it. It can appear overwhelming at first, but trust me, you'll extract great wisdom from it."

"That's really kind, but you can't stay in business if you give away all your books," I say, feeling obligated to buy something.

"Please, this isn't a make or break kind of job. More a hobby I enjoy while my husband spends days on the golf course. These books come from all walks of life: donated, shared, purchased. Their life cycles are broad. A book is my way of gifting back. Besides, you have the aura of someone searching for something."

Another odd tingle shoots down the back of my neck.

Rubbing it, I say, "Well, I suppose you're right. Close, anyway. The quote I saw reminds me of something my parents said to me earlier this morning. They're retired and live in The Vintage Club."

"As do I. My husband and I retired out here a half dozen years ago. What, may I ask, is their piece of advice?"

Here I am in the middle of a bookstore, in the middle of the desert, in the middle of a minor crisis, admitting my innermost secrets to a complete stranger.

"They told me how distance brings perspective."

DING goes the bell above the front door again.

We both turn to see the older man tossing a wave over his shoulder —a book under his arm.

Turning back, she smiles, "I suppose he found what he needed."

"Wait," I frown, moving. "Did he just shoplift?"

She places a hand on my arm. "It's fine. There are those, uh, customers, who wander in—either from the intense heat or an intense desire for knowledge—then wander back out. It's just a book. And if they can't afford it right now and it serves them well, who am I to stand in the way of understanding?"

We're quiet for a long beat when I realize she's still touching my arm. I look at her hand. It's lightly tanned, perfectly manicured, and adorned with several eye-catching diamonds.

"Sorry." She pulls her hand back. "I'm touchy-feely as my husband says."

"No worries. I'm a hugger," I say without thinking.

*When do I ever say that?*

Heading to the counter, she says over her shoulder, "And your parents are right. Best piece of advice I could give someone," she turns back. "Not saying *you*, but someone who's trying to get away from something, or conversely, is too close to something. Or who knows, maybe trying to figure out something that you haven't had the proper time to process."

While she talks, I return one book to the shelf and take the other to the counter.

"And if you're not getting the right amount of sleep—" she smiles, "Well, it makes it difficult to retain clarity."

I acknowledge with a nod.

"Especially if your journey is akin to hunting."

TINGLE goes my neck.

*Okay, this is getting weird.*

"Do you find that to be the case, Detective?"

*What?*

My expression made her chuckle. "Sorry, occupational hazard."

"But how—"

"Well, you have an intensely engaging stare and appear to be aware of everything around you. Plus, you've checked the parking lot *several* times since you entered. And, when the customer started out with the book, you looked like you were about to run after him. It was charming, actually."

I feel myself blush.

"Ah, and you're sensitive. Like me," she says, leaning closer. "It's a dead giveaway whenever I'm hiding something. Face turns red in a flash and stays that way for much too long."

"You have quite the instincts."

"Been that way most of my life," she says, putting the books into a decorative paper sack. "But the real secret?"

"Yes?"

"The detective shield on your belt and the gun in the small of your back," she winks. "Those certainly helped."

Pulling aside my jacket, I laugh out loud. "That's good."

Handing me the books, she takes my credit card.

"Won't take but another second and you'll be on your way. Much wiser than before."

Her smile lingers as she watches the machine for approval.

BEEP goes the register as she returns my card and a receipt, putting her other hand atop mine.

"And Patricia?"

My eyebrows involuntarily rise.

"Your card," she smiles.

I snort a chuckle, "Duh!"

"My best piece of insight? If you don't mind my being so bold?"

"Yes, of course. Wait, I don't even know your name."

"Angela. But most people call me Moonbeam."

"Really?"

Laughing, she catches her breath and says, "No, no, no. I'm playing with you. Sorry. It's Angela Langstrom."

Shaking my head, I suppress another laugh. "Nice to meet you,

Angela. I have a dear friend who's also an Angela. We call her Firefly."

She chuckles, "What?"

We both laugh.

"Sorry. It's Angie, actually. Now, please, go on."

Still chuckling, she leans against the counter.

"I was going to say, you impress me as having a healthy amount of insight yourself. You have the answer right here," she points to her heart. "And here," she points to her temple. "All you have to do is listen. As far as not sleeping? I would hazard a guess that something, or *someone*, is chasing you in your dreams."

"By the way, how did you know I wasn't getting enough sleep?"

"Intuition is all. Nothing mystical. And that someone is no doubt from your past. Not terribly difficult to decipher. But here's my last little piece of magic." Her eyes twinkle as she smiles. "You've already caught them."

*What?*

"The reason they continue to—well, haunt seems like such a *Woo-woo* thing to say, but it's true. They may be a ghost now, haunting you in your dreams. But I think they want you to catch them."

My expression reads: *Really?*

"In your dreams, anyway. Because once you catch and face and rid yourself of them—however that takes shape—they'll no longer have control over you. Ever."

Absorbed by her words, I realize my heart is racing. I glance out to scan the horizon. Turning back, I can't help but hug her.

Pulling away, I quietly say, "Sorry. Hope that wasn't weird."

Smiling broadly, she says, "Not at all. Heart to heart. That's what souls connecting are all about."

RING goes the phone. She holds up a finger.

"Just one second, Patricia. Deserted Books, this is Angela…" she mouths Moonbeam and stifles a giggle. "Yes, may I put you on hold for one tiny second? I have a dear friend with me and I'm just finishing up. Won't be but two shakes."

As she pushes the button to mute them, I chuckle, "Moonbeam."

"Thought you'd like that. Okay, I've gobbled up enough of your time. I'm sure you have better things to do than to listen to some old biddy spout some—"

"Angela, stop. You've been delightful and just what the doctor ordered, so to speak," I wink.

*And now I'm winking.*

"Of course."

"Seriously, thank you. For the book. The insight. For everything."

"It's been my pleasure. Enjoy your trip back to LA, and next time you're out visiting your folks, stop in and say hello."

I'm nearly at the door when she calls out, "And Patricia?"

I spin around. "Yes?"

"Just remember, if you don't take the time to face your fears, they'll just keep coming back until you resolve them. No greater distance between here and here," she points from her head to her heart, "than the distance *you* create."

# CHAPTER FIVE

THE DRIVE BACK HOME PASSES QUICKLY. HALFWAY TO MANHATTAN Beach, my mind drifts back to the conversation with Moonbeam. I grin, rethinking what she said about people from my past haunting me. As much as I've never thought of myself being into *Woo-Woo*, I have to agree with her on some level. There's something about twisted people wanting to be caught; I've seen it many times working with LAPD. Many criminals—especially serial killers we research—have some secret desire to be caught and more often than not, their subconscious desire lands their wish.

Replaying our conversation, I keep glancing over at the book she gave me, comparing it to events of the past year. It's been that long since my partner, Detective Stuart Brown, and I—along with a small team of agents—surrounded the home of Dr. Darius Tercel. It was a move we'd hoped would end a long career of murders at the hand of a serial killer who managed to evade authorities for no less than two decades. Sadly, our plan missed the mark.

In fact, the near miss resulted in my spending the last 350-plus days kicking myself for not being able to bring the psychopath to justice. Likewise, it's taken nearly all that time to—for lack of a better term— reprogram my mind with the help of a different therapist who has spent weeks helping undo the subconscious programming the "Doctor" performed on me. Was Tercel an actual therapist? Yes. However, some- where along the way he got off track and made his practice the perfect cover where he used the neuroses of his patients to put them out of their misery.

My saving grace, according to the best hypnotherapist in Los Angeles, is two-fold. First, I wasn't under his care for very long which means my programming was not as deep as with his other patients like our mutual friend, Angie Myers. Second, I was—according to several sources with whom I spoke—both extremely stubborn and ultimately teachable. Evidently, my drive helped expedite my "deprogramming."

DRIVING THE 10, I'm halfway between Banning and Beaumont. The San Bernardino National Forest is on my right and Mt. San Jacinto on my left—a ridge I hiked last summer. I suddenly imagine getting lost in the woods and being hunted down by Tercel.

*What's that about?* I wonder, unwrapping another stick of gum.

*Does he want to be caught?* I roll it up.

*Did he start out wanting revenge?* My mouth waters as flavors ignite.

*Did his craving for control turn into a game for him?* I blow a bubble.

POP goes my gum as my phone rings.

"Well, hey there girlfriend," Angie says in her most robust Southern Texas accent.

"Hey, y'all," I answer. Since I'm not much for accents, we enjoy a laugh.

"You must be heading back from your folks. Bet there was a lot of relaxation going on there," she giggles.

It's nice to count on Angie for levity. In fact, ever since the parents moved to the desert, Angie's about the only person I consistently see besides Stuart at work.

She and I talk about her new boy-toy—some software geek she met over drinks at a girlfriend's wedding in Vegas a month back. Prattling on about how sweet and doting he is, I sense something offbeat, but I let it go. After all, at her age I'm just glad she's having fun.

"So tell me, Patty, how're you feeling? Any, you know, better about stuff?"

"Ha!" I stifle a snort. "That's specific, Ang. Give me a little more?"

She lets out a high-pitched cackle. "You know what I'm talking about. Ever since that case, you've been, well, my Daddy used to call it 'run hard and put up wet.' He was into horses, you know."

Gotta love Angie's two cents. But she's right, I've been trying to bury the pain of not measuring up.

"Sorry, Pat. You didn't ask for all that. I'm just worried if you keep running that hard, you'll burn out. But hey, you're still the hottest broad I know. Just tired. And maybe more than a little sad."

"Okay, so I haven't been working out like I used to. Are you calling me fat?"

She cackles again. "Girl, just a little extra something to love on, right?"

I'm not enjoying this as much as she is, so I change the channel.

"Say, Angie, what are you up to tonight? Care to join me for dinner?"

"I'd love to, girl. Just can't make it too late. I'm heading to Dallas first thing tomorrow to see my mother for a day or two. She's finally giving up that big old suburban sprawl of hers and moving into an assisted living community."

"That's nice, right?"

"Oh, hell yes. And truthfully? It's more like a mini Country Club. It's *real* nice. With Daddy gone nearly three years now, it's just become too much for one person. So, yes, it's a good thing. I'm just heading out to help her get settled."

"You're a wonderful daughter."

"Oh, go on," she giggles. "No, really, go on!"

"I will, later tonight," I laugh. "Okay, I'll grab a bottle of wine on the way home, take a quick jog down to the pier—you know, to work off some of this *side dish*—then head over to your place. How's seven?"

"Perfect. See you then."

"Hey, Ang, before I go. Are we still on for that Santa Barbara girl's retreat you planned this weekend?"

Silence.

"Angie?"

"Yeah, uh, I'll have to reschedule. After, uh, Mom's, I've got to head East to take care of some other business."

"Really? Where?"

"New York, for some business."

"Yeah, you said that. What sort of business?"

She gives a long-winded ramble with too many details about attending a Real Estate Convention which I find odd, given she is going to New York when the lion's share of her business is in LA.

PING goes something in the back of my head.

"Hey, Angie before you go, and I know we said we wouldn't talk about this for obvious reasons, but do you or have you ever heard from Darius?"

There's enough silence I have to check to see if there's still a connection.

"Nope," she finally says. "Like you said, he just up and vanished— without a peep."

# CHAPTER SIX

Angie disconnects the call, lets out a long, shaky breath, and sits upright in a living room chair, staring at the ocean in the distance. Her color is pale. Her eyes are jittery and glazed with fear. She squeezes her hands together in a death grip. Silently, she sneaks a quick glance at her guest sitting opposite her.

His dark eyes pierce a hole through her as he quietly says, "I know it's a lot to take in. And I'm certain it doesn't make a great deal of sense right now."

She averts his intense gaze.

"But trust me, it will."

Silence stretches between them before she sneaks another peek, then looks away.

"I need you to listen closely. And to be patient."

Turning back, she forces a hard swallow. Periodic squints punctuate her expression.

"I'm sorry if I alarmed you. It's just I feel it's better to just show up."

Looking down at her hands, she strangles a tissue.

"I was afraid you might ignore a call from a number you didn't recognize. And email is too dangerous these days."

Her gaze returns to the ocean. Nerves raw, her stomach gurgles.

"Frankly, I had to see you face to face. And to come clean with a good many things."

Swallowing hard again, she manages a raspy, "That would be nice. And a good idea. Given our history."

Her Texas accent, while strained, is clear.

His obscure accent, while unfamiliar, is odd.

Everything about the moment feels disorienting.

"Good, let's start at the beginning. And Angie you can relax. I will *not* hurt you. I would *never* hurt you."

Hesitant, she allows her shoulders to loosen.

He takes a quiet breath. "Personal matters first, then business. Will that be okay?"

With a nod, she adjusts to face him, squinting. "It's just so *strange*."

Managing a friendly smile, he says, "What's that?"

She examines him head to foot.

"Well, there's a hint of an accent I don't recognize," her drawl stretches as she squirms in her seat. "Which makes this whole thing even stranger."

"Understood."

She sets aside the tattered tissue, adjusting her chair to face him better.

"But to your direct question." Manufacturing an uncomfortable smile, she says, "Your physique is...I mean, you were always kinda slight, but now everything is so massive."

"It's amazing what hard work can accomplish."

The first crack in her defensive posture discharges her fear.

"Obviously," she says, raising her eyebrows. "But your face is *so* different."

He pushes a long strand of blond hair behind his ear.

"You must've started growing that..." she nods toward his hair, then stares at the floor.

"The day I left."

"Reminds me of Fabio..." she nervously says, "back in the day."

"Although not my original intent," he chuckles, "I'll take that as a compliment."

She squints again.

"And yes, contact lenses. One of the tougher things to get used to."

"I can imagine," she whispers. "I have to admit. If I hadn't recognized your voice when I answered the door, there's no way on earth I would've ever guessed it was you."

He remains silent.

"But why?"

"What?"

She frowns. "Why go to all that trouble?"

Now, he stares out at the ocean. After a long moment, he turns back.

"There was no way I was going to prison. And you and I both know Detective Norelli—as kind a person as she is to both of us—would never sleep until she caught me. She is just wired that way. So," he shrugs, "I had to disappear. First to the other side of the world. Then under the knife."

"Hmm."

"I call it my second chance. And since no one found my DNA at the scene, it's like the real me—or rather, the former me—no longer exists."

She shudders. He notices.

"Frankly," he smiles, "I like the new me better."

After another long silence, her expression shifts from confusion to fear. "And what on earth do you want with little ol' me? I mean, we liquidated all your homes and some of your art. That had to have put a load of cash in your bank accounts…"

"You did. And yes there is, thank you."

"Then what do you need from me?"

# CHAPTER SEVEN

WITH A QUICK RUN UNDER MY BELT, A LONG SHOWER REWARDING MY body, and a bottle chilling in the fridge, I put last touches on my face before heading out to dinner. Just then, my phone rings and, checking the screen, I automatically smile.

"Hiya, peanut! To what do I owe this surprise?"

"Really, Mom? We only talked like last week."

Still my little girl.

"I know, Shay. I'm just missing you is all. What's up?"

I hear noise in the background that sounds like a party.

"Just checking in. Sorry for the noise; we're standing outside a restaurant waiting for a table. How are you feeling?"

*Who's we? My ex-husband? A new friend?*

"I'm good. Real good," I lie. "Just got back from Mom and Dad's. They send their love. And I'm about to pop out for dinner with Angie."

"Well, okay, I won't keep you. I just—"

"Shay, you're not keeping me. Tell me all that's happening," I say, walking into the kitchen to pour a glass of wine. "Honey, I miss you so much and want to hear everything."

She tells me about school, about how her professors are challenging her to think in ways she never considered, and by the time she shares how she has grown tired of living with her Dad--something I completely understand--I've emptied my glass.

"Mom, before I go, I wanna ask you something and you have to tell me, okay?"

"Yes."

"Are you still having trouble sleeping?"

As much as I'm ready to lie so she won't worry, she beats me to it.

"And don't bullshit me just to make me feel better. We owe each other honesty."

Rinsing my glass, I tidy the kitchen.

"True. And honestly, I thought my insomnia was bad before. Now, I'm enjoying some pretty messed up dreams."

"I'm sorry, Mom. I'm sure we both know what that's about. I guess it'll just take time, right?"

Checking my makeup in the hall mirror, I reapply lipstick.

"Right. All it takes is time."

*And plenty of wine and sex.*

"But seriously? It's not as bad as those first few months after I got out of the hospital," I lie.

"Good. That's progress, right?"

"True."

A long beat of silence separates us, then, "Mom, one more thing…"

"Let me guess. She's tall, athletic, and blonde?"

Stepping outside, the temperature is cooler than expected, so I go back in for a jacket.

"How'd you know?"

Grabbing the jacket, I chuckle, "Really?"

Locking the door, I wave to a passing neighbor and head to the restaurant.

"Mom, she's awesome. I mean, we have so much fun. And yes, she's tall and athletic."

"Of course—your type."

"I know, but she's not just a jock; she's like *hella* smart."

Smiling, I take in the sweet moment with my only child blossoming into a woman. This is truly the best part of my life.

"And naturally beautiful."

"What's her name?"

"Natalie. She's from San Francisco. Tiburon, actually. Her dad's some fancy chef with a restaurant in the city."

Suddenly, a flurry of voices distract her. "Sorry, Mom, but our table's ready and I gotta bounce. I'll call you later this week?"

"Sounds good, baby. Have fun. And yes, ring me when you can squeeze me in. I love you."

The cool night air, the slowly fading light, and the echoes of Shay's voice make me a little sad.

# CHAPTER EIGHT

Not far from the restaurant, my phone rings. Checking the screen, I push aside my somber feelings and light up with a smile. "Hey partner, how ya doing?"

Stuart laughs, "I'm good, how *you* doing?"

"What's up?"

"Can't a guy call his best friend to see how she's doing?"

Stuart is a good cop. And an even better friend. The longer we've gotten to know one another, the closer we've become. And that isn't always the case with partners. Having a new daughter has certainly softened him. And with a second child on the way, my guess is life's causing him to stop and see what's important.

"You're right. And you can, anytime. But seriously, everything good? I mean, I'll see you in what," I check my watch, "A dozen hours?"

"Or in your case, fifteen?"

"Screw you. My days of rolling in late and hungover are in the past."

"Okay," he laughs. "Just checking to see if everything's okay."

*Since when does everyone check in to see if I'm okay?*

"All good. Parents are happy and healthy. Shay's good, and I'm just about to head to dinner with Angie."

"Cool, then I won't keep you. Besides checking on you, I had one other reason for the call."

"Yeah?"

"Would you mind swinging by to grab me in the morning? The tank's acting up and I had to put it in the shop again."

"Yeah, no problem. I'll see you at 8."


ARRIVING AT THE RESTAURANT, I see Angie sitting at the bar. I'm about to enter the restaurant when I suddenly feel a chill tingle my spine. Spinning around, I check my surroundings—a habit that's become all too frequent. Seeing nothing odd, I head in.

But a pair of eyes across the street don't miss a beat.


AFTER A DELICIOUS DINNER, two bottles of wine, and a decadent dessert neither of us has any business eating, the server warms our coffee and delivers the bill. I grab it before Angie can.

"Wait just a minute, girlfriend, I'm buying tonight!" She says, reaching across the table and nearly knocking the floral arrangement over.

"No way, Jose. Remember the last time we got together and burned through this much booze? I said I was buying next. And here we are."

She playfully pouts. "All right. But I'm buying a nightcap."

Signing the bill, I look up with a double take. "What? I thought you were going to be a good little girl and get to bed early. What about your flight?"

Taking a compact from her purse, she reapplies makeup.

"Hey, it's been way too long since we got together like this. Just you and me. No boys, no interruptions," she slurs, putting her makeup away and bouncing her eyebrows.

"Okay, but you're the one—"

"Lah-dee-dah," she says, tossing her head toward the bar. "C'mon, let's grab a seat at the end of the bar. Chuckie always takes good care of me," she winks.


HALFWAY THROUGH OUR post-dinner drinks and with softening inhibitions, our earlier conversation bounces in my ears. That's when I feel like stirring the pot.

"Hey, Ang, is it my imagination or did you get a little weird on the phone when we talked about Tercel?"

Clearly shaken, she says, "What's that?" She takes a sip and tries to hide a frown. "When?"

"When I was driving back from the desert."

Looking away, she straightens herself, then turns back to me and sighs, "It wasn't your imagination."

Practicing my craft, I allow the silence.

She looks away again, tightening a mischievous grin. "Look, I'm having as hard a time shaking him as you are."

"I am not!"

She lets out a loud cackle that attracts attention. Lowering her voice, she says, "Oh, really?"

I take another sip. "Yes, really."

"Uh huh," she smirks, leaning closer. "Still sleeping with your gun under your pillow?"

*Shit.*

I whisper, "Sometimes."

"Still locking and relocking all the doors and windows in your place? Repeatedly?"

"It's a new home."

"Right."

I look away. She doesn't.

Her glare is fierce. "Still watching all the exits *everywhere* you go?"

I instinctively check the exit, then catch myself. "Stop."

Now it's my time to smirk; however, it falls flat.

"And tell me this," she dramatically wags a finger. "Still eyeballing every parking lot no matter where you are?"

*Fuck.*

"Yes."

"Okay, just one more thing—"

As I start to respond, she holds up both hands and leans in. "How about the dreams?"

"What?"

She gives me a look: *Yeah, right.* "Still having them?"

I sigh, "Oh, hell yes."

Sitting back, she empties her glass. "Me, too."

"Really?"

"Oh my, yes." She waves to the bartender for another round. "It's the same thing over and over. He shows up to my house, all dressed up nice and handsome, and smelling so very good." She leans close. "Like he *always* did."

"He did, didn't he?"

The second round arrives. We smile at Chuck and, as he leaves, I lean in. "And?"

"And..." she grins, looking around. "We'd sit and talk, have some wine, and then make out a little."

"What?"

"Hey, it's part of my fantasy life." Giggling, she leans closer. "And who'd know better than him, right?"

"*Aaaaand?*"

"And he tells me to get into bed and that he'll be back in a minute. Next thing I know..."

Her wide grin suddenly vanishes. Staring into her drink, she stops talking as a darkness clouds her eyes.

"What happens then?"

She finishes her drink in one gulp, dabs at the corners of her mouth, then looks me dead in the eyes. "Then he takes out a syringe and shoots some shit into my veins." Her eyes tear up. "And just about the time the burning hits my chest—"

I gasp, "Your heart explodes."

With wide eyes, she nods, "And I wake up."

"*Shit.*"

# CHAPTER NINE

THE NEXT MORNING, THE ALARM IS SQUAWKING AT AN HOUR I HAVE TO assume is wrong. Frowning through bleary eyes, I reach for my phone and slap at it until it shuts up. Gaining focus, I try to ignore my throbbing head and dry mouth. I consider a few more minutes of sleep before I recall agreeing to get Stuart. Forcing myself out of bed, I begin contemplating a three miler.

"Something's better than nothing," I say aloud, sliding on shorts and a tank top.

As I bend over to tie my shoes, I feel my heartbeat in my temples.

Splashing my face in the kitchen sink, I try recalling when we shut it down last night—no such luck. Before heading out, I check myself in the mirror, then put on a ball cap to block the sun—and hide my face.

FINALLY WARMED UP, I'm moving at a good clip along the Veterans Parkway, aka Hermosa Valley Greenbelt. As I approach my turnaround, I replay last night's conversation.

*Is she still as possessed with Darius as I've been?* I keep running.

*Was or am?* I pick up my speed.

*Am I still?* I run even faster.

I'm at a full sprint by the time I reach the end of my block. Gasping for air, I realize it's been too long between consistent runs and decide to walk the rest of the way to my place.

. . .

AFTER A SCALDING SHOWER, a dab of makeup, and a dose of eyedrops, I grab an apple and head out. Within minutes, I'm pulling into the township of Culver City where Stuart and Janine live in a cute bungalow facing Carlson Park, only blocks from Sony Pictures. Pulling up to within feet of the curb, I toot the horn and check my face.

Exiting his front door, Stuart hands off his little girl to Janine as we exchange waves.

"Hey," he opens the door. "Can you park any further from the curb?"

"Morning to you, too. And as you'll see—when not so intent on balancing your bagel—this car is lower than the last one. Makes them prone to getting nicked by curbs."

Squeezing his six-foot-four-inch frame into my Corvette is fun to watch.

Balancing a breakfast in one hand and a briefcase in the other, he cuts me a look as I imagine trying to get garlic cream cheese out of my soft leather.

"I'll be careful, Officer *Tidy*."


PURSUING full recovery at the coffee shop, I power through a third double Americano while Stuart gets a haircut next door. Australia? I replay for the thousandth time, considering the "love letter" Tercel delivered to my hospital room after nearly killing me with a paralyzing narcotic.

*Would he really have told me exactly where he was going?*

I can't seem to let go of the one case plaguing me for entirely too long and seeing Angie last night reignited my need for justice.

*Right, Norelli. It wasn't Angie. You're just freaking obsessed.*

Whenever I spend too much time fixating on Tercel, I'm supposed to use an app to replace those thoughts, a "prescription" from my new doctor. Each time it happens, I'm supposed to take 60 seconds to run the test.

Spinning my iPhone on the table, I watch the timer count down.

*Would he have really gone there?* I monitor the parking lot.

*Am I being watched?* I look to see if Stuart is done yet.

*Did he kill only eight?* I ask my constant critic, glancing at the timer as it nears zero.

My ex-husband, of all people, recommended Dr. Josephine Proctor to me. She is a middle-aged, African-American woman with more degrees on her wall than Tercel could ever imagine. According to Proctor's instincts, she said somewhere along the way—and amid a slow and likely severe breakdown—Tercel simply lost touch with reality.

I reset the timer and click the stem of my AirPods to listen again.

*We are never certain what causes us to lose touch with reality or to lose touch with normalcy. For many psychopaths, it's a chemical imbalance while others suffer a trauma so deep they never recover. There are those who have an inciting incident that literally breaks their social code—rendering them weaker than others to withstand their primal urges. Like a muscle pushed too far past its normal abilities, they snap. And in that snap, someone can often repair the tear through counseling and medication. Left untreated, that muscle may never operate as it once did. Functional? Yes, but not performing at maximum capacity. Then again, many people choose never to return to such a state. They enjoy the manic phase. They find pleasure in the pain they cause others. It's as though they satisfy an itch somewhere in the depth of their psyche that also provides a sense of pleasure unlike anything else.*

*BZZZ, BZZZ, BZZZ, BZZZ.*

Tapping the screen, I silence the vibrating timer. My 60-second allowance is up. Again.

"Shit."

"What's that, partner?" A voice says from behind.

Startled, I spin around and snap on a smile, admiring my partner. "Just mumbling to myself. Hey, I like what your stylist did. Looks so metrosexual."

Shaking his head, he can't stifle a grin. "Can always count on you for just the right compliment."

As I start to get up, he puts a hand on my shoulder.

"Pump the brakes, Norelli. We're in a posh coffee shop with dandy treats of which I'm going to avail myself of both. Cool?"

"Sure, and then—"

"Yes, and then we leave," he says, taking my empty cup. "Refill?"

He's at the counter before I can decide if I want more.

*New Zealand*? I start again. *Europe*? Without thinking, I reach to reset the timer and then stop and bury the phone in my pocket.

"I know that look," Stuart says, placing a coffee in front of me before taking a seat. Biting into a hot croissant, he stares at me, raising his eyebrows.

"I know," I grin, blowing the top of my coffee. "I should be further ahead by now, but—"

"But nothing. C'mon girl, I said I'd help. All you have to do—"

"Is ask, I know," I try to smile with conviction. "Thank you."

Silence grows from seconds to minutes. Stuart wipes crumbs from his mouth and leans forward.

"Patty, there's nothing wrong with taking your time. Especially in matters of the heart. Or the mind. Time is time. It takes what it takes."

I can't help but grin. "You should be the doctor here."

"Nah, I have enough trouble just being a Detective. And in your shadow? *Fuhgeddaboudit.*"

I sip my coffee, mindlessly eyeballing the perimeter of the parking lot. A black car with darkened windows sits under the shadow of an enormous Cyprus tree. A panel van sits in the corner separate from other cars. And an all-black limo has its engine running near a store entrance.

Stuart swipes headlines on his phone and without looking up says, "What're you staring at?"

"Huh?" I start tidying up. "Just thought I saw someone I knew."

"Right." He doesn't look up. "Still looking over your shoulder?"

"A little."

Putting away his phone, he looks at me.

"Here it comes," I mumble.

"Wait a second partner, it's me. The other half of you? The half that never left. That will never leave. We're in this together—thick or thin. You know that. If it happens to you; it happens to me."

I drain my coffee and gather my things.

"Okay, we've got better things to do than sit around drinking five-dollar coffees and munching ten dollar biscuits."

"That's *croissant*, thank you very much," he grins, placing his hand on my arm. "Hang on. Before we go, I just want to be sure of something."

"Yeah?"

"You okay?"

My frown is a reflex. "Peachy. Why?"

"Not trying to mother you. Just want to be sure you're not thinking about doing something crazy?"

My eyes go from him to the napkin I'm twisting into knots.

"There's nothing crazy happening here." I tap the side of my head.

"Cool," he grins, gathering our trash. "Then let's get to it."


THE DRIVE back to the station is quiet, too quiet, until Stuart turns from the window to me, shifting his considerable weight in the seat.

"So, how's the Judge?"

"Funny you should ask. I was just thinking about some advice Dad gave me."

After spending his entire life dedicated to defending and protecting Los Angeles as their premiere Circuit Court Judge, my father is finally spending his days doing what he wants—playing golf and little else.

"He's good. Retirement looks good on him, and I think he's enjoying it. More than any of us imagined, actually. I can't say the same for Mom. Not sure she's as ecstatic about having him around all the time."

"I bet," he laughs. "And how'd the weekend with them go?"

Taking a left onto Wilshire Boulevard, I pull into traffic toward Westwood, glancing at the Los Angeles National Cemetery in the distance. I never miss an opportunity to admire her.

"Ever heard the phrase, *Distance brings perspective?*"

He frowns. "It's vaguely familiar."

"Basically, it means you can't fully appreciate what you're in or going through until you step back and see it from a distance. Or should, anyway."

He looks at me with a lopsided grin.

"What?"

"Just that this is exactly what I've been telling you for weeks, hell, months now. Maybe not that eloquently but certainly the same message. You gotta step back and cut yourself slack before you can get back on track."

I cut him a sideways glance. "Think you're clever, don't you?"

He looks like a bobblehead.

"A real rapper," I shake my head. "And you have. I've been listening."

I turn on the radio for a distraction, flip stations four times, then turn it off.

Stuart eyeballs me. "Still sleeping with your gun under the pillow?"

"Does everyone have to…"

Silence.

Scanning traffic in both directions, I catch Stuart staring at me.

Several minutes pass when he says, "You think just because you didn't solve your first and biggest case…"

"I don't deserve to be First Grade," I mumble, looking out the window.

"What? Okay. First, you earned that badge. You did the work and found—"

"But I didn't *catch* him."

"So?" He snorts. "He's not practicing any longer. He's likely not even in town. And for all we know, he could've pushed his luck so far that—"

"Nah, if my instincts are even close to being right, he's still out there doing the same thing all over again. Maybe not in the exact way, but…"

More silence.

"But what?"

I release a heavy sigh, start to say something, but stop.

"What?"

"As corny as this may sound, a leopard can't change its spots."

"Now who's playing armchair therapist?"

The laugh feels good, so I leave things alone—for now.

# CHAPTER TEN

*HOLLYWOOD, CALIFORNIA—*

ARRIVING AT THE PRECINCT, I have an odd feeling arise from a dark place and take inventory of the surroundings as we make our way across the parking lot. We're about to enter when Stuart's phone rings. Checking the screen, he holds up a finger signaling he needs a minute. I return a thumbs up and head in.

At my desk, I flip through a stack of pink message slips and am about to slide into a pair of worn mules I keep under my desk when our boss comes charging down the hall.

Captain John Nelson has softened over the past handful of months and, being the last of the old guards, that says something. His rarely racist, but often sexist, attitudes have slowly dissolved; the current environment demands it. He had planned to retire about the time we closed the Meredith Johansen case, but sadly those plans—along with any hopes of spending his retirement years with his wife of forty years —disappeared when she lost her battle with cancer. Her death has taken all but the last gust of wind from his sails.

"Norelli," he barks in his inimitable style, glancing at Stuart's empty desk. "Where's boy wonder? I've gotta talk to you two."

Stuart appears from behind. "Morning, Captain. Just wrapping a call—"

Turning, Nelson asks, "Do I look like I give a shit about what you're doing or with whom you're doing it, Brown?" He looks to the clock across the room and continues. "About the only thing I give a shit about is the fact you're late. I mean, look," he points to me. "Norelli's here. On time. *Ish.* And from the looks of it, I'll bet she's not even hungover."

I shrug, holding up a fist full of slips, planting a ridiculous expression on my face.

"Okay, no need to gloat," Nelson frowns. "Ever since the Johansen case, you've both been doing excellent work. And Norelli, while your attitude seems saltier than usual, you've been closing cases at an insane level. I don't recall a time when I've seen such a run on copycat murders. Geez, popping up like dandelions. Thing is, both of you can pump the brakes every once in a while." He looks directly at me. "Working constantly can make one worn around the seams, if you know what I mean."

About to speak, he holds up a hand.

"And before you blabber about how it's been a long time and you still haven't found Tercel, I want to say we don't always catch the bad guys."

As he stops for a slurp of coffee, a new Detective named Brooks comes running into the room with an orange folder. Catching his breath, he stops short of a slide.

"Sorry to interrupt, Captain, but one of our team got wind of a situation. Thought you'd want to see it."

Taking the folder, Nelson says, "Thanks, Brooks."

As Nelson opens it, Brooks doesn't move.

Nelson looks up. "Anything else, Detective?"

"Uh, no, sir. Well…" he looks from me to Stuart and back to me.

Suddenly, I feel like I'm in the principal's office, as I watch Nelson start reading. A frown slowly grows, then quickly morphs into a slack jaw. Next, the color leaves his face as he looks up at me.

*What the hell?*

Burying his eyes in the folder, he waves at Brooks. "Okay, Brooks. I'll take it from here."

As he leaves, I ask, "What is it, Captain?"

"Yeah, you look like you've seen a ghost," Stuart adds.

Rubbing his nose, he clears his throat. "Ah geez, Norelli…"

My monkey mind kicks in.

"Sir?"

While the Captain isn't much for drama, this moment certainly looks like he does. Looking from me to Stuart, he stands and stares at the ceiling like the answer might be there. Grinding his jaw, he hands the folder to Stuart.

Scanning the page, Stuart stops to stare before his jaw goes slack as well.

"Stuart?"

As our eyes meet, I'll never forget his expression.

When his eyes begin to pool, I whimper, "Stuart, what is it? C'mon, guys, you're killing me here."

The Captain looks at me. "I'm sorry, Norelli, there's no simple way to say this."

I look at Stuart whose expression is cracking.

Nelson says, "A neighbor found your friend Angie in her home this morning."

Now, it's time for the wind to leave my sails.

My ears ring and my vision narrows as my mind fights to process the news.

Sounding like he was at the back of a long tunnel, Nelson says, "Norelli?"

When I don't answer, he waves a hand in front of my face.

I look up and whisper, "What the hell, Captain?" Trying to catch my breath, I say, "This, uh, that can't be."

"It's too early to tell, especially without specifics of an *official* autopsy, but early indications suggest heart attack."

I freeze in place.

Then he mumbles, "Could also be a suicide."

"What?" I shout. "No fucking way, Captain. I was just with her. Last night. As in only hours ago."

The Captain looks from me to Stuart and back again, shaking his head.

I stand. "Fuck this!" I grab the folder from Stuart and start flipping pages. "When?"

Stuart remains frozen as Nelson says, "Sometime around one, maybe two, this morning."

"That's impossible, I left her house sometime around…"

That's when it hit me—as did the punch in my gut.

The air escapes my lungs—along with the oxygen in the room.

My head—throbbing from before—now spins.

My balance is completely off.

That's when my stomach…

SPLAT!

Luckily, I make it to a nearby trash can just in time. Stuart runs out of the room and returns seconds later with a handful of damp napkins. I wipe my mouth with one napkin while he places another one on the back of my neck.

Sitting, I feel thoroughly disoriented. As my mind races to Angie's face, Captain is in the tunnel again.

"Norelli? You hear me?" He waves his hand in front of my face again.

"Yes, sir," I push it away. "I hear you. Just trying to—"

"Of course. It's a lot to process. I'm sorry, Patricia. I know she was a good friend."

Stuart squeezes my shoulder.

"Pat, you said you two were out for dinner. When exactly was that?"

Suddenly and for no reason, I feel like a criminal, but I push aside the thoughts.

"We had dinner, drinks, and closed the restaurant. Then I walked her home. Exactly? Not sure, but could've been around 11:15. Maybe a little later? No, wait; we closed The Strand at 11 and left a few minutes after. It took us a good twenty minutes to get to her place, so I'd say 11:20? That's right because I was home by 11:40. I remember because I set my alarm early to get you. I went straight to bed, so I was out by 11:50, maybe midnight at the latest."

Captain and Stuart exchange looks, saying nothing.

"This is impossible," I whisper. "Fucking horrible."

Angie and I had known each other forever but had only recently become really close. She sold my parents their first house on the West side where I grew up and set me up with my current house at the beach. She always treated me like the sister I never had. And ever since Tercel vanished, I spend more time with her than my family.

"Look, Norelli, why don't you take—"

"No, Captain," I snap. "I don't need to take time off. I need to find out what the *fuck* happened."

Reaching for the report, I double check their estimated time of death; it appears to be between midnight and 3:00 a.m., Sunday into Monday. A chill scatters down my back.

*Just like Meredith.*

The report shows no signs of foul play, no breaking and entering. There was a bottle of sleep aids on the nightstand, but plenty remained. No empty bottles of booze. I shake my head, handing Stuart the file.

"Whaddya say we step outside for some fresh air?"

Nelson's face is dark with sadness. "Listen to Brown. Get some fresh air. And let me know...you know."

The three of us are silent before I lean over to hug Nelson. His embrace is genuine and his aftershave reminds me of Dad when I was younger.

As we release, he quietly says, "I'm sorry, Patricia. Please let me know what I can do to help. Anything. And look, you're bound to come across something in there," he nods at the folder. "Hell, you knew her better than anyone. You'll figure it out." Turning to Stuart, he adds, "Both of you will."

"Thank you, sir. And you're right, we will."

"Let me say this before you head out and I head upstairs," Nelson says.

Upstairs means the 9th floor. Management. They're always pulling his strings.

"Something I want you to be ready for. It probably isn't, uh, suicide, but at the very least consider—"

I'm about to speak when he holds up both hands. "Like it or not, lots of people just can't take it anymore. Whatever it is. Sad, but true. Just, you know, prepare, okay?"

I barely nod.

"The other side of the coin—the one I'm 100% sure you're considering right now even if it's been a year since that bastard disappeared—we have to at the least consider it."

"True," Stuart whispers.

"Oh, hell yeah, Captain. Hundred percent," I say, wiping my eyes.

He looks around. "And as much as I hate putting you through this

Patricia, it isn't the worst idea, you know, you taking this case. With Stuart, of course. But only if you think you're up to it."

"Miles ahead of you." I stand. "And as much as it hurts—and it really does—like you said, nobody better than me to get on top of this thing."

Taking the folder from Stuart, Nelson double checks several pages.

"I know it's not our jurisdiction, but one detective knew you two were pals and neighbors. So, we're all going to play fair in the sandbox, right?"

We both nod and he looks at Stuart. "This'll be plenty tough on her, so be sure to, you know, buffer matters. You get what I'm saying."

"Copy that."

"Best start doing what you do." Nelson forces a smile. "Just keep me in the loop. And if you wig out…"

His overprotectiveness is sweet.

"Got it, sir."

"Good. I need to get upstairs, so carry on," he says before walking away. At the door, he stops and looks back at me. "Hey, Patricia, I'm really sorry."

He leaves before his aftershave does.

Waving the air, Stuart mumbles, "You think he knows how much of that he wears?"

With an absent nod, I force a phony smile and grab my coffee mug.

"Let's get another cup on the way to that fresh air."

As we head out, I bury my emotions, knowing I can face them later. Right now, I need to find what really happened.

# CHAPTER ELEVEN

STUART AND I ARE IN THE BACK LOT OF THE PRECINCT WHEN HE considers an early lunch. He has a burrito; me, another coffee. My stomach—not to mention my heart—is too sensitive for a food truck. We're an hour ahead of the main crush, so the crowd is negligible. Across the way, our friend McCloud from Surveillance is burning smokes end to end while ogling a young blonde in a tight skirt. Stuart's attention is more focused on catching hot sauce before it drips onto his tie than much else. I hand him a napkin in anticipation of the obvious.

"Thanks," he says between bites. "And I'm sorry."

"Huh?" I say, staring at a scuff on my boot. "Why?"

"I know how hard this is. And how much she meant to you."

All I can do is nod.

"You wanna—"

"I *want* to see her. Or, maybe see the *scene* first." Looking up, I squint. "No, let's go see her. Morgue's closer. We can hit her home at the end of the day," I mumble, fighting the urge to cry.

Tossing his trash, he puts an arm around me and we stand in silence. As I look up, McCloud grinds out a butt and heads our way.

Approaching, he quietly says, "Good to see you, Detectives."

"McCloud." I manage a half-hearted smile, "Haven't seen you in a while."

"Yeah, late hours 'n shit. Heard about Angie. Really sorry for your loss."

*News travels fast.*

"Thanks."

"Anything I can do? Just let me know," he says, reaching for a fist bump.

I return the gesture. "Thanks."

After a moment, he gives an awkward nod and starts walking away. "Okay."

"Hey, McCloud," I shout. "There is one thing."

He spins on a heel and returns. "Yeah?"

"Stu and I are going to look at the crime scene. After we leave the coroner's. Care to join us?"

"Sure. When?"

I check my watch. "Say 2? No, make it 3, in case traffic's hell. I know it's a hike. I'll buy you a coffee."

Grinning, he says, "Thanks. See you then."

"What're you thinking?"

"Just a hunch," I shrug.


BEFORE WE HEAD OUT, we swing by the Captain's office to give him a heads up we won't be back today. As we round the corner, I recognize a face in his office. The two appear in deep conversation.

Lowering my voice, I say to Stuart, "Isn't that…"

Slowing his roll, Stuart stares. "Oh yeah, same guy nosing around the Johansen case. Remember how he kept showing up just moments after we did? Never spoke to us."

"Or us to him."

"We also never asked."

"But our hands were full."

As three cops pass, I nod and smile, lowering my voice, "Gotta be Internal Affairs."

"That'd be my guess."

Just then he notices us and abruptly closes Nelson's door.

"That's a fine how-do-ya-do," I frown at Stuart.

"No shit." He takes my arm to move us on. "I wouldn't spend any time worrying about it."

I instinctively reach for my timer, hesitate, then leave it in my pocket.

"Hey, is it my imagination—you know, all caught up in my *depressive anxiety*—or is Nelson avoiding us."

"Huh?"

"Just then. Notice how when...*what's his name* saw us and closed the door, Nelson just stared at the floor?"

Stuart thinks for a moment and frowns. "Could be. Maybe. Who knows?"

Approaching the exit, I push aside Stuart's hand and get the door myself. "Well that's fuckin' specific."

We are silent on the way to the car—and most of the way to the morgue.

During that silence, I can't help but think of Angie. It's as though a film reel is playing all the highlights of our best memories together. Between suppressing tears and managing anger boiling in my chest, I try enjoying the happy memories. Unfortunately, I'm having a hard time finding peace.

I also find it odd how *the face* shows up the day we get this news—especially since we haven't seen him since the Johansen case—and needs a private pow-wow with our boss. It makes me wonder if he's looking over my shoulder again.

# CHAPTER TWELVE

PULLING UP TO THE MORGUE, STUART PUTS THE CAR INTO PARK AND I grab his arm.

"Stu?"

"Yeah?"

"I'm sorry. Back there." Deep breath. "When I shut you out."

"No worries. She was your best friend."

"Thanks. Actually...*second* best."

Smiling, he turns off the car.

"You *do know* this is some fucked up *bullshit*."

"Yeah," he snorts. "We've...*you've* just got to trust your instincts."

Fiddling with a charm on my keyring, I close my eyes and roll my neck. Taking a breath, I look at him. "Thanks partner. For always having my back."

"Always."

INSIDE THE MORGUE, I'm not prepared for what comes next.

On more occasions than I care to admit, I've seen victims in their vulnerable state of finality. However, not once in all my years, have I seen someone who was or had been close to me lying dead on an autopsy table. The pain is crushing—and more than I can handle.

While I'm trying hard to disconnect emotionally, Jackie—the coroner on duty and a close friend—prepares a quiet place so we can have time with Angie before her mother is contacted. As much as I want to be strong for Stuart, myself, or Jackie, I simply cannot do it. That's when I lean into the shoulder of my partner.

After several excruciating minutes, I pull away from his soaked shoulder and attempt to regain my composure. Returning his soaked handkerchief, I force a smile. "So much for not losing my shit."

As we approach the table, I hesitate pulling back the cover, but I know I must do it in order to get to a place where I can better understand it.

"You okay?" Stuart whispers behind me.

"Yeah..."

"Understood."

Walking to the other side of the table, Stuart watches as I pull back the sheet. We both examine her face and all I can think is, *If only the dead could talk.*

Stuart and I share more than a cubicle and a service car in our line of work. Besides the professional aspect, we share a deep friendship. It's deeper than mere co-workers; we're more like soulmates.

"What I don't get..." he begins slowly, "and this is where you can call me Captain Obvious, is the *why*. Was she drinking too much? Were pills involved? Did she exercise? What'd she eat like? I mean, given the evening you two just enjoyed, not to mention the fact her business was *banging*..."

Nodding, I remain quiet.

"I suppose it could be a heart attack—between her weight and the stress of work—but on the other side of the coin, I recall you mentioning something about a new man in her life she was enjoying."

Another nod. More silence.

"She had it all: a thriving business, plenty of money, companionship, and best of all, a great friend in *you*."

Our eyes meet and I smile.

"Thank you. I agree. And the real kicker? We had the sort of friendship where we told one another *everything*. I mean, as far as I know, we didn't have any sec—"

CLANG!

Whipping my head toward a tray behind me, I see a scalpel coming to rest on the floor. Stuart and I look at one another, and I involuntarily rub both arms.

"Yeah, me, too," he smiles nervously.

"That's pretty whack," I mumble. "And not—"

"Nope."

Entering, Jackie asks, "You two okay?"

She approaches with a hug.

"Yeah, girl, we're okay. And thanks."

Nodding, she smiles. "She was one of the good ones."

The three of us look at Angie and remain silent for a long moment.

"I appreciate your taking care of her. And I know you have to, well, since she doesn't have any siblings, her father's passed, and her mother just landed in an assisted living community, I'm more than happy to help with all arrangements."

She nods.

"And even though all facts seem to be pointing to natural causes, I just, I feel like maybe we should…" I drop my head, feeling the weight of sadness overtake me. Not sure what to do, I look at Stuart.

"Pat, take your time," Jackie says. "There's no rush."

"I know, but this is important. I mean, what if *it's not* natural causes."

Jackie's eyebrows raise. "Right. I mean, it's possible," she says, flipping pages of a clipboard. "The officer on duty reported nothing out of the ordinary. And without examining deeper, it all *appears* normal."

"But we don't *really* know," I mumble.

Stuart nods. "Agreed."

She shrugs and looks from Stuart to me.

"We read the report's initial assumption of heart attack. Any reason we couldn't double check, you know, to be sure it's not something else."

Jackie's expression slowly morphs from curiosity to recognition. "Tercel?"

"Maybe," I say, crossing to pick up the scalpel that had fallen to the floor. "And not to get too *Woo-Woo*, but for starters, would someone please tell me how this knife just up and falls off your tray? Across the room. With no one around."

She shrugs. "You've got me there. Although I have some thoughts about it."

"And I'd love to hear all of them. But first things first. We have to move forward. Time is of the essence and all that. Look, *if* Tercel were to be behind this—which I have very strong feelings about, and you know how rarely I use the word *very*—then it's critical we find those answers. Sooner than later. Stu and I are heading to her place now to see what clues we might find. We'll be just blocks from my house, so it doesn't make sense to drive all the way back out here—"

"Of course not. And you know what?" She smiles. "I can start an autopsy. Soon. And see what we can learn. I should have all the info I need by the end of the day."

"Perfect, Jackie, and thanks," Stuart says. "And do us a solid?"

"Of course," she nods. "Under the radar."

"We're gonna solve this, girls," I squeeze Jackie's hand. Then turning to Angie, I lean close and whisper, "But I'm gonna need your help.

# CHAPTER THIRTEEN

THREE CITY BLOCKS FROM MY HOUSE, WE ARRIVE AT ANGIE'S HOME and park out front. There is no crime scene tape, but across the front door is a statement declaring it illegal to proceed without proper credentials. I slide a credit card into the seam and pop it apart before using a key Angie gave me.

Entering Angie's home makes me feel odd because I half expect to see her coming down the hall—a broad smile across her face, waving like she always did—asking us in for a glass of wine or a cocktail.

The place smells of her Chanel perfume.

Inside the great room, I glance out the wide picture window, knowing Angie and I would never again enjoy girl talk out on the back deck—glasses of wine in hand—watching the sun set over the ocean.

"You okay?" Stuart asks from across the room.

"Not really," I say before turning to him with a forced smile.

"Take your time. I'm gonna hit the head. I'm guessing it's—"

"End of the hall on the right," I toss a thumb over my shoulder.

As he leaves the room, I sit in her favorite chair and recall the talks we enjoyed over the past year.

Closing my eyes, I listen. "*Angie Myers, Southern California's Premiere Real Estate Agent, how may I be of service?*"

The number of times I heard her say that phrase when she didn't know I was calling numbered in the dozens. Another phrase for which she was known, especially when flirting with waiters decades younger,

"*I could so hurt that young boy.*" And my favorite, usually imparted during many a girl's weekend, "*Two cocktails are socially acceptable, and three never hurt anyone, but four is how you get the* real *party started.*"

Looking around her immaculate home, I notice several picture frames stacked atop one another and pushed to the back of a shelf. Knowing her obsession with tidiness, I'm certain that was something she'd never do. I cross the room and pick up the stack. One photo is of a bunch of us girls on the beach not a mile from here; it was a weekend we got together for a wine and cheese sunset. Several others include a variety of real estate events she attended. There's a collage of boyfriends she dated over the past decade, and one of her favorites is a large frame of her and her parents just before her father passed away.

I'm about to set the stack aside when a photo slips out and falls to the floor. Picking it up, I look closely.

My stomach drops for no reason whatsoever. It's Angie standing with a man I've never seen before. He seems oddly familiar, but I don't know why. *Must be the guy she met at her girlfriend's wedding in Vegas.*

Built like a bodybuilder, he was handsome as hell with long, blonde hair and a deep tan. *That's odd.*

Looking out the picture window to the deck, I know the exact spot where that photo was taken. Crossing the room, I'm not sure why it catches my eye, but I notice how the position of the sun in the photo is about the same as it is now. Plus, the plant behind them appears to be exactly the same size. Holding the photo up, I compare the photo to the actual scene. *Wait, if we haven't met, but he was from Vegas—*

A flush down the hall snaps me back and an odd sensation sends chills down my back as Stuart enters the room.

"What's up?"

"Just thinking. Why?"

"You look odd."

"Thanks."

"No, I mean—"

"I got it," I smirk. "I know this sounds crazy and won't likely make any sense, at least not this minute, but two things seem *particularly* off. First, a *very* similar thing happened exactly the same way a year ago."

Catching myself, I shake my head and start pushing the image away.

"What? And when you say *year,* do you mean—"

"Yes. And I know this is *completely* random, but when I heard the toilet flush, I had this sudden flashback to that moment I was in Tercel's home—there in his art gallery—just before he came down the hall and caught me discovering his *artwork.*"

"Hell yeah, I remember. I mean, I couldn't actually *see* you two because Jackie and I were in the bushes waiting to come out and arrest that mother—"

"Right, and of all the random moments to recall."

"Things come back to us when they do. Doesn't need a rhyme or reason. What's the second thing?" he asks, nodding toward the picture in my hand.

I hand it to him. "Tell me what you think," I say, returning to the window, trying to place the significance of the buzzing in my head.

"Handsome dude. Guessing a surfer? Her neighbor?"

"You're probably right. Just…" I wave him over. "See that plant?" I point to the deck. "It's the same in the photo."

"Yeah?"

"It hasn't grown an inch."

"*Okaaaaaay.*"

"That's California Morning Glory. My mother grew them in our yard when we were kids. I distinctly remember how they grow wicked fast—like inches every couple of days."

Stuart looks from the photo to the plant, then heads out to the deck. "Come with me."

Outside, the ocean breeze smells nice, the sun is warm, and happy memories of Angie flow over me.

"Okay, talk to me."

"All right," I take the picture. "And it's probably no biggie, but Angie bought that plant *maybe* two weeks ago. On my recommendation. I also told her the exact plant food to get. As I said, I've been around them all my life."

Stuart looks at me like I'm wearing a lampshade.

"Okay goofball, I'll cut to the chase. First, that plant should be, I don't know, three, maybe four inches taller than it is—if say two weeks have gone by. And no, she didn't trim it because she has the worst green thumb ever."

He looks at me: *And?*

"Okay, which means the photo was taken inside the last day or two. *Maybe* three, but doubtful."

"Yeah?"

"And there's a *hella-gorgeous man* standing here with Angie."

"Established fact," he rolls his eyes. "*Sooooo?*"

"So, he pops into her life out of nowhere. More importantly, I'd've known about him!"

Rubbing his brow like it's being crushed, he takes a deep breath. "Okay, let me see if I understand. So, a handsome dude…likely a surfer from…" he says, waving his arm like a gameshow model, "anywhere in this *entire* Manhattan Beach community, stops by to say hello to Angie."

"And just *happens* to snag a photo with her?"

"Could. Why not?"

"Except that—"

"What?"

I snatch the photo from his hand. "Okay, Mr. Panties-in-a-bunch, except look at her expression. That's not an expression of, *Hey, I'm a neighbor who just wanted to swing by and snag a pic of me and you.* No, that's a photo of two people who know one another *very well*. See the way they're holding one another's sides? Comfortably. Closely. *Intimately.* About the only thing *off* is that she looks—I don't know— maybe a bit scared? I mean, I've known her a long time and…"

Stuart just stares at me.

"Not to mention the bunch of flowers on the table behind them," I point. "Tied in a red ribbon. With a card attached. *That's* two people who know one another very well. And while I don't *know* him…I know who he *reminds* me of."

Stuart's expression slowly shifts from impatient confusion to instant recognition.

# CHAPTER FOURTEEN

AN HOUR PASSES AND I'M SITTING ON THE EDGE OF HER BED GOING through what I quickly assume is a journal or diary when I hear Stuart in the other room. For the most part, he's mumbling. I continue reading and flip to a section dated nine months ago where Angie describes how much she misses her time with Darius, and how she wasn't feeling as grounded as she did when they were having sessions.

"Oh, boy," Stuart mumbles.

I hesitate a second, then return to my reading.

"Not good," he mutters much too loudly.

Still trying to ignore him, I leaf ahead several more pages—representing another month or two—finding an entry where she discusses returning to anxiety meds because she wasn't feeling as level-headed as she would like.

Pages later, I get an inside look into my friend. In one section, she describes in exact detail about recurring dreams she was having about Darius. They involve a lot of sex.

Angie's steamy secrets are suddenly interrupted by, "Oh shit, Patricia," Stuart says, coming down the hall.

"Come here," he motions me to follow.

In her office, he sits at a desk with a stack of ledgers spread open. The closet door is open and in the bottom sits a safe. The door is open.

Looking up from paperwork, he follows my stare.

"Stuart, tell me you didn't open that yourself."

"Actually, I did," he grins.

"And when did you become a safecracker?"

"McCloud."

"I thought he got caught in traffic," I say, walking to the window to see if he's arrived.

"He did. Should be here shortly. But no, remember during the Johansen case when he told us how he cracked her phones?"

Now, I grin. "You sneaky little devil."

"Yeah, right?" He taps his pad with a finger. "You know I write *everything* down. Okay, that was so ingenious, I thought I'd try it. And since I knew her birthdate from the death certificate report and her pet's name," he points to a framed photo of her cat on the wall. *Baxter* was written in sparkly letters on the frame. "I just plugged in her house number and added the pound sign."

Looking at his notes, I read: 020869Baxter#.

"Think you're smart, huh?"

"Yes. However..." His expression darkens.

"What?"

Laying aside a document, he turns the bank ledger in my direction and points to a column of entries.

"Her savings account. See this first column? It's what she saved and/or invested. See this one?" He points. "It's the *source* of that allocation."

At first, all I see are numbers. "Okay." After a moment, "Wait."

He nods.

"Oh. Shit."

"Yep. That $250,000 dollars is directed to one Shay Norelli. And as you'll see in the memo, for her college education. But—"

"I had no—"

"I know you didn't. But it gets worse."

"*What?*"

"That is," he snorts, "if becoming *rich* is your idea of getting *worse*."

Picking up the document, *Last Will & Testament*, he turns to the last page.

"Direct your attention to *whom* the house in which you're currently living belongs—upon her death."

I squint.

"That $4.2 million dollar home? Belongs to *you*."


STUART and I are staring at one another in shock when a knock at the front door jolts us. We walk down the hall as McCloud enters. He approaches Stuart first, extending his hand for a fist bump.

"S'up, buddy," he says to Stuart while looking at me oddly.

"Hiya, McCloud," Stuart says.

"And what's up with Detective Looks-Like-She's-Seen-A-Ghost?"

Lost, I stare.

"Sorry, that was, uh, in really poor taste. I am truly an asshole."

Ignoring the comment, I approach for a hug. After a warm embrace, I pull away, kissing his cheek.

"All good, McCloud. Being an asshole is just part of your charm," I wink.

"Thanks. I think."

Stuart dismisses the comment with a shrug and says, "Okay, we've got some good news and some not so good. Which do you want first? And nothing can leave these ten square feet," he says, drawing an imaginary square at our feet.

"Let's start with the good," McCloud looks up from our shoes. "There's been enough bad going around the past month."

"The good? We think it's *not* suicide."

McCloud squints. "And that's conclusive?"

"Nearly," I say.

"The bad, on the other hand…" Stuart continues, "is that *we think* it's murder."

"Shut the front door," McCloud says. "For real? Wait, I heard it was a heart attack."

Realizing how tense I've become, I roll my neck, popping it several times.

"Here's where some of this went slightly off the track," Stuart sighs. "A neighbor shows up early this morning to return Angie's cat. Evidently, he'd gotten out and was next door aggravating their dog. Neighbor knocks. No answer. She checks to see if her car was here—which it was—and knocks again. Still no answer. Knowing Angie was both an early bird and a severe creature of habit—like OCD level—she uses her key and enters. After calling out her name, seeing the house untouched, and hearing nothing, she proceeds to the master where she finds her still in bed. After getting no response, she calls the cops."

"It gets better," I chime in. "A local cop arrives and investigates. He doesn't see anything that suggests any trouble and *assumes* it's a heart attack. He calls his patrol Sergeant. They decide, or perhaps better, they again *assume* it has all the markings of a heart attack. Then, after speaking to someone who knows I'm a neighbor, they bypass calling the coroner and instead put in a call to our precinct whereupon someone is called to pick up the body. However, as soon as I get wind of it, I redirect them to see Jackie who's currently awaiting further instructions."

"And here you are," Stuart smirks.

"Wow," McCloud mumbles. "That's concise."

"So, as you can see, while it *wasn't* officially a murder investigation? It is *now*."

"And all we now need is the killer," Stuart adds.

McCloud stares at both of us for a long beat. "Yeah, that'd help. Like a lot."

# CHAPTER FIFTEEN

STUART, MCCLOUD, AND I SPEND ANOTHER TWENTY MINUTES searching the place but come up empty. There was no break-in, no mess left behind, nothing valuable taken, no suicide notes, no odd medicines laying about. Nothing.

In fact, the only thing of note is a photograph of a handsome, obviously friendly, and mysterious stranger Angie hadn't told me about.

*Unless he's the realtor from Vegas, aka new boy toy.*

We give McCloud the mission of wiring her home with tiny time-lapse cameras to watch over the place for the next several days. While I can't imagine the killer—if there is one—returning to the scene, I'll feel better safe than doubtful. The three of us agree to circle around tomorrow morning when Jackie will be available to complete the reunion.

After McCloud leaves, Stuart organizes and photographs the documents. We decide it's smart to have a personal backup, especially since we have little clue what *the face* is up to. If Internal Affairs is watching us—for whatever reason—we want to be ahead of and not behind any potential challenges. And considering there's about four-and-a-half million dollars in cash and real estate potentially heading in my direction, there's no doubt I'll soon be under a microscope. I doubt anyone will care, much less believe me, when I tell them I had *zero* idea about any of it.

It never ceases to amaze me how no matter how long someone

works with people and no matter how diligently they keep their integrity intact, there is always someone somewhere who will attempt to soil that reputation. Tracing the events of the past week, I try putting the pieces together.

*The photo is clearly a clue, but who was it? Why was he here? Why was the photo hidden among the frames? Or was it? Had the photo been taken within the past several days? Whoever took the photo would be a key to the puzzle.*

We're wrapping up and ready to roll when I ring Captain Nelson to tell him what we found. He isn't available and, given the sensitive nature of the findings, we don't leave a message—except to have his secretary tell him we called and to call us back immediately.

As we lock up and head out, I stop Stuart on the front stoop.

"Okay, let me address the elephant on the porch," I smile. "Tercel's been gone a year. But something tells me, and tell me if you think otherwise, that if he were to have stuck around, we would've seen him by now."

Stuart frowns deep. "As big as LA is?"

I shrug.

"Not sure if I *completely* agree," he mumbles, looking out at the beach.

"Way I see it…" I continue, "he cashed in all his chips which means he has all the money he needs and is or has been trying to figure out what to do next."

"And just maybe he's not within a hundred miles of us right now. Hell, maybe not within three thousand miles of us."

*PING!*

It's a text from Jackie saying she just got called in on a case and will chat with us first thing in the morning. I text an affirmative, and since logic suggests we call it a day, we head to Stuart's home.

AFTER TEN MINUTES of silence down the road, he finally says, "You okay, partner?"

"Yeah," I mumble, staring straight ahead. "Stu?"

"Yeah?"

"Something started coming to me—mostly in a subconscious way —when Nelson first shared the news about Angie."

"What's that?"

"It was weird, but about the time you two were asking me questions, I had this feeling, and I know it's crazy—maybe even paranoid —but..."

"Talk to me."

I stare out the window before turning to face him. "You *know* there's going to be some serious questions coming my way. *Some*where, *some*one will put me in the spotlight."

He confirms with a nod. "Look, I know you didn't have a thing to do with it. No way, shape, or form. But to your point, here are my thoughts, *especially* in light of what we've just found. And I gotta say again, I'm heartbroken for Angie and her family. And for you. Just tragic. And as much as we secretly hope it was a heart attack—which Jackie'll confirm—it does feel wonky."

"Just the word I was going to use."

"And c'mon, the bank statements and college tuition? The deed? Is it nice? Of course! Could it all be legit? Maybe. But will it look good? No huffing way. Will it draw massive attention? Hell, yes. And as much as I hate to say this..."

"What?"

"As cliche as this sounds..." he snorts, "it's gonna get worse before it gets better. And when Nelson finds out?" He whistles.

"No shit. And about Nelson. You think there's any way we can sit on—" I stop mid-sentence as a thought hits me. "Oh shit!"

"What?"

"What's-his-name, *the face*? What if he's—"

"Internal Affairs," Stuart nods. "Of course. And when he puts it together—"

"I'm double-fucked!"

*PING!*

It's McCloud's text: *The Face's name is Jonathan Davenport. New York office.*

Staring at Stuart, I rub both arms and hum the Twilight Zone theme, "*Woo, woo, woo, woo....*"

# CHAPTER SIXTEEN

PULLING UP TO STUART'S HOME, I PUT THE CAR IN PARK AND LEAVE IT running. We're silent for a moment as Stuart fiddles with a pen, and I, my key ring.

We simultaneously say, "I think—"

He snorts, "Go ahead."

"There are only two ways for me to approach this. I can stay put, work the facts, hope for the best, and see where that gets me—with the understanding that the situation is likely to blow up in my face. Maybe ours, but *certainly* mine."

"Or?"

"Or, I can hop a flight and see if I can track down—"

"Wait, what?" He says so loudly, I jump. "Track down who, Tercel? Who could be—who knows where?" He laughs. "Are you insane?"

"Really?" I squint, rubbing my ear. "Just hear me out. Before you throw me under the bus."

"You know better'n that."

"Yes, I do. But look, there are things we know and things we don't."

"Brilliant."

"Trust me, I have more insights into this lunatic's mind than anyone. And it starts with the love letter inside the book he delivered to my hospital room nearly a year ago. Seems more like a month," I mumble.

He rolls his eyes. "Don't tell me that's still on—"

"Would you please stop interrupting me? After I share thoughts, you can shoot holes in every one of them."

He grins.

"I'll run them in the order I think is most likely. *Hunches,* anyway, okay?"

He waves for me to proceed.

"Thank you," I grin. "One: the letter *specifically* names Australia. *Not* Hawaii. *Not* Costa Rica. *Not* Bali. *Not* Indonesia, which would be the *second* choice, but no, he said *Australia*. And before you give me a history lesson on how large it is, I already know the entire country is roughly three million square miles."

He shakes his head.

"Two: there are actually only five *major* cities in the entire country. Sydney, perhaps the most *obvious* choice and the biggest—as the capital of New South Wales. For now, it's among my two top picks. A solid second choice would be Melbourne, southwest of Sydney and the capital of the state of Victoria. Third is Adelaide, a cosmopolitan coastal capital, but not on my hit list. Not *sexy* enough. That leaves Perth on the west coast which *could* be my second choice because it's the *furthest* away, but I'm saying no. Bottom line and inside my top two choices? Brisbane. Why? As the capital of Queensland, it's modern, hip, and best of all, has some of the world's most beautiful beaches. And women."

Stuart starts to say something but shakes his head and stops.

"Also, he *specifically* mentioned *beaches*. And Brisbane, or better yet the neighboring city of Gold Coast, attracts some of the best *surfers* in the world."

"What's surfing got to do with it?"

"Part gut, part research. He often talked about what he liked to do on his time off and there were only two things he ever mentioned. Visiting museums because of his love of art and how he had taken up surfing. In fact, he mentioned having hopes of being able to master it someday. He began surfing when he moved out to the Malibu house, but because of a hectic work schedule, he didn't have time to perfect the sport as hoped. I figure now that he has all the time and money he could ever need, he'd go to the place where legends are made."

"But what about Hawaii?"

"True. A potentially good *backup* choice. As it's closer, but perhaps *too* close to home. Too easy to predict. Don't you think?"

He shrugs.

"Okay, now for the research. Brisbane is known for the Queensland Gallery of Modern Art, one of Australia's major contemporary art museums."

"Okay, so you mentioned his love of art. Aren't there other cities that—"

"Excellent, and yes. So, Sydney has the Opera House where it's more about music while Melbourne has an impressive performing arts complex but *not* the museums. Adelaide has museums, but they're mostly indigenous work, not fine or modern—the sort he *collects*. So, again, it's mostly hunch but grounded in logic."

"This has been a great geography class," he smirks, "but it's still a wild-ass hunch. And I probably shouldn't ask, but just how long have you been percolating on this?"

"Uh, pretty much...this past year."

He scratches his chin, trying to hide a grin. "I'll give you props for doing your homework. And for listening to your instincts—one of your finer traits. But you do realize and will agree with me—along with pretty much anyone else on the *planet*—that it's *more* than a stretch."

"Ridiculous, yes, but I think—as the saying goes—it's worth the stretch."

He gives me a sideways glance. "And because I know you so well, what's the remainder of your wild-ass scheme?"

This feels like the moment of truth. While I'm uncertain and even a bit confused, there's a part of me that knows deep down my instincts are right—or at the very least, close. Besides, if Internal Affairs gets ahead of this and me, I'll be in a situation without any control.

"Wild-ass? Yes," I sigh. "Ridiculous? Likely. But if my gut is right about Davenport being part of the trouble that is to come, then what do I really have to lose?"

"And you've considered the costs?"

"Sure. It'll be expensive. And will take time—most of which would be difficult to get permission for *if* I were to ask. But Stu, all I'm asking is for you to listen to my process, and if you think I'm completely out of my mind, I won't give it another thought and completely play it your way. Fair?"

Shifting in his seat to face me, he stares with an expression that says *No*—until a nod gives me the go-ahead.

"Look, I know I'm, uh, more than a bit all over the place, and it's a high-risk, potentially low-reward situation. But, I don't know, it just feels like the right thing to do. Well, for me, maybe the *only* thing to do. Besides, I'd rather get ahead of things, circumventing permission, than to be in the thick of things and having to get permission. And knowing they'd never give it to me. Does this make any sense, my voice of reason?"

His tiny grin gives way to a nod.

"Besides, I have plenty of vacation time accrued and more than enough miles saved to go anywhere I need. And I've got a little cash—"

"Uh, *more* than enough cash, if—"

"I'm not *even* considering any of that," I roll my eyes. "But look, I can be there in fifteen, sixteen hours, sniff around, and get back—who knows, probably in a long weekend."

His expression says he doesn't buy it.

"Okay, maybe a day or two more, but I'll pick *one* city, two at the most, and if I can't find any evidence of him by the third, I'll come back."

"Uh huh."

"Stu, I have a *very* strong feeling about this. And you know I've got the chops to find him."

"And you're using that word again."

"Huh?"

"*Very.*"

I smack his arm. "Don't forget I sat on his couch and had way too many long conversations. Plus, I've studied him relentlessly."

"True."

"And named him *The Poser.*"

"True—with help from me."

"Hell, it wouldn't have happened without you. We both know that."

"Okay, I get it. I'm with you. Just…" he sighs, "be sure to tell me what you have in mind."

"Of course."

"And give me an idea where to find you. Not if, but *when* the proverbial shit hits the fan."

"It won't."

Giving me his best Dwayne "The Rock" Johnson eyebrow raise, we enjoy a laugh.

AFTER LEAVING STUART, I swing by my favorite wine store Manhattan Wines on Artesia and pick up two bottles. Once home, I'm out of my company clothes and into a pair of worn jeans and a comfy sweatshirt in a flash, snacking on Italian salami and cheese. Into my second glass of wine, I think of Angie and how she was always able to cheer me up no matter what. Sadly, that will never happen again.

I can't seem to escape the emptiness, so I grab my glass of wine and go out to the deck for some fresh air. Climbing into the oversized beach chair, I enjoy a view of the ocean over the rooftop of my neighbor's house. Within minutes, I realize how the adrenaline of the day is keeping me from winding down and, taking that as a sign, grab my second bottle of wine and head to Angie's house.

Within minutes, I'm going through the diaries I found earlier. One series must've been made at the direction of Tercel because they feel more systematic than soulful. Next, I run across a medical diary on her mother who is evidently suffering from early Alzheimers—making me wonder if Angie might have suffered in a similar way.

Finally, I find a small diary dedicated to just Angie and our friendship. It's pink and has a pocket on the front where she inserted a photo from one of our beach outings. It's super sweet and I cry through the entire book. Near the end, I find an entry that could help me should Internal Affairs push me into a corner. It's a note about how she wants to do something special for me and Shay in light of the significant financial windfall she received from selling all of Tercel's properties. The entry was made a week ago and contained no specifics, but I need something that links her with Australia.

I go to her bedroom and begin snooping through the master closet. It is full of handsome and expensive clothes and enough shoes to make Imelda Marcos blush. Finding nothing significant, I'm ready to give up.

*PING!*

Startled, I see it's a text from Stuart, checking to see if I was okay or needed anything. I tell him no, blowing him an emoticon kiss. I then slide the phone into my back pocket. But because I'm tired, buzzed, or both, I drop it. Getting down on all fours, I find it under the bed—along with something that catches my eye.

Under the bed is a shallow storage container. Instead of plastic, it's wooden. I slide the box out and see a four-digit combination lock, currently set to 0000.

Channeling my "inner McCloud," I try the first four digits that come to mind: her birth month and year. It doesn't work. Next, I try her house number—luckily only four numbers. No go.

Returning to her office, I rummage through documents, recalling I've never seen her social security number. I return and try the last four digits. No such luck.

Frustrated and thirsty, I go to the kitchen for some water and, while drinking, recall the photo of "mystery man."

Taking down the stack of picture frames, I look through them again, but find nothing new. Putting the pictures back, I recall the photo I kept —the one of her and the long-haired guy. Taking it from my jacket, I stare at him, trying to make sense of it. Nothing comes to mind, so I disregard and return to the bedroom. That's when an idea comes to me.

Crouching down, I enter 1078. It's Tercel's birth month and year, something I learned in last year's research. Odd coincidence: we share the same birth month while Tercel is three years older.

*Bingo.*

Opening the box, I discover how profound that revelation is. Inside are stacks upon stacks of newspaper and magazine clippings of Tercel, along with photos from a wide variety of sources and numerous articles referring to his impressive "Therapist to the Stars" legacy. It's a scrap-book of his life history.

"Takes obsession to a whole new level," I mumble aloud.

I'm about to text Stuart when I consider the hour and decide to catch up tomorrow. Returning the photos, I suddenly spot something buried in the bottom corner. Digging, I remove a paper clipped together with a stack of postcards from Hawaii, Switzerland, Germany, Hong Kong, Bora Bora, and *Australia*. Each locale is represented by one card, except Australia which has three: Sydney, Melbourne, and Brisbane.

*Thanks, Angie.*

# CHAPTER SEVENTEEN

THE NEXT MORNING—AFTER A SOBERING RUN, A SCALDING SHOWER, and a half pot of coffee—I pick up Stuart from his home and brief him on what I found last night. Taking him through the process step-by-step, he listens intently while making his way through an "all the way" bagel. As I finish my notes, we look at one another with matching nods.

"Right?"

"Certainly adds some...perspective," he says.

"Stu, when I leave town, would you take care of my baby?" I smile, stroking the dash like it's a purring kitten.

"What kinda question is that? Hell yeah."

"But you put one little dent in her and our friendship is over. Forever."

"I promise not to pull a stunt like Jesús did with your first baby."

"Good, 'cause it'd be terrible for your new son to grow up without a father."

This is one time I don't mind facing thick traffic because it gives us time to discuss next steps. My emotions have been a roller coaster, but Stuart's good at keeping me on point. My discovery releases significant tension for both of us, and even though it means I'll have a great deal of area to cover, it provides us confirmation.

"Back to your question, and I get where your head is," he says. "Disappearing during an investigation will certainly raise eyebrows, but I'm sure they'll cut you slack because of your relationship to Angie."

"The fact IA shows up a day *before* our discovery baffles me, though."

"Could be any number of things. Could also be paranoid we think his appearance has anything to do with us."

Bypassing the 10, I jump on Washington Boulevard, and by the time I hit the intersection at Western, traffic is at a standstill. Checking my watch, I take a deep breath.

"We're okay. And I promise, today's the last day. Car'll be outta the shop tomorrow."

I'm silent, thinking back to the photo of the mystery man.

"Where's your head?"

"Still wondering about the guy in the photo."

"You're just pissed because you didn't find him *first*," he winks.

As Western Boulevard opens, the traffic releases. With that brief respite, my thoughts return to Angie before shifting to Tercel.

*RING!*

It's Captain Nelson. I look at Stuart and frown.

*RING!*

Checking the screen, he shrugs. "May not be the worst news."

*RING!*

I take a deep breath. "Norelli."

"Morning, Detective. How ya holding up?"

"Good, sir. As best as can be expected. Thanks for asking."

I look to Stuart and mouth, *What the fuck.*

"Of course. I'm guessing Brown's with you? You two heading in?"

"Yes, sir. What's up?"

Stuart reaches over to hit mute on the dash. "Someone's in the office with him. Play along."

Unmute.

"Just checking in on you. And Norelli?"

"Sir?"

"I need you and Brown to swing by my office the moment you arrive."

"Of course, sir. We're running behind because of an accident—"

"Don't need a traffic report. Just stop in when you get here. Okay, gotta run."

I suddenly fight the urge to vomit.

"Don't do it," Stuart looks at me and grins. "It'll never come out of the carpet."

"I'm fine."

"So that band of sweat on your forehead is what exactly?"

"Funny," I smack his arm. "What do you suppose that's about?"

"Davenport was standing there. Which is—wait—Nelson *does* know about, I mean, you *did* call and fill him in last night, right?"

Silence.

"Pat? You told me that—"

"No, I didn't."

Cocking his head, he smirks.

In my distress and exhaustion last night, I finished both bottles of wine and vaguely recall making a nightcap.

He stares at me.

"Or two."

His stare doesn't shift.

"Oh shit. I called you, didn't I?"

"I wondered what..." he slowly offered a nod. "Well, it was a helluva day."

We let the silence guide us to the next intersection of Santa Monica Boulevard.

"Pat, do me a large, will ya?"

I roll my eyes. "Stu, you heard the Captain."

He shakes his head.

"What?"

"Look who's worried about being late. This time last year, you couldn't be *bribed* to get to work early."

"Oh, shut it. And let me guess, Trejo's?"

His goofy grin always makes me laugh.

Trejo's Coffee & Donuts is the invention of Danny Trejo, an actor who stars in hyper-violent B-movies. People say he's an incredibly nice guy who makes remarkable donuts.

"Thought it'd help, ya know, grease the skids."

Now, I grin, "Just be sure I get a couple *Da Berry Bombs*."

# CHAPTER EIGHTEEN

A HALF HOUR LATER, STUART—A BOX OF DONUTS IN HAND—AND I stop at our desks on the way to Nelson's office. I transfer coffee to my mug and check myself in a mirror on my file cabinet while Stuart grabs a fistful of napkins.

"We're not auditioning for a commercial," Stuart says between licks of a donut.

"It's called nerves, *bitch*," I wink.

Arriving at Nelson's office, we offer a donut to his secretary who asks us to wait because Nelson was called upstairs. She declines with a smile, and Stuart takes a seat, proceeding to scroll headlines on his phone. I get caught up on texts. Shay checks in with a sweet note, and Dad asks how my week has been. I haven't shared the news yet.

"Okay, before we head in…" Stuart leans in to whisper, keeping an eye on the secretary. "We know Davenport's gonna show up, so just, you know, keep your cool. We're doing everything by the book."

A smile belies my nervousness. "Which means I'm suspended pending further investigation. Or, would it be insane to think—"

Just then, Nelson comes barreling down the hall—Davenport in tow. Nelson has an uncomfortable expression: less nervous, more strained. Davenport has an odd expression: less friendly, more snarky. I feel my energy disappear as a wave of anxiety washes over me.

"Detectives," Nelson nods. "Join us," he waves us to follow.

Inside his office, he says, "Officer Davenport, these are Detectives

Pat Norelli and Stuart Brown. This is Jonathan Davenport from Internal Affairs."

Nelson pours a cup of coffee from a thermos on his credenza. Motioning for us to sit, he takes a slurp. Davenport stands at attention off to the side.

"Okay, let's just dive in. Detective Norelli, would you get us started by sharing the chain of events from the moment you received the news of your friend, Angie, up until let's say, end of day yesterday. And Detective Brown, feel free to jump in as you see fit."

I SPEND the next twenty-plus minutes giving a play-by-play of exactly what happened from the time we met for dinner, through when we walked to her house, and then where we ended up at my home. Stuart pipes in occasionally, mainly to clarify a timestamp in the procedure. Davenport doesn't speak and listens closely, periodically shifting his gaze from us to his notepad. My intention is to remain factually specific without coloring with emotion. It's difficult, but I keep tears at bay for nearly the entire time.

When I finish, Davenport releases a dramatic exhale, returns his notepad to his pocket, and completely shifts his energy by sitting on the corner of Nelson's desk, a move that apparently doesn't please Nelson.

"Nicely done," Davenport says plainly. "And from what I've learned, completely on point."

I feel my shoulders begin to relax.

"Mostly."

*What?*

"However…" Davenport squints at the ceiling as though overhead lights were blinding him, "several facts have come to my attention that were *not* included in your description."

He looks over his shoulder from Nelson to both of us.

I look from Stuart to Nelson and back to Davenport.

The four of us stare as though awaiting a ball to drop.

"*And?*" I finally say.

"And Detective Norelli, the several missing facts are infinitely more *significant* than you can imagine."

*Oh, for fuck's sake, spit it out.*

"Captain Nelson, would you kindly share with Detectives Norelli and Brown what we have learned..." he pauses, turning to eyeball Nelson, "that makes this apparent tragedy more than it appears."

As Davenport turns back to face us, Nelson—behind Davenport's back—rolls his eyes and shakes his head with an expression that says, *Sorry about this.*

Rounding his desk, he positions himself in front of Davenport. The move appears to upstage Davenport and, as he begins to stand, Nelson places a hand on his shoulder and forces a smile.

"To begin with, I've known Patricia for many years. She came aboard straight out of school, quickly showing promise as a boot, and worked her way up through the ranks until becoming a detective. Her brother also worked here. And he worked his way up through the ranks from street cop to Sergeant, spending most of his later time managing detectives. There's also her father, the now retired Judge Samuel Norelli. So, as you can imagine, I have a long history with the Norelli family."

Davenport's expression shows impatience. Knowing Nelson, he relishes the annoyance.

"But to Officer Davenport's point, and in order to progress matters, Detective Norelli, were you aware that a sizable amount of Ms. Myer's estate was designated for your daughter?"

*How'd they learn that so quickly?*

I consider acting shocked, getting defensive, or playing it as it lies. Option three won.

"Yes, sir. I was aware of that."

Looking at Davenport, I can't tell if he's surprised at my candor or disappointed his surprise is blown. I keep going.

"Within approximately thirty minutes of our arriving at the victim's —to the home of my *friend* Angie—Detective Brown and I discovered a short stack of documents that, for lack of a better term, appeared oddly coincidental."

As Davenport is about to speak, I hold up a hand.

"That is to say, I can imagine how this looks, but for the record, I had absolutely *no* idea about it."

I want to slap the smirk off his pompous, sallow, fair-skinned face but decide to save the energy—and up the ante.

"In fact, Officer Davenport, let me offer how both of us were made aware of some real estate property that was to be—or *is* to be—

bequeathed to yours truly. And again, I had *zero* prior knowledge of this fact. I'm sure you will *not* find my signature confirming such transactions anywhere. And finally, there isn't a single inch of this story that makes sense to me. Why did my best friend—who was in good health —die suddenly and for no *proven* reason? One thing I can say with clarity is how Detective Brown and I will learn the reasons for Angie's death immediately following this meeting because we're seeing CME Jackie Corazon."

*Take that.*

In the time it takes Davenport to stand and adjust his tie, I calculate he must've gotten someone from IA into her house to find those documents. He drapes a faux smile across his face.

"That notwithstanding we, rather you, must face the fact that only days before your friend's death, not one, but *two* significant and rather sizable *donations* were to be paid to you. Yet, and pay attention because herein lies the crux of the story, *you* are the last and only person to see your friend alive. In fact, you were with her only *hours* before she passed. Not only that, because of your in-depth knowledge—thanks to lengthy research of the same—*you're* the only person, perhaps in the division, with the *specific* knowledge of how to make it appear a person dies from a suici—"

"Wait a fucking minute!" I jump up, causing both men to flinch. "That *same* knowledge works to make *anyone* believe death was from *natural* causes. And besides, a half-dozen people in our department are aware of the same thing."

If it wasn't for the fact Nelson is feet away and my partner grabs my arm, I would've enjoyed clocking that clown so hard he'd be searching the floor for his teeth.

"Okay, back in your own corners, people," Nelson says, motioning both of us to retreat. "This isn't a courtroom. Nobody's been charged with anything—"

"Not yet," Davenport mutters.

"Won't happen," I fume.

"Stop! I'm the Captain, and here's what we're going to do. First, and only because an investigation is underway…" Nelson sighs at Davenport, then turns to me, "Detective Norelli, I'm sorry to say but I have to suspend you. Just until we get several things straightened out."

"But Captain—"

He stops me with a hand. "One thing at a time, okay? You know I've got your back. As does Brown. But this is a distinctive situation where substantial facts at the very least, imply otherwise. So, effective 10 a.m. *tomorrow*," he gives me a certain look, "you're suspended until further notice."

"But I have yet to—"

"I know, there's still a lot to do. You and I will chat again today, and then you'll take a few days to just, you know, lay low—"

"And stay within city limits," Davenport mumbles.

Nelson looks like a crossing guard as he whips a hand into Davenport's face. "I'm handling this, Davenport. We discussed what you need. This is what *I* need. We're all adults here and playing by the rules. Norelli's one of my very best, so please let's wrap this meeting, and Davenport, you and I will head back upstairs. Norelli, you hang around long enough for me to handle a few things. Then you, Brown, and I will meet me back here, yes?"

Stuart takes me by the arm and says, "Yes, sir."

"Thanks. Meeting adjourned."

I waste no time brushing past Davenport with nothing but a death stare.

# CHAPTER NINETEEN

"I HAVE HAD IT!"

Still jacked-up from the meeting, I feel the heat in my pits. Officer Davenport managed to push all my buttons—no doubt putting me in the exact frame of mind he intended—creating enough doubt with our leaders that anyone with half a nugget of intuition would question my motives. Back in our office, I prop my feet on my desk and stare at the floor.

"Just look at my track record, fuck-stick."

Slouched in his chair and twirling his pen like a rock drummer, Stuart stares, looking from his shoes to my face and back again in an unconscious loop.

"C'mon, does anyone *really* think for one minute I have what it takes to do anything *remotely* close to harming my friend? And for what, *money*?"

Stuart absently nods.

"Hey, earth to Stu."

"Huh? Yeah, I know."

"You weren't even listening."

Snapping alert, he sits up straight, returns his pen to his breast pocket, and slaps his hands. "Okay, here's what I think." Looking around, he leans close. "I say we talk to your dad."

"What?"

"And your brother."

The first suggestion makes me question; the second makes me nervous.

"Wait. Why my brother?"

He looks at me and stares.

All my brother Pete ever wanted was to be a cop. He grew up in the LAPD and is a hard-working, well-respected soldier to the system where the world is black and white, and grey doesn't exist. In the beginning, he ousted anyone who bent rules to accommodate their desires; however, by the time he became Captain—moving to and becoming entrenched in the dark underbelly of Manhattan—his perspective changed dramatically.

I suddenly feel nauseous again.

"C'mon." Slipping his cellphone in a pocket, he grabs an iPad from his briefcase and waves for me to follow. "Let's grab a snack out back. Ring McCloud and tell him we need him on a Zoom call in thirty minutes."

Not waiting for me, he heads for the door. I grab my phone and follow.

Making our way down the hall, he adds, "Next, call your dad and tell him the same thing. While you're doing that, I'll ring Jackie." Punching in her number, he says, "Time to get the band back together."


Minutes later with a burrito in Stuart's mouth and a diet soft drink to my lips, we're sitting in my car with an iPad propped on my dash, waiting for others to join the call.

"You wanna tell me what's on your mind?" I sip.

"Look, there are *three* people who have the power to help us. Potentially four." Slurp. "Jackie has an inside scoop we don't—but will soon. McCloud has tech savvy we only dream about and will gladly give." Munch. "And your dad has insight we're likely missing." Burp.

"Really?" I frown, waving aside his breath. "And my brother?"

Wiping his mouth, he turns to face me. "And Pete has connections none of us have. Including Nelson."

"I'm still moving forward with my plan."

Before he can start, I stop him with a hand. "I know, you think I'm still trying to prove myself to him. That may be, but it's my reputation on the line. And yes, it's a lot of ground to cover, potentially dangerous, and all that *happy horseshit*, but I'm a Detective, for crap's sake, and this is what I'm supposed to be doing!"

*PING-PING!*

Stuart connects the call as I say, "Hey, Jackie girl."

Waving, she says, "Hey, Pats. How ya feeling?"

"Good. Confident. Yeah, pretty—"

"That shitty, huh?"

We laugh.

*PING-PING!*

It's McCloud. He waves at us as he waves away smoke. "Hey, kids!"

Frowning, I say, "I thought I told you to quit!"

"I know, *Mom*," he smirks, grounding out a butt. "Just been harder than I thought."

Stuart wipes salsa from his chin and says, "Hey, Jackie. S'up McCloud."

They wave.

"Thanks for hopping on the Zoom," Stuart says. "Reason we're calling—in a sentence—is we need help from each one of you. And the only reason I'm doing the talking is because our friend is about to do something pretty whacked. We all know she's gonna do what she's gonna do, but we can't stand by and do nothing."

"Bring it on," Jackie says.

"Let's hear it," McCloud adds.

Fighting to keep my head in the game, I take a deep breath and force a smile. "Our friend was a one-of-a-kind friend. We became particularly close over this past year. Which is why, like Stu said, I'm taking matters into my own hands. It helps that I now have some spare time."

"What?" Jackie says.

"I've been suspended, pending a full investigation. But it doesn't start until *tomorrow.* Nelson gave me until 10 o'clock. I'll run down the details in a minute, but I'd really like to start with you, Jackie, and apologies for not being there ringside, but we've had our hands full, and frankly, I'm not sure I could, you know..."

"I get it. And don't you worry; she's in my hands. What can I do for you?"

"Tell me everything."

Taking a deep breath, she says, "Okay, and to put it right out there
—she *was* drugged."

My heart feels like it stopped. I desperately fight to catch my breath
and keep tears at bay.

After a deep breath, I say, "So for sure it *wasn't* a heart attack."

Shaking her head, "99-percent and change? No."

More silence while I struggle to quiet my monkey mind. "What
else?"

"She was drugged with a chemical called Succinylcholine. More
specifically, Suxamethonium Chloride, aka, Sux. No joke. It's actually
a medication used to cause short-term paralysis. Most often, as part of
general anesthesia."

"Like for an operation?" Stuart asks.

"Yes. And more specifically, to help with tracheal intubation. Basically, it's used to provide skeletal muscle relaxation during surgery.
Muscle *paralysis* is actually what's happening. It's used to stop a gag
reflex. However, in this case, it was used to basically stop the heart.
And *without* indications of foul play. Unless you know what you're
looking for."

Recalling Angie's face, I mumble, "To *look* like a heart attack."

Jackie nods. "And like I said it provides *negligible* traceability."

This is breaking my heart—but driving my rage.

Stuart squeezes my knee and gives a comforting smile, then turns
back to the screen. "Jackie, how was it administered?"

"Syringe. It's ordinarily injected into a vein or a muscle; however, I
found an injection site between her toes. It's an easy…"

I suddenly tune out as my mind races to the nightmares haunting
me for the past year. "…so you can see it would be easy to miss.
Thing is—"

"Wait! Sorry to interrupt, Jackie…"

"No, go ahead."

"But looking at this from the outside in, and knowing what we
know about our serial killer, I'm guessing it's safe to assume that it'd
be easy for him to acquire this drug, right?"

"Sure. I mean, all you'd need is access to a doctor. An anesthesiologist would be better. Easier, anyway."

My mind is reeling.

"And Pat? It's been administered in pretty much *every* operation since the '50s. And it's on the World Health Organization's list of *essential medicines*."

"Okay?"

"Meaning, it's *easy* to get."

*Access to a doctor or anesthesiologist. I wonder if—*

"Jackie, what about a veterinarian?" I lean closer to the iPad screen.

"Sure, that'd work. Makes it easier to put your pooch to sleep—say, to remove a tooth or such."

Looking at Stuart, he sees I have all I need.

"Thanks, Jackie, that's exceptional info," he says. "We'll circle back shortly. Hey McCloud, we need your help with some surveillance. You available—"

"That'd be *while* I'm on the road—which starts immediately."

"I'm yours," McCloud says, "whenever you need."

"Wait, Patricia," Jackie interrupts. "Do you really mean *immediately*? And will you tell us where you're going?"

Stuart and I exchange looks, then turn back to the screen.

"Australia."

# CHAPTER TWENTY

WITHIN MINUTES OF HANGING UP WITH THE GROUP, STUART GETS A text from Pete and sends him the call-in information.

*PING-PING!*

Pete connects and jumps right in.

"Hi, Sis. Long time no chat. How ya doing, besides the painfully obvious?"

After the initial shock of seeing his face for the first time in ages, we drop into stride as though we spoke yesterday and do a quick catchup on his family and my friendship with Angie. I then transition to an abbreviated description of my plan, and as usual, Pete gets to it.

"Are you out of your mind?" He snaps. "Do you have any idea just how —not only dangerous—but *ridiculous* your plan is? I mean if it were—"

"Pete, stop! The purpose of this call—well, first of all, it was Stuart's idea, and while not necessarily a bad one, not one I would've gone with—but the purpose is…" I sigh, turning to Stuart, "Why not jump in here, partner."

"Hiya, Pete. Okay, so my idea is—"

"Wait, wait, wait," Pete interrupts. "Stuart, as much as I appreciate your suggesting this idea, it sounds like my bull-headed and rebellious sister has ideas of her own that *don't* include me, so unless—"

"Okay, this won't get us anywhere," I snarl. "I get it. Sibling rivalry and all that bullshit, but here's the thing, Pete. *I'm* the one who figured out who the killer was. *I'm* the one who pulled together the team to catch him. And I'm the one—"

"Who didn't bring him in," Pete snaps.

Even though true, I don't need my brother smearing it in my face.

"You're right. And trust me, I've lived with that fact, along with the knowledge he killed at least a half-dozen people over a long period of not getting caught, so yes, you're right. I didn't catch him."

Silence.

"Which is why this is so important to me. And why I must do this. For me, the Force, but mostly? For Angie."

Taking a deep breath, I look back and forth between Stuart and Pete.

More silence.

"It's something *I* have to do, Pete. Now, I'll have my partner in close contact, and I plan to have teammates helping along the way. And trust me, Pete, I'd appreciate any help you can provide."

"Aside from sibling advice perhaps."

I manage a small grin. "I was going to say especially because you've had ample experience dealing with *nut-jobs* like this. And sorry for appearing to be a prima donna but, odd timing as it might be, I have the time off, thanks to being suspended. Might as well use that time to track this *psychopath* down."

I see Pete check his watch.

"And if you need to bounce, I get it. You're in the big time now and—"

"Patty, will you stop? I'm just checking the time. I have to pick up the kids from daycare. Steph's working late. And yes, I'm happy to help. I'll do anything I can. And I get it; I remember my first big case. You take it personally when it doesn't go right. So, I understand. Truly I do," he says with a sincere smile.

That helps ease my foot off the gas.

"Thank you."

"Way I see things…" he says, rubbing his face like it itches—a habit since childhood— "is that you have to consider all the angles. You know Stuart and I are on your side. We *want* to see you get this *asshole*. So, trust me when I say we've got you."

I smile.

"But you've got the lead," he says. "which means if it goes south, it's on you."

"You just had to add that, didn't you?"

"Pat, I know we've covered this already," Pete sighs, "but I'm going to say it one last time. And before you can interrupt me, I'll tell you specifically why I think it's the best idea. Remember how Tercel gave you that drug that nearly killed you?"

"Of course. But it wasn't—"

"I know it wasn't the concoction he told you it was. I read the transcripts. But he knew the *exact* chems to mix in order to do the job he *implied* he would do. And, I might add, had your entire team believing he would do it if they didn't follow his orders."

"Right."

"However, and this is what scares the shit outta me, it's what he's *likely* to do once you get close to him again. Let's face it. If he'd gotten caught—which was damn close to happening—he would've gotten burned for multiple murders and that means he'd be serving consecutive life terms. So, I can't imagine given all the money he amassed and the freedom he stands to lose...that he would hesitate for one second. Therefore, if you show up—whether it's Australia or Hawaii or—"

"But I've already said—"

"I know what you said, but seriously, you just don't know."

Silence.

"Do you? 100%?"

"No," I say quietly. "But then *nothing's* a hundred percent."

"I got it. But *practically* speaking."

"Agreed."

"So, at the very least, let me give you something. As back up."

"What?"

"I've got just the guy to follow you. Trust me, you won't even know he's there. You think you'll know he's following you, but you won't. Not only is he one of the savviest fuckers I've ever known, he's a..." he chuckles, "well, he's got a reputation as a master of disguise."

I roll my eyes at Stuart.

"I saw that," Pete barks. "And Stuart, I know you want to go, but you can't. I know Nelson, and he won't back you. He'll *want* to, but he can't. Besides, I think Davenport's in the works to jam you up—in more ways than one."

"What do you mean?"

"Look, you're the one on suspension. The department would never in their wildest dreams pay for your partner to join you on this *safari*. And let's not forget you're not even supposed to…" he lowers his voice, "leave the county, much less the *country!*"

I lean close to the lens. "You're getting a sick pleasure out of this aren't you?"

"What? Of course not. But I am anxious to see my little sister get back home in one piece and outta this whole damned thing alive."

A coworker suddenly interrupts Pete. He says he has to go, but before we ring off, I impress upon him how my clock is ticking and that I'll be packing soon. He pleads for me not to leave until we speak. I promise him that much and we disconnect.

Sitting back in my chair, I stretch. "Well?" I say to Stuart, popping my neck from side to side. "Dollar for your thoughts."

"Price's gone up, huh?" He grins. "You want my real answer or one you want to hear?"

I frown dramatically.

"I think it's a no-brainer. Since I can't go, you should at the least have someone we trust tag along."

"But Stu, what if Tercel—"

"Pat, you asked. I'm telling you. Take it. It can't possibly hurt. Besides, if this guy's as good as your brother says, you won't even know he's there."

I let out a long sigh, burying my face in my hands, and try to picture Angie's smiling rosy face instead of the blue-gray face I saw on Jackie's autopsy table.

Next, I see Tercel at the foot of my bed—about to inject death into my veins.

"You're right," I nod, looking out the window for a ray of hope. "Probably not the worst idea to have a shadow—*if* he'll let me do my job."

Turning to Stuart, I see a half-smile and what looks like tears as he gathers his things.

"Hey, what's up partner?"

"Nothing," he mumbles.

"Really? Cause it looks different from this angle."

"I just don't want…" he straightens his tie, "to see my best friend get hurt."

With a catch in my throat, I stand and hug him. "C'mon here, ya big lug."

As I bury my face in his chest, I realize the only other time I've seen him even pretend to cry was the birth of his daughter. I can hear his heart beating strong in his chest and hold onto the moment.

Finally, he lets me go—or I, him.

# CHAPTER TWENTY-ONE

*Meanwhile*—

A fit jogger wearing a baseball cap and sunglasses runs down the street and stops in front of Norelli's home to catch his breath. He takes several moments to stretch before climbing the steps to the front door, then removes something from his pocket, unlocks the door, and enters.

Removing his sunglasses, he puts them in one pocket, retrieving a plastic bag and an envelope from another. With little wasted motion, he makes his way through the house and down the hall, stopping in the bathroom to hide a bag. Next, he goes to the spare bedroom and tucks an envelope out of sight.

Returning to the front of the house, he searches a kitchen cabinet and removes a plastic cup, filling it with ice cubes from the freezer. He removes an item from his pocket, places it in an empty slot, and fills the tray with water before returning it to the freezer. Pouring a sports drink into the cup, he puts away the bottle and takes a hand towel from a nearby rack. Next, he removes a photo and a folded note from his pocket and tucks them between picture frames on a shelf in the living room.

Finally, he wraps the towel around his neck, removes and buries a pair of latex gloves into a pocket, puts on his sunglasses, and leaves.

*FIFTEEN MINUTES EARLIER—*

Carrying out his mission of wiring and monitoring Norelli's home, McCloud enters the Manhattan Beach neighborhood and pulls to the curb. Rolling down a window, he turns off the car, lights a cigarette, and waits for anyone to approach the house. Turning on the radio, he changes stations repeatedly before turning it off.

He waits a little longer.

Scanning the street in front of him and behind him via the rearview mirror, he bounces a knee, twirling a Zippo lighter in one hand.

The next several minutes feature knuckle popping, tune humming, people watching, and more smoking.

Lost in thought, he sees a young couple pushing a stroller approach his side of the street. They cross the street and, as they land on the side-walk, an obviously fit jogger approaches. They share a smile and the couple goes in one direction while the jogger runs in the opposite direction. At the last second, the jogger glances in McCloud's direction but keeps running.

With the couple and jogger out of sight, a homeless guy walks out from an oversized trash bin squeezed between two buildings. McCloud sits up straight on high alert. The bedraggled man stands on the side-walk's edge, looking up and down the street.

*Nice camouflage, Tercel.*

McCloud reaches for the door handle. Checking the side mirror for oncoming traffic, he holds back when he sees the man vomit on the sidewalk, then shuffle in the opposite direction and disappear around the corner.

Grimacing, McCloud leans back in his seat and sips a fountain drink.

Tapping the steering wheel, he checks the rearview and, just as he looks back to the house, a delivery truck pulls to the curb and blocks his view. He can't see the driver or the house. As he's about to grind out the cigarette, the truck pulls away and speeds down the street. Hand still on the door, he hesitates.

*What if the driver dropped a bomb on the front stoop?* He twirls his Zippo.

*It could make sense.* He checks the rearview again for oncoming traffic.

*I've got to do something.* He pulls the door handle.

Just then, a man opens the front door, picks up the package from the stoop, and returns inside.

*What?*

Closing the door, he scrambles for his notepad—eyes darting back and forth between the street in front of him and his rearview mirror. Reaching in his backpack, he finds the crumpled paper and double checks the address: 114 17th Avenue.

Looking back to the house, the number is 117.

*What?*

His eyes dart to the cross street: 14th Avenue.

"What the fuck?" He mumbles.

Frantic, he pulls up a map on his smartphone. Scrolling, he tries to keep an eye on foot traffic on the street. He spreads his fingertips to zoom the map, and that's when he notices the cross streets.

*How the fuck did I—*

Tossing his phone in the console, he starts the car, checks oncoming traffic, and waits for another approaching delivery truck who is now blocking his ability to pull forward. Putting his car in reverse, he scoots back until he touches the bumper of the car behind him, then inches forward.

He checks his watch.

*Shit!*

Without being able to see oncoming traffic, he pulls out anyway and, just as he's about to maneuver around the truck, a horn blows and a car screeches to a halt, narrowly missing him. Tossing a wave over his shoulder, he guns it down Highland. Looking at his phone, he sees the blinking red dot of where he's supposed to be.

PING!

He looks from the traffic light to his phone's incoming message. Looking up at the last second, he narrowly misses a passing cyclist who sees him *just in time* and shoots him the bird. With his heart racing, McCloud tries to calm himself.

The light at 16th turns red. Not being able to make the light, he hits the breaks.

RING!

Checking the screen, he hesitates.

Looking up, he sees the familiar jogger and, before he considers anything, the phone rings again.

"McCloud."

"Hey, McCloud. Stuart's running me home then to the airport. Just wanted to check in. How's it going?"

Mouth dry, he tries to speak, "Uh…"

"You okay?"

"Yeah. I'm good. It's just, uh..."

"McCloud? What's wrong?"

"I, uh, fucked up."

"How's that?"

The light turns green, and he slowly pulls away—now only blocks from her house.

"Talk to me."

"Fuck! I was sitting at the wrong address."

Silence.

"I know, I know—a bonehead move. Especially since—"

"I was counting on you. Exactly. Okay, take a breath. Not the end of the world. Hell, may not even be a problem. Could be. Not sure. Anyhow, where are you now?"

Pulling up to the corner of 17th, he parks alongside a red curb.

"Your house."

"114 17th Avenue, right?"

"Yeah. But, um, I was at 117 *14th* Avenue."

"Uh, McCloud?"

"Yeah?"

"That's Angie's place. You're supposed to be rigging my house."

"I know. I'm sorry, Norelli. I, uh, I had two notes: Angie's house and yours, and for whatever reason, I grabbed hers and not—"

"Got it. Again, no big. You're there now. Wait, huh? Hang on a sec, McCloud."

He lights another cigarette with shaking hands. His knee bounces. His fingers strum. His eyes dart up and down the street, repeating the same front to back sweep he spent the past twenty minutes doing.

"Okay, sorry, I'm back. Stuart was reminding me how you may want to, and I know it's not part of what we talked about, but what do you think about installing a motion detector light on the front and back porches?"

*Like that'd stop anyone.*

"Sure, I can do that."

"It's just a thought. I know you're doing cameras and such. Never mind, you're the pro in this department. You do what you think is best."

"Thanks. I've got this. Seriously."

"And McCloud?"

"Yeah."

"Don't freak. Easy mistake."

"Okay."

"But do this for me?"

"Yeah?"

"Text when you've left. Then do me a solid, will ya?"

"Yeah?"

"Go check on *117*. I'm sure you know where that is."

"Smartass," he mumbles.

"True, but you love me anyway. All right, I'm heading back, but you'll be gone by then. My night's gonna be short. Gotta pack and catch a redeye where—as you know—I'll be off the grid for a few days. But Stuart's on call 24-7, so you need something, call him, okay?"

"Copy that. And Norelli?"

"Yeah?"

"Sorry."

"Forget it. See ya."

Ringing off, McCloud takes several more drags, checks traffic before opening the door, and grinds out the cigarette on the street. Grabbing his satchel of electronics from the back of the SUV, he heads in.

LESS THAN FORTY-FIVE MINUTES LATER, McCloud has a series of tiny, wide-angle cameras installed. The first is placed in a thick palm in the main room that also covers the kitchen and part of the outside deck. He hangs a second one in an overhead heating vent in the master bedroom. He places another one atop a bookshelf between a sloppy stack of fitness magazines in the spare bedroom office. The final camera is attached to the garage door motor, giving a 180-degree view that faces the street.

Before leaving, he wires one of his homemade contraptions to the back of her cable modem that will allow him to monitor anyone who might enter and access her wifi. Snagging a cold beer from her fridge, he looks around a final time and leaves.

# CHAPTER TWENTY-TWO

THE STRAND HOUSE IS A SWANKY FAMILY-OWNED RESTAURANT IN THE heart of Manhattan Beach. They have great views of the Pacific, some of the best food in Southern California, and the tastiest cocktails around. I would know because I've spent plenty of time getting acquainted with all of them for nearly a year.

Taking my favorite spot—where Angie and I spent many an evening—Stuart and I order drinks and stare out at the stunning view. As our drinks arrive—a beer for him and an Old Fashioned for me—we clink glasses.

"Here's to Angie."

"May she rest in peace."

Fighting a tear, I take a sip.

"Last time I was here, we talked about, well, mostly girl stuff but also Tercel."

I feel a chill run down my spine.

"I'm sure."

The somber moment is interrupted by a text from my travel agent. My non-stop United flight is officially booked for later tonight, a good thing because I'm hoping to sleep a lot of the way.

When I see the price of the flight, I nearly choke.

Stuart looks at me. "What?"

"Nothing," I take another sip. "Just the price. It's fifteen grand to fly to Sydney!"

"Wow." Sip. "That's a lotta cash."

"And a lotta *cocktails*," I grin. "But that's what I get for last minute booking. And if I'm going that distance, it's got to be First Class, right?"

Stuart nods as his phone buzzes. When he ignores it, I look from the phone to him.

"Aren't you gonna check your electronic umbilical cord?"

"Huh?" Sip.

"Your phone. What if it's Janine?"

"It isn't." He puts down his glass. "So tell me. Why did you pick Sydney?"

"Figured it was a safe choice. One of the bigger cities. Logical starting point. I'm only targeting three: Sydney, Melbourne, and Brisbane."

*BUZZ!*

I look from him to his phone and back. "All I've gotta do is pinpoint the biggest, swankiest hotels. The way I see it, he likes the finer things. And he's got money to burn. Like I say, I doubt he'll be inland because I'm certain he's trying to master the surf. Which is why my money's on Brisbane."

He frowns. "But you're starting—"

"Like I say, start big, work my way back."

"Hmm."

"You have a better suggestion?"

"No. Guess that makes sense. I gotta pee," he says, sliding his phone in his pocket. "How 'bout some calamari? Be right back."

Waving the bartender over, I order an appetizer and another beer for him. Out of habit, I check my phone for messages. Scrolling, I find an email from HR with some crap having to do with my upcoming suspension and an official letter from Nelson about the same.

*Covering his bases is all.*

I let it go because I feel sure we'll speak before I leave. Just as I'm taking a sip, I see Stuart out of the corner of my eye.

As I turn around, I come face to face with Captain Nelson—and behind him is my brother Pete.

"Holy shit!" I shout, nearing spilling my drink. Standing, I slap Nelson's high five as I pull Pete close for a hug.

"What the hell? And how in the world did you pull this off?" I ask, smacking Pete's arm.

"Ow!" He laughs.

"And *you*," I turn to Nelson. "What are you—hell, who cares," I say, kissing his cheek.

"I'll tell you why in better detail in a second, Norelli," Nelson smirks. "Suffice it to say, I've got a dog in this hunt, too. And since we're all in this shitstorm in one fashion or another, we've got to work together."

"Right on, Captain," I say, patting his back.

"And I'll share more in a second," Pete says, looking around. "But how about—"

"I've got a table, Pete," Stuart points to a table in the corner where a waitress waits.

"And you…" I stick a finger in Stu's face, then point to the phone in his hand. "No wonder."

Grinning, Stuart shrugs and pays the bartender while I grab the arms of both Nelson and my brother.

"This is freakin' amazing, Pete. I can't believe it," I say as we take our seats. "First, how'd you get here so fast, and second, how long's it been?"

"Christmas, three years, I think," he says. "Doesn't matter, I'm here now. And while I was pushing you off on the Zoom call…" Pete says, "I was en route to the airport for a private charter. I just couldn't imagine your taking a plunge like this without seeing you. I mean," he looks down for a second, "I nearly lost you once, and I'm not going to get that close again, you know," he says, rubbing an eye.

"Oh my God, you and Stuart," I say through tears. "Now, will ya stop?"

Nelson really surprised me. In fact, this may be one of the few times since working for him that I step back and genuinely feel his commitment to caring about me and my future. He spends several minutes explaining how he had to make himself scarce to me and Stuart —as well as Davenport—so he could coordinate our meeting.

For once, I'm speechless.

. . .

Several drinks in and halfway through our meal, Pete leans forward. "I gotta tell you something, and it's probably a good thing I've got a buzz." Stuart and Nelson laugh. "I'm *so* proud of you."

Here's the thing; he could've stopped there and not said another word. In fact, he could've finished dinner and returned home because that tiny phrase did it—all I've ever wanted was to make him proud. I'm not sure how long I've wished to hear those five simple words, but it feels really good.

"If you keep making me do this…" I point to my teary eyes, "I'll smack you silly."

We all laugh.

"Seriously? Thank you. I mean it."

Taking my hand and squeezing it three times, he smiles. "I know you do, Sis."

As kids, we'd squeeze one another's hand three times to say *I love you*—another thing I miss about this lug. And it's been way too long since I felt that connection.

# CHAPTER TWENTY-THREE

"Now, as far as the *other* thing I told you about..." Pete says, looking over our heads and toward the entrance. "I want you to meet your, well, let's call him your *shadow*, for lack of a better term," he says, waving someone over. A man waves back.

*Hello, Shadow.*

"Pat, meet my old friend and your new shadow, Carter Matheson. Carter, this is Detective Norelli and her partner, Detective Stuart Brown."

"Hello, Detective Norelli," Carter says, shaking my hand. "And just call me Carter. Nobody uses my last name."

*Is that a southern accent?*

"Hello, Carter," I flash my best Rembrandt smile.

*Maybe this won't be such a bad idea after all.*

He turns to Stuart. "Detective Brown, Pete's told me a lot about you."

Stuart looks from Carter to Pete. "Can't believe everything you hear, unless it's good, of course."

"Probably told him what a pussy...*cat* you are," I laugh.

"Have a seat, Carter," Pete says, adding a chair to the table while waving our waiter over. "What's your poison, Bourbon, right?"

With a smile that could melt butter, Carter says, "Usually yes, but club soda's fine for now. Thanks."

I try hard not to stare, but his Robert Redford handsomeness is distracting.

"Pat, I wanted to say how sorry I am you're in this position," Nelson says with a lopsided smile. "But it was out of my control. Trust me."

"I do."

"And for the record," he looks at each man, "you're right about Davenport. Even back to the Johansen murder. There was a power play in motion; one I didn't know about—then and now."

Staring into his drink, he lets out a long sigh and starts to say something, then stops.

"What is it, Captain?"

"That's another thing," he snorts. "Won't be Captain much longer— if I don't play my cards right."

"What?" Stuart and I ask simultaneously.

"Ain't that a kick in the balls?" He motions for the bartender to bring another round. "Between my continually pushing back and Davenport continually pushing in, upstairs gave me a choice. I can either play along—letting him take the lead while I take a few steps back—or quit. And risk losing my pension."

"Shit," I mutter.

"Exactly. So, I agreed. Figured what the hell. Besides, I figured I could just take more of my free time to *steer* my attention in your direction. Help you in any way I can. Shit's not worth fighting sometimes. Besides, with the wife gone, I got nothing else to do. And I need the pay. Just less hassle this way. Anyhow, somehow it all started in Internal Affairs and someone not wanting you to succeed."

"Why me?"

His glance goes from Pete to me. "Not exactly sure, but he's the guy who finds *just* the right dirt. On just the right cop. The real truth will shake out eventually."

"Shit's as old as law enforcement itself," Pete says.

All the men nod.

"Let them play their bullshit games. I'll pull the pin anyway— sooner rather than later. But in the meantime, that's why I'm sitting here. To help you."

I feel a tear coming. He sees it and rolls his eyes.

"Now, c'mon, Norelli, I don't need to see the waterworks for crap's sake. And I certainly don't wanna get all sappy and shit, but I'm just gonna lay it out there and say that what's happened is horrible. But as long as I'm Captain at the helm, the bunch of us," he stops, looking into the eyes of our group. "As long as I'm helping lead this thing, we're sticking together. I know, I know, cornball shit and all, but c'mon, you're my gir—, I mean, you're one of my best detectives," he says, rubbing his nose. "Now, let's discuss how I, we, can help cover your ass and get you what you need. Because we're gonna set this shit straight!"

"Thanks, Captain. And I can say without hesitation—even though it is a corny cliche—this gal's not going down without a fight."

Carter, Nelson, and Pete raise their glasses, "Hooah!"

Stuart and I join with "Boom!"

Pete holds up a hand. "Okay, now that we're sufficiently liquored up and shouting our mating calls," he laughs. "I've got points to discuss." Turning to me, he adds, "Plus, hanging with my kid sis."

"I'll drink to that."

"Okay, Patricia's bound for Sydney in five hours and change. That's enough time to shore up details with you clowns before spending what little time I have left before these two," he waves a finger between me and Carter, "to catch the redeye down under."

As Stuart eyeballs my drink, I lean forward. "Not to worry, slugger. I'll be sleeping the *whole* way there."

Pete continues. "My intel tells me that our target's first location— where he began—was indeed Sydney."

"What?" I nearly choke on my drink. "How'd in the hell did *you*—"

Pete tosses a thumb at Carter who shrugs. "I had a little time on my hands. Just thought I'd get the ball rolling."

"Woooah, before you start swinging," Pete says with hands in the air, "I *know* this is your case, and you're *definitely* in charge. However, Carter has a *vast* amount of experience in tracking people and I thought it could be *exceptionally* helpful to you."

He feigns pouting with puppy dog eyes.

"Okay, I'll hear you out," I snarl, looking at them. "Only because you flew all the way across the country for one meal. And because he's easy on the eyes."

"Nice," Carter says.

"And Sis, I've known Carter for *many* years. In fact, remember when I entered the Reserves right out of high school before I changed course and entered the Police Academy?"

"Yeah."

"I met Carter then. He was enlisted, but our paths occasionally crossed over the years. Then, when our Mayor had a problem recently. Turning, he says, "Hell, Carter, you tell the story. It'll serve as a good background."

I know Pete is only looking out for me. How can I be hurt when Carter wants to help protect me? I wave for him to take center stage.

"Thanks, Pete. And I have to say, thank *you*, Patricia. I'm honored—"

"You can call me Norelli." I wink.

He grins. I bat my eyelashes.

"Okay. And I'll keep this short. Last summer, an old friend reached out to me when their daughter went missing. Claire is the wife of Lukas Burton, Mayor of New York City. Their nine-year-old daughter Abigail was kidnapped in broad daylight in Central Park."

"Oh my god."

"Yeah, it was a well-crafted abduction led by a man named Donovan Blair who, besides being a successful real estate investor in Manhattan, was one notorious drug dealer. Our paths had crossed once before in Havana where he was not only dealing drugs but illegal arms."

"Shit."

"What you said. Anyway, because Claire and I had a friendship from way back when, I was called in to help. I worked directly with the Mayor while orchestrating back channels with your brother Pete. I tracked Donovan and his team down with the help of my best pal Mack McKenzie."

"Wait, you said *was*," I lean in. "As in..."

He nods.

"That's what Carter does," Pete says. "Tracks bad people. And if he can't bring them in, well, he—"

"Yeah, I got that, brother. Thanks."

"Truth is," Carter says, leaning on his elbows, "I was trained in surveillance but ended up being a pretty good shooter."

"Pretty good? *Right*," Pete says. "As in *well* over a thousand yards. Across a handful of streets and avenues. From one high-rise to another.

*And* in less than ideal conditions. Took out the asshole with a single shot."

*Woah, Nelly.*

"Yeah, it was a long shot, but like your brother says, my real forte is huntin' people," he says with a thicker country drawl.

"Which is why I'm here, Norelli. To help you hunt down Tercel."

# CHAPTER TWENTY-FOUR

SAYING GOODBYE TO STUART AND NELSON, I PROMISE TO KEEP IN touch and ask Pete to drive Carter and me to my house. Over a couple of beers, they talk while I pack.

Later at LAX, we move quickly through security and, after being upgraded to First Class thanks to Pete, Carter and I board our 16 hour flight from LA to Sydney.

NINE HOURS and more than a dozen periods of broken sleep later, I jerk awake from a nightmare. A man who looks like a cross between the photo I found on Angie's bookshelf and Tercel was chasing me with a long spear.

*At least this time, I wasn't bound, gagged, and facing a syringe.*

I take several long breaths before appearing from beneath my blanket.

"Hello, stranger," I say, peeking from behind my sleep mask.

"Hi, yourself," Carter says, putting aside a paperback. "I hope your mind slept better than your body."

"Huh?"

"You jerked about every twenty minutes, then you'd fling an arm back and forth for I don't know how long. I can only imagine who you were fighting in those dreams."

"Yeah, well, some things never change," I say, reaching for a bottled water. "Sorry to keep you up."

"No worries. Took me a movie and half a paperback to finally pass out. Haven't been awake long."

Waving for the flight attendant, he orders two breakfasts for himself and asks if I want anything. I tell her I'll have half of what he's having and, as she's about to leave, he asks if he can have a pot of coffee.

"How about I bring you a *cup* first," she smiles with a hand on her hip. "Then you just flash that handsome smile of yours whenever you need more."

"Sounds like a plan," he smiles.

As she walks away, I say, "I'm guessing that happens everywhere you go."

"That a question or a statement?"

"Both?"

MINUTES LATER, I catch Carter staring at me as I pull a steaming towel from my face.

"What?"

"Haven't known you long, Norelli, but you're a unique woman."

"True." I return to the hot towel. "Mmm, how does something so simple rank as one of the best feelings ever?"

"Dehydration and stale air?"

With my face still in a towel, I mutter, "Are you always the optimist?"

AFTER BREAKFAST, I order a Bloody Mary and, as the attendant waits, I look at Carter. "Hey, we're only halfway. Plus, I might be able to snag another nap if I play my cards right."

Carter smirks, holding up two fingers.

"Excellent choice," I smile.

A long stretch of quiet hovers over us. Then, halfway through our drink, Carter leans close. "You seem to be holding up pretty well if you ask me."

I guess I don't suppress my mood very well because his expression looks terrified.

"I'm sorry. I meant, you know, all things considered—what with losing, well, and the job and…"

I look at him from the corner of my eye.

"Sorry. Never was good at small talk."

"Really? Wouldn't have guessed it." Smacking his leg, I say, "I'm fucking with you, Carter. And thanks for noticing. I think I'm probably still in that denial stage. That's the first one, right?"

He nods.

"Let's see if all my months of *therapy* have paid off. Okay, we start with denial, followed by anger. No, maybe I'm already there because I'm pretty f'n pissed right now—even though it doesn't show. I mean, who kills their best friend, right? And for no other reason than, I don't know, because they got in their way? That's the one thing I'm still having a difficult time with. I mean, why?"

He says nothing; I keep going.

"Let's see there's still bargaining and depression, although I'm feeling a good dose of that about now. No, that's not here yet. Not fully, anyway. But it's coming. That's for damn sure. Let's see, that leaves acceptance. Fuck! I don't see that coming anytime soon, do you? I mean, I'm fully in the denial stage. Although I'd say I'm straddling the anger fence. Yeah, that seems about right, you know? With just a *dash* of depression."

Suddenly, I feel a blush erupting.

"Patricia," he says, resting a hand on my arm, "it's *all* good, wherever you are. Doesn't matter. Just be there. If it helps you at all, and I know we've just met, and I'm *not* trying to, you know, get in the way of your routine, but—"

"Wait, what? How'd you know about…" I react without thinking. "Oh. Pete. Of course."

"No, actually I saw it in your report."

"The Johansen case?"

"Just as background," he shrugs. "On you and this whole thing. Pete wanted me to be up to speed."

I stare out the window and am quiet for several long moments before turning back and adjusting myself so we are face to face.

"Okay, here's the thing. And you might as well get up to speed on *me* as much as you are about that case. Or Angie's death. And/or Dr.

Tercel. I've got to stop calling him that. Or anything else for that matter. And that's this. You ready?"

Grinning, he nods.

"And for the record, that smile of yours is going to get you into as much trouble as it does into favor. You follow?"

Another grin.

"Okay, stop and just listen." Frowning, I look at the empty Bloody Mary. "Okay, I'm stopping with *two*. Otherwise, I'm gonna get silly."

"Get?"

Smacking his arm too hard—which gets a grimace from him and a look from an elderly woman directly behind us—I grab his hand.

"Sorry, that was harder than I meant." I release his hand. "Okay, enough of this tender bullshit. I'm cutting to the chase on the off chance there's something you missed. You know, in all your *intel*."

The grin again.

Playfully ignoring him, I continue with my background. It's rapid-fire, but he follows along with the appropriate smile or nod or sad look —whatever's required. I tell him about getting married too young, and then pregnant almost instantly; how I have a 19-year old daughter who's attending law school at Stanford and living part-time with her father—my ex-husband, a practicing therapist.

Next, I cut to the Johansen case, sharing how I devised the "notorious eight" suspects and how that came about. Then, I share details about my nearly non-professional relationship with the man I've come to call "The Poser."

He asks why that phrase and I explain how he posed all of his victims to look like they had taken their own lives. The second reason for the nickname is because he'd been posing as a well-respected therapist in Hollywood for nearly two decades.

Asking very few questions, he stops me only once to ask for more details about Bobby Shapiro's background, specifically his upbringing. He also asks what I think about the length of time Angie had been a patient and what sort of relationship she had with Tercel besides that of doctor and patient.

"That's a really good question, because to be honest, I didn't really know just how deep their relationship had become. Besides the doctor-patient angle. I'd say she remained his patient for so long because of several reasons. Tercel had a very *seductive* way about him. He somehow managed to get *all* of us to peel away all our inhibitions and expose not only our deepest weaknesses or neuroses but also our deepest *secrets*. And then he preyed upon them.

"With Angie, even with her take-no-shit attitude, she was weak and vulnerable. She had anger issues she couldn't handle and a number of dependencies she couldn't control; pills being the worst. And the booze? Well, I can't toss any stones there." I say, looking out the window.

Turning back, I look at Carter. "You're still listening."

"Is that a question or—"

"Very funny. I think their relationship began as any standard doctor-patient agreement, but one going in an entirely different direction. Tercel was expensive and greedy. And he made you believe his talents were even better than they were. Anyhow, Angie was making a *lot* of money, and he preyed on that *and* her weaknesses. Which I think kept her on the line."

At that moment, I think of how much I miss her and wipe my eyes.

"I'm sorry Pat. And if you don't want—"

"No, that's fine. I mean, I'm fine. This is good, actually. Kinda like I'm on your couch. Wait, that didn't sound right."

As we enjoy a laugh, I realize this is part of my healing and embrace it.

Carter nods toward the attendant who was scanning the cabin and holds up two fingers. She flashes her pearlies in return and spins to fetch our drinks. All I can do is shake my head.

"What?" He looks incredulous.

"Really?" I smirk. "Anyhow, I'm going to finish one point, then we're going to talk about *you* for a change."

"Fine."

"I didn't know just how *obsessed* she was with Tercel. I mean, what I found in her home—"

"You mean the photos?"

"No. Well, yes, but what I'm talking about is letters, journals, and love notes. It was more than a doctor-patient thing for sure. And she had *way* more than a crush on him. He was her, I don't know, hero? Boyfriend? Savior?"

*PING!*

I look around, knowing our phones aren't supposed to be on and wonder if it's mine.

*PING!*

Searching my backpack, I dig to the bottom to find my phone with a message from a number I don't recognize. Looking around, I mute the sound. The message reads: *Please don't tell me you're actually trying to find me, Patricia. You're good, but you're not that good.*

It feels like a thousand spiders suddenly crawling down my back.

*Why would Tercel be reaching out after all this time?*

My heart begins racing as I try hiding my shaking hands. Burying them between my legs, I stare out the window.

"What is it?" Carter whispers.

I take a long deep breath so my head doesn't explode. Turning to Carter, I hand him my phone.

"It's *him.*"

# CHAPTER TWENTY-FIVE

*SYDNEY, AUSTRALIA—*

SEVEN MORE HOURS, four cocktails, two meals, and one nap later, our plane lands in Sydney. Between the jet lag and the booze, I'm not my sharpest while Carter appears fresh as a daisy. As we taxi, I turn my phone on to find a series of messages. Stuart shares how Davenport is spending time snooping around the office—making everyone nervous in the process. Shay's sweet message is about how she and her new girlfriend are getting along. Jackie's discovered something new and says to call when convenient. Nelson leaves a semi-cryptic message: *Call ASAYL.* It takes me a second to decipher: Call As Soon As You Land. And McCloud lets me know the coast is clear.

THE LATE AFTERNOON sun feels good on my face and the weather reminds me of Los Angeles but with more humidity. The vibe, on the other hand, is electric like Manhattan. As my driver loads my car, Carter's driver loads his car directly behind mine. During the flight, we discussed how once we landed we should keep our distance on the off chance Tercel might be nearby.

En route, a billboard advertising several hometown actors being nominated for films in the upcoming Oscars captures my attention.

"That's it," I say, slapping my leg and recalling the significance of Tercel's reaching out.

*The anniversary of Meredith's murder and the case that merged our paths.*

I text check to see if Carter is close behind. He isn't.

Then I shoot a text to Stuart: *Stu, do you realize today's significance? Anniversary of the Johansen case. BTW, I've landed. How are you?*

Checking my watch, I calculate it to be nearly 11. Last night.

*Time change is a bitch.*

Scanning my environment, I need a quick lay of the land.

*PING!*

Carter texts: *Did you see the billboard? About your text. Tercel's toying with you. Perfect. It'll only help us catch him faster.*

The drive from the airport to The Sheraton Grand takes all of twenty minutes. In the same amount of time, we check in and head to our rooms on the same floor. Given the hotel recently reopened after a long respite from the Covid pandemic, management is doing everything in their power to fill the hotel. Carter's nose is buried in a local newspaper when my phone vibrates.

Checking it, I see Stuart's emoji smiling big. The text reads: *Yeah, that's me. Jan's got me hooked on these stupid emoji-cons. Anniversary? Makes total sense. Duh! Family: Everyone's good. I'm exhausted. Circle around first thing?*

I catch myself smiling at his embrace of technology and text: *Good to hear. Landed safely. Tomorrow's good. Hugs to all. Nite, P*

We arrive at our floor and, as the doors open, Carter waves for me and a couple with their child to step out. They head down one hall while we venture in the opposite direction. Carter walks behind me and, as I take out my door key, he whispers, "Text me when you're ready to venture out."

AFTER A LONG HOT soak in a tub overlooking Hyde Park, I feel as good as new. I'm at the front desk waiting for the manager on duty when Carter arrives, wearing a navy suit, dress shirt, and tie. On his breast pocket a badge reads: *Sydney Private Tours.* A leather portfolio, a neat mustache, and horn-rimmed glasses complete the look.

Looking straight ahead, I whisper, "Very handsome."

"Thanks," he smiles, handing me a brochure he picked up at the airport.

A tall and attractive woman with a broad smile appears.

"Welcome to the Sheraton Grand Hyde Park. I'm Ms. Fillmore, the manager."

We spend the next several minutes getting her opinion on the top five-star hotels in Sydney, then share several photographs of Tercel.

There isn't a blip of recognition in her expression. When asked how many other managers were on duty at the property, day or night and inside the past twelve months, she provides all necessary information and adds that if he were a guest, she would've known about it because she takes great pride in knowing every person who stays in the 558 room hotel. I believe her.

As we're about to move on, she offers something more.

"By the way, there are a number of very fine establishments within minutes of this location. Two in particular would be my choice. That is, *if* you don't prefer our accommodations and you're someone who desires impeccable accommodations with the budget to match. You did say he could be spending as much as a month at a time at any of these, correct?"

"Absolutely. On both counts. He has great taste and money to burn," I say.

"Understood." She takes out a pad and pen. "Here are the two I'd start with. They're located within blocks of each other. Oh, wait, there's a third," she smiles. "I've spent many an evening watching sunsets at this bar," she taps the pad. "Perhaps you could end there. You'll see why."


IF TERCEL IS IN SYDNEY, I feel confident he'll be in one of the proposed establishments. If I know anything about him, it's how his ego needs to be fed lots of attention—even more than his carnal desires. With Carter's disguise and me playing tourist, we exit the front onto Elizabeth, taking a left to Market Street. Carter has the idea to take a quick ride up the Sydney Tower Eye, just a block away, because of its reputation as an iconic tourist trap with a platform offering a bird's eye view of the city.

He is right. It is spectacular.

On the deck—over a thousand feet high—Carter sketches out a quick map of our destinations, reminding me of the story he shared at our first meeting involving the criminal Donovan Blair and his penthouse in midtown Manhattan. When I ask him the distance of the shot, he scans the nearby high-rises and points to nearby MLC Centre—two city blocks away.

"The height's about the same as that tower." Looking around before pointing South, he adds, "See the Opera House between those two towers?"

Leaning closer to him, I squint to see Sidney's quintessential landmark far in the distance.

"Yeah?"

"That's the distance. Just over a mile. Give or take."

He's close enough I can smell his cologne. Regaining my focus and clearly impressed, I say, "You've got to be kidding."

Tossing away a shrug, he says, "It's what I do."

## CHAPTER TWENTY-SIX

SEVERAL BLOCKS DOWN PITT STREET MALL, WE DECIDE TO GRAB A CAB and get dropped at The InterContinental Sydney. It is gorgeous and feels like the kind of place Tercel would land, but he didn't in this case. After speaking to several people—showing them the same photos we'd shared with the manager at The Sheraton—I tell Carter we've come up with Emu eggs.

My joke falls as flat as my enthusiasm. Then, it gets worse.

After learning that some of the nicest places in town—Pier One Sydney, The Sheraton, The Hilton, and Spicers Potts Point—also have no record of a man matching Tercel's specifics, I am officially dejected.

Deciding to merge business with pleasure, we take a taxi to find our next potential candidate: The Park Hyatt at the foot of the Harbour Bridge.

Upon entering, I'm floored by the elegance and views. It feels right.

While Carter works his charm to snag us hard-to-get dinner reservations, I work my own magic at The Bar, taking a seat in front of a bartender named Jack. His eyes are the color of the bay and his hipster beard is groomed within an inch of its life. I can see how his easy manner and athletic build could create a living as handsome as his face.

I order a drink and after a short education on Archie Rose—a distillery twenty minutes south of us—I proceed to enjoy the best gin and tonic I've ever had. Jack bounces his eyebrows as if to say, *Am I right?*

I mirror the expression when Carter arrives.

"I see you're mingling with the locals."

"You know it," I smile. "Got seats?"

"You betcha."

Jack approaches and begins his gin pitch, but Carter politely waves aside the history class and says, "I'll have the same."


THE THREE OF us enjoy a slight lull in bar traffic and, after small talk about beverages and the beauty of the country, get down to specifics. I share with Carter what I learned from Jack about management and people traffic over the past year. His decade-long experience combined with an expectation of learning all names matched with cocktails makes him a valuable asset. Just as the hostess arrives to tell us our table will be ready in five minutes, Jack asks to see the photo again.

He stares at it as though attempting Calculus.

"What is it?"

"Well, he looks like any other American. But I realize if it's the mate I *think* it was, he would've been here about nine, maybe ten months ago. Wait, actually, it was just about this same time of year. I recall how he spent a good deal of time out there," he points to the deck overlooking the harbor. "And with several striking *Sheilas*," he winks.

Carter gives a nod. "Ladies' man, huh?"

"Truly. And now that I'm remembering the mate, I recall he was a good tipper, too."

Carter and I exchange looks.

"So, you're sure," I reach toward Jack for the photo. "This is the guy, Darius Tercel."

Nodding, Jack spots someone down the bar waving for his attention and holds up a finger. Leaning closer, he frowns. "Don't recall *that* name—which is odd because I remember everyone's name—but another thing I recall is his accent. It was odd."

"How's that?" I ask, knowing Tercel doesn't have an accent.

"It came and went. Meaning, he sounded and acted American; you know, a real *yakker*, but then his Aussie accent would come and go. Who knows, maybe he was just practicing. Alotta yanks do that. Listen, I need to grab this, can I—"

"No, it's good, go ahead. I'm sure we'll chat again."

. . .

AFTER A SPECTACULAR DINNER, Carter and I return to The Bar for a nightcap, hoping to see if we can learn anything more from Jack. Nothing new is offered until one of his co-workers, Lisa, arrives for a nightcap. We ask her the same questions and she shares how she hung out with someone who resembles the photo.

"Something's different, though, I think. And the only reason I even begin to remember this guy is because I told him I was working here part-time while studying to be an actress. He said it was a coincidence because he was a Hollywood producer. When I told him I wanted to get into films and would eventually move to the States, he asked what I had done. I'm only a couple years into the business so I didn't have a lot to *Wow* him with, except a commercial or two. I asked his name and if he had produced anything I'd seen. I don't recall the name, but I'm pretty sure it *wasn't* David Tercel."

"Darius," I correct.

"Okay, Darius. And honestly, we got to drinking pretty hard and I just don't remember. Plus, it's been a long time—and a *lot* of cocktails since then."

"I feel you, sister," I grin. "Did you get the impression that he was, you know, for real, or just bullshitting you in order to..."

"Oh, he was for *sure* bullshitting me. But that didn't stop me from enjoying the drinks he was buying—which went well into the night. But you know, a girl's gotta play along sometimes."

"Right," I fake a smile, looking at Carter.

"And did you keep playing?" Carter asks. "You know, into the night?"

Her waffling expression is interesting, and just as Jack is about to jump in, she snaps her fingers.

"That's it. I knew I'd eventually pull his name. Last name was Mickelson. First name was Chris, I think. Reason I recall is my two older brothers are big into American golf and they love Phil Mickelson," she chuckles. "That's right, because I recall him saying they weren't related but how they'd become friends after shooting a commercial together."

She lights a cigarette, takes a drag, then says, "I think it was shortly after that I exited stage left. Yeah, he was *so* full of shit. And yes, wanted to, well, you know."

In fact, I do. And she's right; he *is* full of shit.

*And he would've done more than just* you know.

# CHAPTER TWENTY-SEVEN

AFTER A FEW HOURS OF SLEEP, I'M READY FOR ANOTHER DAY OF hunting. After a run around nearby Government House and adjoining Royal Botanic Gardens, I join Carter—already a half pot of coffee in—for a hearty breakfast downstairs. Thanks to bartender Jack who put in a good word for us with the concierge, we gain several insights.

Whoever booked the Harbour Suite paid $155,000 for the month of April in advance. While that seems staggering to me, I recall Angie telling me—in no uncertain terms—how Tercel made over $50 million by selling both his Bel Air home, an inheritance from his mother, and his Malibu home purchased shortly after beginning his business. Stuart and I figure he can easily have half that amount in savings and investments, especially after all the years of such a successful business.

Also, whoever leased the property was extremely private—hiring a service that allowed only one person to manage all the cleaning of his room while the butler tended to a host of other duties, including a private limousine car and driver.

*Tercel.*

I soon discover how the suite was paid with a Black American Express card, but there was only a negligible chance I'd get a lead on a paper trail. Then again, since Tercel was or is traveling under an assumed identity, all cards and identity would have to match across the board, thus making it all the more difficult to track.

*I need McCloud's expertise—starting with Chris Mickelson.*

Something I'm finding odd is how I have yet to find anyone who can say with 100% certainty the man in the photo is Tercel. Why his image can't be verified better than 90%—a number each person quoted —stumps me.

I need my team to meet Carter, so after breakfast and before we check the remaining hotels, we go to my room for an 8:15 Zoom call— 1:15 p.m yesterday back home.

"Nice digs," Carter says, following me into my suite. "Doesn't look like anyone's been here."

Setting up my laptop, I mutter, "Yeah, I'm kind of a neat freak."

"Copy that." At the window, he admires the view of Hyde Park. "I see your old man was in the service too, huh?"

Surprised, I look up just as Jackie and McCloud connect.

"Hey kids, how are you two?"

"Just another day in paradise," McCloud says.

"Not the same without you, girl," Jackie says. "Stuart said he'd join shortly. Something about trouble he's having with a Pink's chili dog?"

"Same old story," I laugh as Carter pulls up a chair, leaning into the frame.

"And this is Carter, my *shadow*."

After explaining the connection Carter and I have via Pete, we make small talk until Stuart can join us.


TEN MINUTES LATER, Stuart steps into the picture behind Jackie.

"Hey, Pat, sorry I'm late, I—"

"Yeah, we got it. Pink's reference told me everything. Let's cut to the chase with some things I must know. So if I may, I'll get to it with three questions."

"Stuart, I'd love to hear the latest concerning Davenport. Jackie, what's your news, and apologies for not getting back sooner. McCloud, let's talk surveillance and credit cards. Who's first?"

"Let me start," Jackie says, "because I've got two cases I need to jump on."

"Shoot."

"Okay, the element I found, as you know, was the anesthesia product, Succinylcholine. That's what stopped her heart. She also had a healthy blood alcohol level—"

"Yeah, we got over served at The Strand."

"Right. But what caught my attention was the amount of Ambien in her system. Do you know if she had trouble sleeping?"

*Don't we all?*

"She did. In fact, she said it was a challenge that began a while back when work got stacked up and she got stressed out. But I can't imagine she would need it *that* night. I mean we had enough wine to put all of us out. I'm curious, how much was in her system?"

"Well, to borrow your inference," she raises her eyebrows, "enough for all *five* of us to get a solid night's sleep."

Everyone's quiet.

"Now, that's just *odd*. Isn't it?"

"It is. But *somewhat* understandable. Here's why. People will often take one, maybe two, but then an hour later—if they're particularly *aggro*—take another one, without even remembering they took the first ones."

"Shit."

"Indeed. Okay, hate to do this, but that's all I have right now. I gotta bounce, but I'll circle back with you inside the next 48. Cool?"

"Sounds good. And thanks, Jackie," I say as she steps away and Stuart takes her seat. "Hey, Stu, why are you at the MEC?"

"I want to see the report Jackie just shared," he says. "Just to double check things."

"Copy that. Okay, McCloud, I need you to do me a favor, but first tell me what you've learned with surveillance."

"Nothing much. I mean, you've only been gone a day and change, but as it pertains to anyone being in or on the premises, not much."

"Okay?"

"However, your wifi has been tapped a number of times, like—"

"You mean, like a neighbor. Yeah, there's a kid next door who regularly bogarts my bandwidth."

"Nice reference," he chuckles, "but no, this is different. I saw that and shut him out because of your ridiculously simple password. Evidently, you didn't learn that lesson from me a year ago when I unlocked your phone?"

"Okay, so I'm lazy. And yes, my birthday, month and year,

followed by my dog's name, should be changed. Which I will change—"

"Already did. I'll get it to you later. Here's what I found. It's like someone is *inside* your house. But like I said, nobody's been there. Cameras don't lie."

*There go the spiders down my back again.*

"So, what is it?"

"Best I can tell? There's *something* in there—could even be a laptop —that's tapping your service. *With* your password."

"What?"

"My guess is it's being operated remotely."

I don't know what to say. I look at Stuart, then Carter; both shrug.

"Do you want me to—"

"YES! I want you to get in there, toss the place, and find what the hell's going on. This isn't fucking cool!"

My heart feels like it's going to jump from my chest.

"I'll check for bugs while I'm there, too, because—"

"What? You didn't do that before?"

"No, you said get in, plant the cameras, and get out, but you didn't say—"

"Okay, yes, right. My bad. Just assumed you would is all. Please do. It certainly can't hurt. Hell, I'm sure it will help. And thank you, McCloud, I didn't mean to bite your head off. I'm just—is edgy a good word?"

"Duh," McCloud mumbles.

"Agreed. Look, I, uh, got a text from Tercel."

Each mouth drops just as I'd expect.

"Yeah, pretty cocky to reach out, but the text said, *Don't tell me you've come looking for me* or something close to that."

"Wow," Stuart says.

"What he said," McCloud mumbles.

"Yeah, so that's why I'm more than a bit aggro."

McCloud says, "Understood."

"Let me jump in here for just a second," Carter says. "McCloud, I've heard great things about you, so I know you're on top of this. Something I'd like to suggest—which I'm sure you've already thought of—is for you and Stuart to go there, either tonight or first thing tomorrow, and..." he stops and raises his eyebrows at me.

"What? Yeah, keep going. You have a plan; we're all ears. What're you thinking?"

"Go there and, for lack of a better term, play a little game for me, okay? I don't want to tell you *exactly* how to play things for fear of making it feel or sound phony, but I think I may have an idea how to go at this."

# CHAPTER TWENTY-EIGHT

*MANHATTAN BEACH, CALIFORNIA—8:00 P.M.*

THAT EVENING, Stuart and McCloud meet up at Norelli's home. McCloud arrives early and sits across the street watching for unusual people traffic while monitoring the inside of her home on his laptop. Punching a key, he activates a grid of web activity on the screen filled with small boxes representing his hidden cameras.

*What?*

The software he installed shows the house wifi is being tapped, but only in pulses.

*Someone toggling a switch? Maybe it's a faulty connection?*

Just then, Stuart pulls up to the front of the house.

Closing the laptop, McCloud buries it in a shoulder bag and gets out.

"What's up, SB?"

"Hey, McCloud! Grab this, will ya?" he says over his shoulder, taking a sack from the back and handing it off. "I've got a pizza on the front floorboard."

McCloud looks inside to find two six packs of craft beer. "Hello, ladies."

"Been here long?" Stuart asks, unlocking the door.

"Nah, just long enough to burn one. And to see we've got action."

. . .

As Tercel exits the elevator, he receives a text alert.

With a swipe of the screen, he sees someone entering Norelli's home. A sneer crosses his face as he puts in a pair of EarPods to listen.

Approaching the town car, he hands his bag to the driver and gets in.

*Hope you like double sausage 'n double cheese.*

Tercel hears beer bottles being opened in the background.

*Who doesn't, bro? So, did you ever think Pat would steal from her best friend?*

A sudden sound of television nearly drowns them out.

*No f'n way. And now that she's off the force, no telling what she'll do next!*

Tercel pushes the EarPods deeper into his ears.

*Just goes to show how you never really know somebody.*

Tercel waves for the driver to go.

*But the hardest thing to absorb? If anyone seriously thinks she had anything to do with killing Angie.*

Staring out the window, he frowns.

"*No shit. I did NOT see that coming. Then again, she was seeing that shrink; maybe she dug so deep it got to her.*

Tercel admires his perfectly buffed nails.

*True. But does anyone think she'll get away with it?*

Tercel cocks his head as static appears on the line.

*Look at her family tre...ou kno.. they al...ook out for...ne another.*

He squints.

*Hand me a napkin, will ya? And lemme ask you, 'cause you know her better'n most. Do you think there's any way she'll try to find Tercel?*

A grin swells on his face.

*Who the hell knows. The million dollar question is...*

He unconsciously leans forward.

*You think she's going after him for almost killing her?*

Tercel's eyes shift back and forth rapidly.

*Oh hell ye... You kno...'s a ball brea...and...l stop at no... to ge...
hat...e wan...*

Looking at the screen, he frowns again, refreshing the page.

A moment later: *I don't thin... many peop... know ... about her. For real.*

He stares at the screen, chewing the inside of his cheek.

*The bitch is Bat Shit Crazy! And for the record, I don't care how much money's involved—who'd kill their best friend?*

He pushes the volume to the limit.

*For that kind of money? Hell, I'd kill YOU!*

THEY'RE HALFWAY through the pizza and beers when they step out onto the back deck. McCloud lights a cigarette while Stuart sips a beer. Grinning, Stuart shakes his head and turns toward the ocean.

"What?"

"Just thinking how if Norelli were here now, she'd be busting your chops."

"I know," McCloud says, taking a drag. "I'll quit." Exhale. "One day."

"Sure."

After some silence, Stuart tosses his chin toward the house, "Think we're doing any good?"

"For sure," McCloud nods, blowing a trio of perfect rings. "I've got one eye on the game, but the other on my monitor. Someone's definitely been pinging the hell outta my grid."

Stuart nods.

"And whoever it is did a nice job hiding the mics. I've found at least seven which I'm sure is all of 'em. Looks like they all talk to a hub attached to the back of her internet box. The average bear wouldn't notice, but the panel has been expanded to half again the thickness. Pretty smart little transponder rig."

After a sip, Stuart says, "Where're the mics? I was on my phone when you did the scout."

"Three in the living room. One in the light stem of that big arc lamp hanging over the couch. Another is under the lip of the end table between our chairs. The last one that I know of," he winks, "is on top of the doorbell box at the entrance. Covers the whole room."

"Nice work. Where're the other three?"

Blowing a cloud, he grinds out the butt.

"In the master under the lip of the picture frame over the bed. Bet that provides plenty of entertainment," he snorts. "And the office? Just inside the overhead light. Took me forever to find it. It was painted to match the glass perfectly. Last one's in the bathroom attached to the frame of the medicine cabinet. Fortunately, it's closer to the door than the *shitter*."

Stuart laughs.

"All in all, whoever's listening knew what he was doing. And has to have heard it *all* by now."

Looking around, Stuart frowns, "But what about out here?"

With a scared look, McCloud freezes. "Hadn't thought about that."

Stuart stares.

Grinning, McCloud waves the air. "Nah, they wouldn't bother with out here. Too much ambient noise."

Finishing his beer, Stuart waves for him to follow. "Come on, let's bury the rest of the brews and head out."


*Sounds good, bro* is heard on the other side of the world. *And Stu? This time, let me drop the hammer on Norelli. You've been having all the fun.*

Shoving the phone in his pocket, Tercel mutters, "We'll see who's having fun soon enough."

# CHAPTER TWENTY-NINE

AFTER MAKING ARRANGEMENTS TO MELBOURNE, CARTER AND I PACK up and move out. I have a newly shortened list of places I want to check and, given we have one location all but locked, it's enough to satisfy me. The next few hours will also give our team back home a chance to put Carter's plan into place. There's a part of me that may have felt silly at one time for traipsing all over the world trying to find a needle in a haystack. However, now I feel perfectly competent to do whatever it takes to find the nutcase who killed my best friend. Sanity is sometimes overrated—my brother used to say—especially when it comes to cracking a case. What he meant was that in order to find a criminal, one must think like a criminal and use every morsel of a clue one has.

So, that's what I'm doing: taking every smidge of clues I have. In this case, it's the love letter Tercel delivered after putting me in the hospital at death's door. It's also the wooden box underneath Angie's bed full of love letters and postcards shared between Angie and Tercel. These combined clues make it a lock in my mind.

AFTER A SHORT RIDE from our hotel, we make it to The Sofitel Darling Harbour in minutes. Pulling up to the front of the tower, I see the allure of both the building and the location. The structure reminds me of the eccentric hotel The Standard on Sunset Strip in Hollywood.

As for location, it offers convenient shopping—steps from a shopping mall; meeting space—thanks to the convention center next door; a place to unwind in the city—courtesy of several parks; and a place to enjoy local history—thanks to the Maritime Museum. Points of egress include boats via the harbour and a rooftop helipad reserved for premiere clients.

*Exactly what a millionaire with a hefty ego needs.*

On the way to the hotel, Carter goes in one direction while I approach the front desk. There I'm told the General Manager will join me after wrapping a production meeting. The Assistant Manager shows me to the outdoor bar where I have a coffee overlooking the pool, harbour, and Sydney Opera House.

"I could get used to this," I mumbled to myself, flipping open a notepad with one hand, sipping an Americano with the other.

*A tube of sunscreen and a frosty drink would be nice.*

I'm about to text that daydream to Carter when I hear a pair of heels coming my way.

Judging by the name tag and professional swagger, I assume this is my contact. If her long legs and shapely figure don't get one's attention from a distance, her thick mane and bright eyes will up close.

"Hello, I'm Savoy Hendricks," she says, extending a firm handshake. "Sofitel's General Manager."

"Hello, I'm Detective Pat Norelli."

She waves for me to take a seat.

"Mrs. Hendricks, let me begin—"

"Sorry to interrupt, Detective, but it's *Ms*," she smiles. "I'm much too busy for marriage."

"Understood."

*Eat up all your gym time?* At nearly six feet, her chiseled figure and added reconstruction read: perfection.

After we exchange pleasantries, I proceed getting *Ms.* Savoy up to speed by producing two photos of Tercel: one, a website headshot; the other, a more recent candid photo from the Oscars last year.

"A tuxedo certainly makes the man, doesn't it?" She says, raising an eyebrow. Then switching photos, she adds, "Handsome. And certainly a face one would remember." She returned the photos. "However, I've never seen that man before."

Since I was a kid, I could tell when Pete lied. While not obvious, he had a tell. And I'm pretty sure I had a tell. Hell, everyone has a tell.

*I'll bet he's seen plenty of her.*

After the abrupt wave-off, I'm about to attempt other angles when, on cue, Carter exits the building and approaches our table.

Without substantial progress, I stand. "Fair enough, Ms. Hendricks. I certainly appreciate your time and will let you get back to it."

"Sorry to interrupt," Carter says in a perfectly honed Aussie accent. "G'Day, Ms. Hendricks," he nods. "Front desk said I could find you here along with my afternoon touring companion. Detective Norelli, is it?"

"Yes. Nice to see you, Dwight."

Turning to Savoy, I hand her a card. "Thank you again for your time and please feel free to reach out if anything comes to mind. In the meantime, I'll be on my way. Thought I might take in the sights while I'm here."

We three make our way back toward the lobby when Carter says, "Looking forward to a quiet tour. Just wrapped the morning at the Taronga Zoo with a family from the States. South Carolina, I believe it was. Can you imagine how fun it was straddling a couple *bogans* and four screaming kids?"

"I'm sure," Savoy smiles. "You're a far better bloke than I'da been."

"Well, lucky for me I packed a roadie," he gestures, taking a drink. "But apples she'll be, we're off to a splendid afternoon," he says, extending his arm for me.

"Good onya," she nods then sashays away.

As we exit the lobby, I ask, "What'n the hell did you say back there?"

"Spent the day with some rednecks, but fortunately had a couple beers to help, so it'd be all right."

"You're just full of surprises aren't you, *Dwight*?"


BACK IN HER OFFICE, Savoy kicks off her designer stilettos and sits in a white leather chair behind her glass and chrome desk. Rubbing her bare feet, she dials a number and waits, eyeballing the main security camera on the far wall. Watching the detective and her tour guide await a car at the front drive, she hears the line connect.

"Hello," a smiling voice says on the other end.

"Hello, yourself. How're the waves?" Savoy purrs.

"Hard yakka, but gnarly!" (*Hard work, but awesome*)

"You were right. Your guests finally showed up inquiring as to your whereabouts."

"And?"

"And I told her I'd never seen you before. She was quite something."

"What do you mean?"

"Well, besides beautiful—which she is—she's persistent. And as much as she worked to be coy, going around in a couple different directions, she kept trying to find center. I gave her nothing."

After a long silence, a tiny frown pinches her brow. "Hello?"

"I'm here. You said guests. Plural. Who's with her?"

"Not quite sure. But he's handsome."

He chuckles, "Handsome as me?"

"Darling, no one is as handsome as you."

"You're a peach. Anything else?"

She swivels in her chair, stretching a long leg to admire a perfect pedicure. "Yes, actually," she grins. "While good, his accent wasn't *nearly* as good as yours. It was off. Just a pinch."

"Really?"

"Yeah."

"Not one of *us*, you mean?"

"Right," she giggles. "Not one of us."

"When can I see you again?"

"Any time you like," she coos.

After a short silence, "Do you think they'll be around a while?"

Spinning toward the monitor, she sees they've left. "That's a good question, but I can't say. She did mention taking in the sights."

"Hmm."

"But then, this tour guide, named Dwight," she mumbles, typing Sydney Private Tours into her database. "*If* he's for real and really a guide, I likely would've seen him before. The tour companies are such a tight-knit group." Several results pop on her screen. "Love, let me give this a look and I'll get back to you, okay?"

"Don't keep me waiting. You know how I can be when I don't get what I want."

# CHAPTER THIRTY

AFTER THEY HANG UP, TERCEL SENDS A TEXT TO A PRIVATE NUMBER: *Are you available? Start ASAP in SYD. 2 days tops. 911$*—code for *answer immediately, job in Sydney*, and *handsome payment*.

In less than 60 seconds, a response reads: *Call when ready.*

He engages *Nord VPN* on his phone, providing an extra layer of security, and waits to speak with Noah Taylor, a former cop and current private investigator, of sorts. Their relationship began last year when Tercel relocated to Australia and needed an extra set of eyes on trails he might leave on the way to becoming invisible.

"How are you, Noah?"

"Good, thanks. What can I do for you?"

Tercel likes Noah. He's a no bullshit guy with no agenda. He's divorced, his kids are grown and gone, and he's nearly always available —often, at a moment's notice. He's also a brute of a man; big, strong, and ugly—a good combination for his line of work. Being a former cop, Noah knows how the system operates. Working as a bail bondsman for a couple of years, he learned how to handle felons and any sort of law-breaking idiot. Now as a current self-contracting P.I., he's able to work both inside and outside legal lines. He fears nothing, embraces danger, and is skilled with a weapon. Plus, he never loses information—he only finds it. And he likes cash—lots of it.

For Tercel, he's the perfect combination.

"There's a Detective looking for me. She's from Hollywood and wants to take me in—or who knows, maybe finish me here. Either way, I need an extra set of eyes before she finds me. She also has a sidekick, but I don't know anything about him."

"Okay."

"According to my source, they just left the Sofitel Darling Harbor and are heading out for a tour of the city. No idea how long they'll be there, but I assume until they find me. And it's just a matter of time before they end up here."

"Okay."

"She's got something to prove. And she's...tenacious."

"Copy that."

"Where are you now?"

"Golf. Well, attempting. New South Wales Club."

"Nice. Hard course."

He snorts. "Thought you were a surfer."

"It's a good place to do business, but yeah, I'm better with waves than a nine iron."

"Understood."

"They left maybe ten minutes ago. Like I said, no idea what's next. I'll text you a photo of her as soon as we hang up. Name's Patricia Norelli."

"Okay."

"How soon can you move?"

Noah checks his watch. "15?"

Tercel thinks a moment. "Okay."

"What's her pal's name?"

He checks a notepad. "Dwight, with Sidney Private Tours."

"Okay," Noah says.

"I'll be there shortly, but you get started. I'll text where we can meet."

"Anything else?"

"Nope, that's it."

"I'm on it."

As they disconnect, Tercel accesses his Dropbox where his collectible photos and docs are encrypted and stored. He flips through a folder titled, NORELLI. Scanning through several dozen photos, his desires are instantly ignited. While he especially enjoys the full-length nude of her outstretched body bound to the bed in his Bel Air mansion, he selects a more discreet shot and forwards it to Noah.

*Hard to believe it's been a year—won't be long before I see you again.*

# CHAPTER THIRTY-ONE

COMFORTABLY SEATED ABOARD THE PRIVATE GULFSTREAM G650, Tercel is lost in thought, staring at the earth below. He wonders if it had been smart to text Norelli—even using the encrypted texting service. The ball is in motion, so it doesn't really matter. There are many ways to look at it, but given it is approaching the anniversary of the day he nearly ended her life, he feels it apropos to let her know he is thinking about her.

*So I'm a little obsessed.*

Placing her in the crosshairs of LAPD management makes for a poetic gesture, especially after she has spent a career working for a stellar reputation. He has a perverse pleasure seeing her in the middle of shit.

*If I can't have her, no one can.*

His mind spins after hearing the conversation between the two cops at her house.

*They stood out on that deck and mocked me.*

Twirling the phone on the side console, he runs through his plans: past and current. He understood Angie's neurosis but never fully appreciated the depth of her obsession with him.

*Guess it happens, especially to someone who's wired like her.*

The fact she threatened to leak his whereabouts to the police if he didn't confess not only pissed him off but also bored him.

*If she's not loyal, how can I be?*

He recalls her expression when he arrived at her house after nearly a year. She didn't even recognize him. He grins at the thought.

*Did anyone expect me to disappear knowing I still had entanglements?*

He spots a passing jet and watches until it is out of sight.

*Why else would I move to the other side of the world?*

Looking up, he watches the flight attendant's skirt tighten as she bends over.

*Does Patricia understand just how close to death she came? Two syringes—one would shut her down for a few hours; the other, forever.*

As the attendant delivers his drink, her open blouse invites a peek.

He smiles; her gaze lingers.

He watches as she returns to the front of the jet.

*I've loved before, but I only* wanted *one.*

Aroused, he relishes replaying the crime scene.

*One had to go—one I wanted to save.*

He can't pull his gaze from her striking curves and tanned legs.

*You could've been the one, Patricia.*

Thoughts flash to Norelli being tied up in silk kimono ribbons.

*The One*, he smirks. *Cliche, but true.*

He recalls the phrase he used with Bobby the last time they were together: *Ours for the taking.*

And the words he used to trap Bobby: *Merely for your entertainment.*

The obsession for power, lust, and greed was used to seduce Bobby.

*And it worked.*

Recalling his well-orchestrated escape plan, he grins.

*Not good when they don't give love in return.*

His inner therapist kicks in to decipher hidden meanings and, as thoughts turn to his mother, he sips his drink and watches the attendant who lifts her glass to him.

*Cheers, Mum.*


SUDDENLY, the Captain announcing their intention to land awakens Tercel. He was dreaming how he was the one tied up with kimono sashes as Patricia held the lethal injection. A tiny whisper of terror shoots through the back of his mind and he suppresses it immediately.

*Be sharp. The game is still afoot.*

Checking his watch, he reviews the plans. Satisfied, he retrieves his smartphone and opens *Wickr,* a military-grade encryption app that sends untraceable messages.

Watching the approaching city below, he contemplates the note he will send to Norelli. Then, with the message crafted, he sets the message to evaporate immediately after opening and pushes *SEND.*

# CHAPTER THIRTY-TWO

*MELBOURNE, AUSTRALIA—*

LANDING IN MELBOURNE, we waste little time getting to work. My phone is dead, so charging it will have to wait, but I have plenty to keep my attention for a handful of hours. My list of hotels is shorter—half the number of those in Sydney, thanks to the intel we gathered—so I want to get in and out as quickly as possible.

With that in mind, we begin at the Sofitel Melbourne on Collins. Having spent time with Savoy and feeling certain Tercel has an attachment to that hotel—if only by way of a relationship with her—I'm confident it's worth the inspection.

As soon as we arrive, it doesn't feel right. But given it's on our list, we go in, run the same chatter we've been doing all along, and leave before we can finish our coffee.

In the town car, I check my list. Seeing there is a Grand Hyatt, I double check the website, see it isn't plush enough, cross it from my list, and instruct the driver to take us to the Park Hyatt.

The moment we enter the courtyard, I know it will be our homebase. The building is immaculate; the ambiance, elegant; and the people, friendly.

Once checked in, I begin working on the outspoken and flamboyant concierge, Carson Robicheaux.

Carter enters several moments behind me, then disappears.

Within twenty minutes, I learn three valuable things. First, no one matching Tercel's description stayed here; however, Carson shares how he and a co-worker saw someone who resembled him spending a good deal of time in both their bar and the Cricketers Bar of the Hotel Windsor, just blocks away.

The second thing I learn—thanks again to Carson—is how I can save time; that is, if the Adelphi, the Grand Hyatt, the Sofitel, or the QT Melbourne are on my list. He informs us they aren't up to the par for our "person of interest." As Carson puts it, "This industry, as big as it is on an International basis, is quite small and many of us know each other because we spend a fair amount of time fraternizing with certain patrons."

And the third item he shares is how the people with *real money* stay at either the Windsor or the Langham. He also tells how many celebrities come to Australia to get away, only to find themselves in the dead center of as much gossip as they experience in Hollywood. Carson's about to dish some sordid details when his eyes shift to behind me—and his jaw drops.

I turn to beat his explanation to the punch. Carter is walking straight toward us, scanning the room like he's searching for a target. He's dressed like an Army Colonel: clean-shaven, spit-polished, and eye-catching.

"Hello, *Soldier*," Carson says under his breath.

As he approaches, Carter tips his hat to me, "Ma'am," before turning to Carson. "Sir, I trust I'm not interrupting."

I hold my grin as Carson barely holds himself together.

"Yes, of course. I mean, no, you're not. We're just chatting about, um, a tour my friend here is going to take. How may I be of service?"

"I have an appointment with a..." he checks a note in his hand, "Detective Norelli, and I'm wondering if you—"

"That's me," I say, extending a hand. "You must be Colonel Scott."

"Yes, Ma'am, Colonel Carter Scott at your service."

Turning to Carson, I say, "My escort," then whisper—putting a finger to my lips—"And top secret."

.  .  .

AFTER SOME INNOCUOUS chatter and a quick pint at the bar, we stroll out to Parliament Place, passing through Burston Reserve, a quaint park just outside our hotel. Crossing Macarthur, I say, "Another ten minutes back there and Carson would've likely…yanked your doodle dandy."

Carter's expression says: *Don't you ever stop?*

Downtown Melbourne has an old world charm and begs tourists and locals alike to enjoy the many historic facades and parks around the city. We wait for the light to change at Spring Street and moments later enter the majestic and handsome Hotel Windsor. The lobby is stunning with its high ceilings, broad arches, and lush accoutrements. The air of sophistication is reminiscent of a bygone era.

Approaching the front desk, we're immediately introduced to a Mr. Phillip Shepparton. Tall and immaculately dressed, he reminds me of Robert Crawley, Earl of Grantham, on the show *Downton Abbey*. His accent is soft, but his diction, exact. I keep my detective badge in view and Carter's getup speaks for itself. When we show him the photos, he studies them methodically before passing them back.

"And you say this *official* business requires your knowing if he stayed with us for any duration of time."

"Yes, it is. And yes, we need to learn if he spent time here." Leaning forward, I lower my voice. "He's part of a murder investigation. One that, I'm sad to say, spans quite a length of time."

His eyebrows raise just enough to reveal shock but not enough to cast judgment.

"Understood. Well," he sighs, "I can offer you two pieces of insight. Please follow me."

He shows us to a side counter to wait while he retrieves a large leather-bound book from beneath the counter.

Putting on a tidy pair of reading glasses, he leafs through the book.

"Ah yes," he stops several dozen pages in. "It was May, a year ago. Hmm…" he frowns. "But you said…" he looks up. "Name was Darius Tercel?"

"Yes," I say. Carter doesn't budge.

He flips a page.

"Ordinarily, well, not *always*, but often, we would have a photo taken of our guests." He removes his glasses. "We're very specific about privacy here. We hold our guests in high regard and protect all matters of privacy."

Although I have a good idea why, I ask anyway.

"And why would you have a photo on file of your guests?"

He allows an efficient smile. "More specifically, it's for our *extended guests*. That way our staff can memorize their faces and recall their names—as a matter of respect—so that as they attend to their wishes, they can address them with proper names. Not just *Sir* or *Madam*, you see."

"Of course," I smile.

"All of that long-winded explanation aside, as I'm sure you have more to do than listen to me prattle on about the Windsor's machinations, is that while your Mr. Tercel does look *similar* to our guest, I can't say for certain they are one in the same. This gentleman was a bit heavier; his face, a bit fuller. And his hair made him appear more rockstar, less accountant." Looking down, he says, "And I see he booked our largest and finest suite. The Royal Suite is rather impressive..."

"But do—" I stop. "No, please go ahead."

With a nod, "What I was going to say was *our* guest's name was..." he double checks the book, "Grover. Mr. Jonathan Grover. He arrived with his daughter."

Suddenly, the excitement of being *this close* is squashed in a flash.

I look at Carter and frown. He replies with a raised eyebrow.

"Mr. Shepparton," Carter applies a tight smile, "you said Mr. Grover booked the Royal Suite. I'm curious. How much does that suite cost and for how long did he book it?"

Shepparton turns to his book again.

"It was booked for the entire month of July. And at a cost of $160, US."

I can't help my expression. "$160,000?"

"Yes. In advance. He also hired one of our car services for the entire time as well as..." he points to the front of the hotel, "that horse and carriage—several nights a week for the duration. I recall he was usually accompanied by his daughter—or other *guests*."

*Okay, there's no daughter. His look seems even different. Wait...*

"Mr. Shepparton, you said July, right?"

"Yes. He actually arrived..." he checks the book, "the last weekend of June, checking out the morning of July 1st. And one thing I recall..."

I'm doing the math, but I don't want to miss anything. "Yes, what's that?"

"Our guests arrive from all over the world. They come here to experience this beautiful city, this magnificent hotel, and they have high expectations—which we always strive to deliver."

*Get on with it.*

"Yes?"

"And nearly all of our *premier* guests are gracious. Mr. Grover was one of them. *Very* gracious."

I let my eyebrows do the asking.

"He was an extraordinarily gracious tipper. To all of our staff. He gave me a rather handsome parting thank you."

"Nice," I nod, smiling at Shepparton and eyeballing Carter.

"Mr. Shepparton, how old would you say Mr. Grover's daughter was?"

He looks to the ceiling.

"Oh, I'd say 20? 23? She *could* have been as old as 25."

"So, not a teenager."

"No, no. And now that I think of it, she reminded me of *you*. In fact, she could have been your daughter."

*What?*

"I'm sorry," he says. "That didn't come out right. Forgive me if—"

"Don't give it another thought," I wave the air. "But tell me, do you recall the daughter's name?"

"Yes," he glances at his book again. "Darcy Patricia."

# CHAPTER THIRTY-THREE

It doesn't take long for "Colonel Shadow" and me to snag a seat in the Cricketers Bar for a stiff drink. I ask the bartender if he minds charging my dead phone behind the counter, and we take seats at the end of the bar, so I can keep an eye on the phone and roaming ears off our business. We stare at one another for a minute before our eyes blanket the room.

"Okay, this certainly takes things up a notch."

"We should've booked this joint," Carter says, eyeballing a table of young women.

"I see what you've got on your mind," I turn my attention to a menu. "I'm starving."

"Me, too."

We put in our order and I excuse myself to the ladies' room. After a splash and a spritz, I return to a bustling restaurant. Across the room, I see Carter helping an elderly woman move her husband's wheelchair under their table. I return to my seat and watch him. The couple must've said something nice because he's smiling. When the old man salutes Carter, I get a lump in my throat. Carter returns a snap of a salute, then removes his cap and leans over to kiss the wife's hand. As he walks away, I see him discreetly slide something on their waitress's tray, whispering something in her ear.

*Wow.*

Returning, he picks up his beer and taps my glass. "Cheers."

"So, tell me a little something about that big old *softy* buried deep within that cold-hearted *hunter*."

"Ha! Just wanted to do something nice," he chuckles. "Move along little lady—nothing to see here."

I decide to pry until I can uncover some interesting background. Come to find out Carter has one sibling—a brother who is a pastor. His father is a retired Lt. Colonel in the Army. His mother passed away years ago, and he doesn't currently have a love interest. However, his best friend is back home guarding his 50-acre compound that straddles the Great Smokies and Blue Ridge Mountains of North Carolina. That four-legged friend is Sampson.

When my prying turns to his business, he says what is most entertaining about it nobody would believe and what is most dangerous nobody will ever know.

Then, he slams shut like a door.

The bartender delivers a bowl of mixed nuts, and we enjoy our next drink with light chatter while pushing aside the underlying angst of our mission.

"And how about you, Darcy Patricia?"

I cut him a look. "Funny, but only my parents call me Darcy. Close friends use Patricia. Everybody else calls me Pat. And just plain Norelli works best...Carter *no-last-name*."

WE LAUGH our way through botched relationship stories, the monotony of nine-to-five jobs—something neither of us enjoys— and another drink along with one of the best Wagyu burgers I've ever had.

We reach several conclusions.

"I can't imagine doing anything else, and there's nothing better than..." he leans to whisper, "chasing bad guys."

I raise a glass. "I'll drink to that. And I like the fact we decided to stay the night," I smile. "You know, instead of trying to rush."

"Agreed."

"I mean, we really only have one more place to check out. And I have a feeling we both know that either he'll be there or in that last place we checked. Or, well, you know—who knows?"

"Well said," he laughs.

With a playful slap, I say, "And I think it's probably okay to drop the cloak & dagger, given we've likely been made."

He looks from me to his uniform and says, "Wait, you're telling me you don't like a man in uniform?"

For the first time since we started this trip, I find myself looking at Carter differently. Sure, he's handsome, charming, and his dark side is oddly alluring, but I've seen that many times before. However, there's something different about him that goes beyond self-assurance. He is grounded to his core.

We continued the stories, the laughs, the drinks, and the flirting well into the night. And the more Carter shares stories from his past, the more I feel pulled to him.

## CHAPTER THIRTY-FOUR

Entering the suite, they slowly begin unbuttoning each other's clothing. Once inside, Carter kicks the door closed behind him. Removing all clothing, they continue kissing before landing on the plush king-sized bed.

In the middle of the night, a giggle awakens Carter.

His groggy voice says, "You know laughing's an odd way to get awakened."

"Maybe. But in this case," I giggle again, "it's a good thing."

He reaches for the light. "Wow, that's mighty bright."

"Yeah, turn it off. I've got a better idea," I say, stretching across the bed.

Suddenly, soft lighting slowly illuminates the perimeter of the ceiling.

"Oh, that's much better," he groans, reaching for my naked body.

"And even better?"

I grab the nightstand phone and roll over to straddle him.

"Room service."

Shaking his head, he says, "Voracious."

. . .

AN EMPTY PLATE of food and a bottle of champagne later, he pats his flat belly. "You are certainly full of surprises, Detective."

"Goes with the business," I smile.

After a long kiss, he props against the headboard.

"And each one of them…as delicious as the next."

I run a finger along the edge of his muscular arm, drawing a circle around the tattoo on his shoulder.

"Well, you certainly shared a few surprises of your own," I say, looking at the mound just beneath the sheet.

"How about some dessert?" He asks with a bounce of his brow.

"Yummy."

JUST AS I'M beginning to regain consciousness—between the noise of the waking city and the emerging call from mother nature—another sound grabs my attention.

I open a sleepy eye and shut off the alarm, attempting to gain my bearings. When I hear heavy breathing across the room instead of on the opposite side of the bed, I sit up to find the silhouette of Carter on the floor.

"Are you—working out?" I ask, pressing a button on the bedside table. Ten foot tall drapes slowly pull back as blackout shades simultaneously rise. Light slowly fills the room and Carter gets up from the floor.

"Just a few pushups," he says, grabbing a hand towel to dry his neck. "Helps get the blood flowing."

"Well, *Yippee-ki-yay*," I grin, pulling a sheet to cover myself.

"Don't do that on my account," he smiles, approaching the bed for a long kiss. Taking a strand of my disheveled hair, he gently wraps it behind my ear. "You are some kind of beautiful, Patricia."

SHOWERED AND DRESSED, packed and booked, we're prepared to catch the next flight to Brisbane. Fortunately, the midnight snack helps keep a crushing hangover at bay; however, we both still need to eat. While Carter delivers our luggage to the town car, I get us a table in the restaurant, Breakfast at One Eleven, managing a table in the corner and a pot of black coffee.

Arriving, he spots the pot of coffee and shakes his head. "Okay, that just about does it."

"What?"

Coming around the table, he gets down on one knee and takes my hand. "Will you marry me, Detective Norelli?"

I start laughing so hard, I get the hiccups. I'm also blushing, thanks to two couples at nearby tables who begin clapping at the sight.

Waving him to sit, I seriously feel about as happy as I have in a long time. Catching my breath, I enjoy seeing Carter get a kick out of kidding me.

"You," I say, turning to my menu.

Pouring coffee for both of us, he says, "That looks good on you."

Surprised, I look down at my blouse. "What, this?"

"No," he smiles. "Happiness."


As we finish our coffee, my mind wanders to items that need addressing. Oddly enough, most thoughts of back home have nearly disappeared, and while I need to make some calls soon, they will have to....

*Wait!*

I suddenly realize I forgot my phone in the bar last night.

"What is it?" Carter snaps, setting aside the newspaper.

"My phone. I can't believe I was so freakin' careless, especially after going to such lengths to keep an eye on it last night."

"Relax. I'm sure it's still there. I'll get it."


Within minutes, he's back with phone in hand and smiling as he approaches the table. A tall blonde is with him.

"Patricia, this is Lizabeth. She's the morning bartender."

"G'day, Miss. How're ya?"

Standing, I say, "G'day," the only Aussie phrase I have. "We really enjoyed ourselves last night. In your bar, that is," I blush. "Please join us, Lizabeth."

She checks her watch. "I suppose I have a minute or two."

As I pour three cups, I think of how she reminds me of Savoy in Sydney, but blonde.

"While I was waiting for the concierge to get your phone—thankfully left by last night's bartender—I ran into Lizabeth," Carter says. "Long story short, I shared a bit about who we're looking for. Come to learn, while staying here he made a lot of friends. Including *her*."

"Interesting," I say, giving her my full attention. "He's a nice man, yes?"

Nodding, she says, "And generous. With tips…" she leans forward, "and attention."

"So you showed her the photo?" I ask Carter.

"You have it, right?" he says, looking for my bag. "I described him and shared his MO."

"Got it right here," I say, handing her the photos.

"Oh," she frowns. "That's *not* him."

"No?" I shoot a glance at Carter.

With a dramatic shake of her head, she says, "No, this man had longer, lighter hair. And his eyes…" She flips to the second photo. "I mean, his eyes are *kinda* close, but different. Sorry." Looking up, she says, "Jonathan was bigger. Broader. Well," she eyeballs Carter and tosses her chin at him. "More like him."

I say, "Well, that adds a wrinkle, doesn't it?"

Without a confirmation, the point feels moot and the moment awkward.

"I'm sorry you two. I wish I could be more helpful," she checks her watch, "but I really must get to it." Taking a sip, she says, "Thank you for the coffee. And the chat."

Standing, we shake hands and she leaves.

As we gather our things, Carter hands over my phone. I turn it on and we walk to the lobby while it powers up. There, Carter speaks to the concierge about our car and I enter my security code. As my eyes fall on the screen, the spiders return—scattering down the center of my back. Suddenly, I catch myself not breathing.

Approaching, Carter frowns, "Patricia? What is it?"

I release the breath I'm holding and turn the phone toward him.

He stares. "That's *specific*."

I look at the UNKNOWN caller's message: *I'm coming for you.*

That's when it hits me.

"Hold on," I say, digging into the bottom of my bag.

Finding what I need, I wave for him to follow.

Heading for the Cricketers Bar, I look for Lizabeth. She looks up from the wine glasses she's polishing.

Approaching, I say, "It's me again."

"G'day," she smiles.

"I found another photo. More recent. I wonder if you wouldn't mind taking a quick peek at it and tell me if this is our friend."

"Happy to."

I hand her the photograph I found in Angie's bookshelf.

Lizabeth instantly nods. "That's him. Jumpin' Johnny Grover."

"Jumping Johnny?" I half smile-half frown.

"Yeah, I'll spare *all* the details, but let's just say, he's handy. And a dandy surfer. Certainly not the *shark biscuit*—uh, amateur surfer—you see around the tourist traps. The *nicky* comes from a jump he performs atop a solid wave. It's funny to watch. Yup, that's him, by cracky!"

STANDING BY OUR TOWN CAR, I release a long sigh. "Guess we no longer have to search."

"Nope."

"He was in Sydney. He was here. And I'm guessing he's in Brisbane—or en route."

"Yep."

"Or parts between."

"That, too."

I look out at Australia and think how beautiful it is—and how I hope to see more of it.

"But instead of us chasing him—now, he's chasing *me*."

# CHAPTER THIRTY-FIVE

*SYDNEY, AUSTRALIA—*

TERCEL LANDS in Sydney and has a car take him to the Sofitel to see Savoy. Given the short ride, he takes advantage of the time and sends a text alerting her of his arrival. Next, he sends a text to Noah, arranging a meeting shortly, and a longer text to a New York connection for what he's calling his "Plan B." Last, he refreshes the page, looking for a text from Patricia. Nothing.

*Not a surprise.*

Entering the front of Sofitel, Savoy greets Tercel and he's dazzled with her beauty. He watches her sashay toward him, imagining her working as a model on New York runways.

"Hello, handsome," she kisses both cheeks, whispering in his ear, "I'll give you the real thing upstairs."

"Naughty girl should be spanked."

"Please?" She says, stepping back to admire his physique. "You look amazing."

"Thanks for noticing." As she turns to lead the way, he pats her curvaceous backside, watching other men gawk as they pass.

*That's right; she's with me.*

In the elevator, she leans close. "It's been entirely too long." She kisses him. "You're making me *crazy*."

. . .

AN HOUR LATER, she says, "I need to complete a few things before I end my day." She grabs a nearby robe and disappears.

He texts Noah: *I'm at the Sofitel. Meet me at the outside bar in 30.*

After a confirmation text, Tercel tosses his phone on the bed and enters the massive dressing room where Savoy is touching up her makeup.

She looks at him in the mirror and admires his physique. "Babe?"

"Yes, love."

"It's really good to see you," she says. "Can't believe it's been six months."

He stops buttoning his shirt and looks at her.

*Oh, shit.*

"Seven, this week," he smiles, returning to his buttons. "What's on your mind, Savoy? You're looking at me rather intently."

She returns to her makeup. "It's just…" she smiles, "you've changed so much since I saw you last."

"You like?"

"Of course. It's just—"

"What?"

"When you arrived in Sydney, you looked *so* much different. It's amazing the physical transformation you've managed."

"That's what having an around-the-clock personal trainer and private chef will do for you. As you'll recall when we met, I was skinny, had a belly…" he flashes a set of ripped abs, "and in order to get in shape for surfing I had to make a *lot* of changes."

"Again, baby, *amazing.*"

After a period of silence, he says, "But you're actually referring to the surgery, right?"

"Yes, but…" she holds up both hands, "trust me, I'm a big fan of transformation. I mean, look at me. I was tired of being flat-chested, and I had…" she chuckles, "what my mother called *chicken lips*. And once you get started, you think there's no harm in creating higher cheekbones, and maybe just a little tweak here and there," she says, turning to face him.

"That's exactly why I did it," he says. "As far back as high school, I had my mother's droopy eyelids and bags under my eyes. And I never really liked my nose." Applying moisturizer, he continues. "Besides, I lived in Hollywood *forever*, and it's hard *not* to get caught up in tweaking oneself."

Savoy knows she's touched a nerve. And given their reunion, she doesn't want to do anything to ruin matters, especially since she doesn't know how long it'll be before they see each other again. Something nags at her, but she lets it go.

Standing, she checks herself and starts to leave the room. Tercel grabs her arm a bit too tightly and it startles her.

"What is it, baby?"

He looks at her without a word. His expression is cold and distant —not the same eyes she just made love to minutes ago.

Loosening his grip, he smiles and kisses her. "We're a regular Ken and Barbie, huh?"

She lets out a nervous chuckle and smiles, "Exactly."


IN THE ELEVATOR, she smiles at the mirrored wall, wiping a tiny smudge of lipstick.

*A touchup is one thing—a complete rebuild is another.*

"You look delicious, Savoy. And thank you for letting me take care of a bit of business while you tie up your loose ends. After we're both finished, we can pick back up where we left off. Sound good?"

"Yes, it does. And thank you for the sweet words, Jonathan."


IN THE LOBBY, Savoy went in one direction and Tercel the other. Passing through the doors, he spots Noah across the patio.

Approaching, he adjusts his tie and gives a terse nod. "Hello, Noah."

"Sir."

"What have we learned?"

Setting aside a glass of sparkling water, Noah says, "They went to Melbourne just as you expected, but my contact at the hotel said they mentioned skipping other stops after they got what they needed. They're on their way to Brisbane." He checks his watch. "Should be leaving inside the hour."

Tercel is quiet, staring out at the harbor.

"I anticipated that. It would've been a waste of your time."

"As for Dwight? Sydney Private Tours doesn't have an employee by that name. Never has. And frankly, I have *no* idea who he is. I reached out for some help but came up empty."

Tercel swats aside the comment. "Doesn't matter. My money's on him being a boyfriend. Or hell, he could be a private dick like you," he smiles.

"Possible."

"I'd like to extend my original deal. That is, if you have the time."

"Always."

"Good. Can we just say open-ended, for now?"

A nod.

Tercel checks his watch. "What say you have a nice meal here on me. Then pack a few things and head on to Brisbane. I'd say we go together, but I'm not sure if I'll leave tonight or first thing tomorrow."

"If it's no matter to you, I'd just as soon head out. Get ahead of the situation."

Tercel smiles. "Good man."

As Noah leans forward to finish his drink, Tercel sees a holstered gun inside his jacket. That answered his next question.

"And Noah?"

"Sir?"

"They'll land in Brisbane. But if I know Norelli, it won't take them long to make their way to the Gold Coast. I may even help them along. I want you to stay on top of them. Don't let them out of your sight. When it was just her, I had it under control. But with this unknown *variable*, well, let's just say I don't like surprises."

"Agreed."

"And for the record…" he looks around at the small crowd, "if things get *complicated,* I'll triple your standard rate."

Noah's tiny smirk said it all.


Tercel bids Noah goodbye, enjoys a pleasant dinner with Savoy, and relishes an even more enjoyable dessert back in her room. After that, his attention is instantly elsewhere, and as unhappy as Savoy is seeing him disappear so quickly, he must stay ahead of matters.

Besides, Savoy is certainly no Patricia, and while he doesn't like not knowing who Patricia's travel companion is, he's confident he'll find a solution for the stranger as well as a way to persuade Patricia to his way of thinking.

Whether she agrees or not, Tercel is her lifeline—her ticket to freedom.

# CHAPTER THIRTY-SIX

*BRISBANE, AUSTRALIA—*

EN ROUTE TO BRISBANE, I go through my email and texts. That's when I get word from Nelson to reach out to him ASAP. Next, is a text from Brown: *Have you spoken with Nelson? If not, I'd suggest you do so soon. Hit me immediately after.*

I glance over to see Carter doing google flyovers on his laptop.

"What are you doing?"

"Looking at Brisbane. From above. Trying to get a lay of the land," he says, shaking his head.

"What?"

"Just thinking about something you said a while back. About you not thinking he's in Brisbane."

I shake my head.

"Me either. I mean, look…" he shifts in his seat, "having seen Sydney and Melbourne—if he's looking for luxury living and all the *action* of a big city, he'd have that there."

"Right."

"But if he's here to—"

"Surf. Then he'd be hanging at either the epicenter of the scene or the outer perimeter. My money's on—"

"Gold Coast," we say simultaneously.

I point to his screen. "Zoom in here."

He does while I flip open my notepad.

"There," I tap the screen. "It's about access to the best waves. More than the prestige of the place. Not too commercial. More of a local vibe. Check Coolangatta."

He whips his head toward me.

"I'd love to tell you I have a solid reason, but the truth?"

His eyebrows raise.

"I dig the name. Sounds like it should be a Police song from the '80s."

With a chuckle, he pulls up places. "No highrises."

"Right. It's chess, Carter. I've sat on his couch for more hours than I can count. And even as much as he let me do the talking, it's what he said *in between* that told me everything I needed. Plus, wait, are you interested in my theories?"

He looks up with surprise, then gives me a look that makes my lap tingle.

"You're looking at me that way again."

A tiny grin appears.

"Like you did when you were preparing for *dessert*," I say, lowering my voice.

"Yes, to that. But yes, I'm very interested in your theories," he says, looking from my eyes to my lips. "Please. Continue."

*Mmm.*

"Okay, as I was saying," I grab my blouse and tug it, letting in cool air. "He's got a few classic tendencies. By the way, did I tell you I was married to a therapist?"

A nod.

"I got two great things from that marriage. The first was Shay. The second? Some really solid insight to the human psyche. Hell, to this day, I think I learned more about psychology and therapy than my ex did—and he's the one with the degree."

"I'm impressed."

"Bottom line to understanding Tercel—just in case you haven't picked up all the nuance yet—is that he's a narcissist. Through and through. He's also a womanizer. But what he really is?"

"A serial killer?"

"Well, yeah, but he's a first-class *mama's boy*. As an only child, he was spoiled beyond rotten and lived in the lap of luxury from an early age. Then he created a career where he was idolized by not only patients but also from studio heads who learned he could take their biggest, most neurotic stars, and return them to—what they call—*green light status*. He had the ability to unlock their inner darkness and turn them around. Made him very successful. And very rich."

"And what's the one secret that makes him tick?"

"Right," I say, tucking a loose strand of hair behind my ear. "It's that even though he worshipped his mother, he actually *despised* her because he felt he never measured up. No matter how hard he tried, he could never please her. And secretly, I believe he wanted to have her, in some strange way, so that he could control her."

Silence.

"I know. Weird, and a bit sick, but also kinda classic. Thing is, he couldn't control her. And that frustrated the hell out of him."

I catch myself fidgeting with a cocktail napkin, then toss it aside.

"And the last bit of therapy before I stop this…"

"Patricia, this is fascinating and helpful. Please continue."

A bit self-conscious, I gave a mocking nod. "When he saw his father kill himself—or rather the immediate remnants because he arrived soon after—because *his dad* didn't measure up, I think he subconsciously feared that for himself. And that's about the time Tercel began his process of taking matters into his own hands."

I sit back and release a deep sigh, realizing it's the first time I've put all those pieces together in one cohesive thought—and it comes without the fear of being wrong because I know I'm right.

Carter gives a tiny golf clap and leans over to kiss me.


WE ARE quiet for close to an hour when I suddenly spring upright, startling Carter. "I just had an idea."

"What?"

"The hotel is more about proximity, less about luxury."

"Right, you said that."

"Right. And he needs quick access to an airport. The place I mentioned earlier has an airport barely ten minutes from the beach. That'll be his escape route."

Carter is now reopening his laptop and doing another flyover search. We don't have much time left. My twisting gut assures me Nelson has bad news which means I'll have to return sooner than later. And if I don't find Tercel and bring him in, there's no telling where he'll go next. If that were to happen, I feel certain I won't have another chance. Tercel is either on our heels or planning an escape. Frankly, I'm not sure which twisted desire is stronger for him: escaping from me or removing me.

*PING!*

I dig in my bag for my phone. The screen says it's from Angie.

*What the hell?*

My heart nearly beats out of my chest until I realize it was the *other* Angie—aka Moonbeam—from the bookstore in Palm Desert.

Swiping the screen, I pull up her text: *Hi Detective Norelli. Just wanted to drop you a note to say hello and to let you know I was thinking of you and hoping you are finding the answers you're looking for. Just remember the quote about the distance between your head and your heart. Trust them both. All the answers lie within you. Okay, that's it. Hope to see you next time you visit your parents. Peace, Moonbeam*

I sit for a moment, absorbing the poignancy of the moment.

*Trust your gut—so far it's been right.*

# CHAPTER THIRTY-SEVEN

*HOLLYWOOD, CALIFORNIA—*

NELSON SITS AT HIS DESK, staring at his phone. He knows he's between a rock and a hard place. He owes his loyalty to The Job, his integrity to those around him, and his conscience to...

*Well, that seems to have dissolved over the years.*

He isn't thoroughly convinced what most believe is "right" is exactly that—not anymore, especially given the way those above him don't follow the rules themselves. For too many, it's more a matter of progressing their careers than perpetuating the truth. He's seen it a dozen times—more these days than when he began nearly thirty years ago. And as much as he knows he can't bend the truth to fit his needs, he can at the very least help one of his own come to a place in her career where it matters. He knows Norelli is doing everything in her power to prove herself. As far as he's concerned, she already has.

He isn't sure what Davenport and his allies are up to, but he knows what his gut is saying: *If it feels off, it probably is.*

Using his cell instead of a landline, he dials Norelli's phone again. She answers instantly.

"Norelli."

"For *Chrissake,* Norelli. It's Nelson. How you holding up?"

"Pretty good, Captain. Considering."

"Norelli, hold on." He stands to close the door. "I just needed to share some urgent matters with you."

"Carter and I *just* landed in Brisbane. What do you mean, urgent?"

"It's Davenport. Simply put, he's out to nail you."

"Why?"

"Not sure. Not yet, anyway. But I will, soon enough. Here's the deal, I'm *supposed* to be calling to bring you in officially."

"What?"

"Remember when I said you'd be put on suspension *after* I confirmed a few things?"

"Yeah."

"Well, he found out you bounced. Brown and I tried to cover, but Norelli, you're in some deep shit."

"What are you saying?"

A long sigh. "Calm down. And before you get too rattled, let me just say, I'm going to call you from my office line. But I won't do that for another hour, okay? At that time, Davenport will be with me and listening."

"Sir, what the hell?"

"Because of the *timing* of Angie's death, what *he's* saying about your knowledge of Tercel's *methods*, and the fact we found documents with your signature showing a Power of Attorney—"

"I never signed anything. You and I both know this is complete *bullshit!*"

"Agreed. And Pat, I thought it was all some kind of smoke and mirrors. But evidently Davenport and his people turned her place upside down and—"

"What the fuck?"

"Yeah. They found two key pieces of evidence that pin Angie's murder on *you*. Listen, just follow my lead when I call you back, okay? Brown and I have a plan, but I need you to follow my lead."


MY HEAD IS about to explode from my conversation with Nelson. Fortunately, Carter is turning out to be a gentler giant than I ever imagined. He jumped into action with all the details of our next move. We're on our way to the Sofitel in Brisbane in a blink where Savoy has kindly set us up with both car and hotel accommodations.

"Take it easy. We'll get to the hotel, catch our breath, and sort this out, " Carter says.

"Easy for you to say," I say, staring at the passing landscape.

All I can think of at the moment is how badly I want to kill Tercel. And that I need to get on the phone with Brown and then with my brother immediately.

*A drink would be nice about now.*

"Someone's set you up."

"You think?"

He turns to the window.

Taking his hand, I say, "Shit, I'm sorry, Carter. You don't deserve my bullshit. You're just trying to help. And doing a great job, by the way."

He replies with a smile.

"Two things I have to do immediately."

"What's that?"

"Follow a hunch on Tercel having a *lot* of plastic surgery since leaving Hollywood. And calling my brother to confirm I have legal counsel."

In that brief moment of silence as I try calming my monkey mind, I notice how the driver keeps looking at me.

"G'day, Miss," he says with an toothy smile.

"Hello."

"I couldn't help but notice that you're both cops. Am I right?"

I look from Carter to him. "Why do you say that?"

"You've got the look, you know?" He nods toward Carter. "He seems more military, but you—you're definitely a cop. I have a good many mates who are cops, and well, you can just tell. Know what I mean?"

"I do," I chuckle. "But him?" I toss my chin at Carter. "He's got the haircut is all. He's my boyfriend, and I'm not even sure if he's ever held a gun." I turn to him. "Have you, hon?"

Shaking his head, he says, "They make me nervous."

"Why do you ask?"

"Well, I heard you mention plastic surgery, and well, it made me think of a client I've transferred *many* times between Brisbane and Gold Coast. On a *number* of occasions. I don't know, it just felt oddly familiar."

Removing Tercel's headshot from my bag, I show him.

"This fella look familiar?"

Taking it, he looks and instantly returns it. "No. That's not him."

Grinning sideways at Carter, I already had the other photo in hand. "How about this one?"

Taking it, he smiles. "By cracky, that's him. Goes by the name—"

"Jumping Johnny," we say simultaneously.

"Oh, you know him?" He looks at both of us with wide eyes.

"Sort of," I eye Carter. "However, that first photo I showed you?"

"Yes, Ma'am?"

"No need to call me that. Norelli is fine. That first photo was his "before" photo. The second? I'm guessing is work he's had done over a period of the past several months."

After a short silence, I add, "And yes, I'm a detective."

Grinning, he bounces his head.

"What's that expression for?"

"Well, Ma'am, I mean, Detective Norelli, that makes a lot of sense."

"Why's that?" Carter asks.

"I recall some time, say in the past six or eight months maybe, seeing him, I mean, actually driving him between the cities I mentioned. That is, when he wasn't chartering a helicopter. Fifteen minutes instead of 60, ya know."

"Wait. Do you suppose this same man's in Gold Coast now?"

"*Fairly* certain. There are only so many of these limo services. And we're all a tight bunch of mates."

Carter and I look at one another.

"But when you throw around as much money as he does? Well, word gets around *fast*."

"Interesting," I say, feeling more upbeat. "By the way, you seem especially *intuitive* for being *just* a driver. And I mean that in a good way. Were you a cop at one time?"

"That's funny, Ma'am. And no. Most of that *intuition*, as you put it, is just paying *attention*. Wife says I'm a good listener. And I guess you have to be when you're a barber. That's my first profession. You have any idea how many heads you have to trim to make a living?"

"I can't imagine."

"And with a wife and four kids, I need a second income."

. . .

PULLING UP TO THE SOFITEL, we realize we need to call it a day after the long trek and decide to book the driver for an early pickup in the morning.

"Last thing. I need to get your number, especially since we'll be spending the next day or so together."

Reaching in his pocket, he hands me a card.

"Noah Taylor at your service, Ma'am."

# CHAPTER THIRTY-EIGHT

*BRISBANE, AUSTRALIA—*

IT's time to call Pete, especially in light of Nelson's recent news. I shoot him a text with Zoom info and we're on within minutes. He looks stressed.

"How's it going, sis? Hi, Carter."

Carter nods and I say, "All good, brother. Just landed in Brisbane. We'll snoop around today, then head to Gold Coast—I'm sure it's his home base."

"Listen, about the—"

"Yeah, some kind of shit," I say, watching him rub his face. "Hey, this isn't your battle, Pete. I got myself into it and—"

"Right," he laughs. "And how's that working for you?"

I bite my tongue. Carter remains expressionless.

"I could sugarcoat things, but you're too smart and I'm too stubborn. Or the other way around. What I do know is that it's *murder*, Pats. And we need all the help we can muster to get you out of this."

He hasn't called me Pats since we were kids. It's always been his way of saying we're in it together. It was sweet then and even sweeter now.

"Thank you. And I know you've got my back and really appreciate it."

"Sure."

"What's dad say?"

He looks off to the side. "Well, he's about as pissed as I've ever seen him. And he's going to move heaven and earth to fix this. So get used to that fact."

"Which means he'll call all the shots."

"True. But that's not a bad thing—especially given the gun he's calling in to do the shooting."

I look at Carter who asks, "Who's that, Pete?"

"Andrew Jacobitz."

"WHAT?!"

"Yeah, the *shark*."

"Bobby Shapiro's guy! C'mon—"

"I know. But he's the best."

"And f'n expensive."

"Don't worry about that. Dad's got it under control."

"Not to mention they're not exactly best friends," I mutter.

"Yeah, but this ain't about friendship. It's about keeping *you* outta prison!"

My simmer quickly becomes a full boil.

Holding up both hands, he says, "Don't shoot the messenger, Pat. And realize you'll be better off if you let this part of the process ride, okay?"

I surrender a nod.

"Good. Now, did Nelson tell you the same thing he told me? About what'll happen—"

"Yes. He'll call inside the hour. Davenport will be with him with instructions for me to come in."

"Right. Good. And that's exactly what you need to do."

"Not yet."

"Pat, you *have* to!"

"Pete, I'm *this* close."

"I don't care. IA's not making a *suggestion*."

I look at Carter. He leans back and out of Pete's view and motions: *Tap the breaks.*

"Okay. What's your best advice—as my brother?"

"Follow protocol, and when you get the call, get home. That's my best advice as a cop. But as your *brother*…" he sighs, "tell me what's up your sleeve 'cause I know you've got a different plan."

OFF THE CALL, I feel oddly disconnected from the whole thing—as though it isn't happening to me. But it is. And there's only one person behind all the madness. I need to clear my name, prove Tercel murdered Angie, and bring a psychopath to justice—that's all I care about. And with the clock ticking even louder, we have to put it into overdrive.

"Babe?" I catch myself, then blush. "Uh, sorry, I mean, Carter, we need to get moving."

Leaning forward, he puts both hands on my knees.

"Call me whatever you like. Look, I know you're in more than one sticky situation. And I don't want to be another…I don't know, element of confusion?"

I chuckle.

"What?"

"Men are so funny. They want what they want but then don't want to get *complicated*."

"Hold on a second, Patricia. I'm just saying, you have enough on your plate right now. As for me? I think you're beyond terrific. Seriously. And I'll do whatever it takes to help you get Tercel, get out of this mess, and whatever else comes our way. I just don't want to get in between something you've already established. That's all."

Staring at him, I consider him to be about the best combination I've ever met: a man's man, a protector who isn't afraid of danger, and although a professional killer, kind and—imagine this—in touch with his emotions.

*But when do I learn he's an asshole?*

"Thank you for that. And to be honest, I *am* a hot mess. I know you're a good man, and I don't take that for granted. I've got solid instincts and don't want to ignore them. And yes, my life has a few, as you put it, *complications*. But I'm doing everything I can to simplify."

He smiles. I melt.

"And we'll see how all that goes," I say.

"That's all anyone can ask." Standing, he looks at his watch. "And given we don't have a lot of time, I say we call the driver—what's his name—Noah?"

Handing him the card from my bag, I add, "Taylor."

Reading it, he frowns.

"What is it?"

"Why isn't the name of the car service on the card? It only has his name and number."

I shrug. "Simplicity?"

Expressionless, he heads toward the door. "I'll call him, see if we can't kill two birds with one stone. Text you when he's here. I'll be in the lobby."

As the door closes, I head to the bathroom.

*PING!*

Spinning around, I grab my phone, see UNKNOWN, and swipe to read: *Welcome to Brisbane, Patricia. Nice of you to join us. Are the accommodations to your liking?*

I assume it's Savoy and begin typing: *Yes, Savoy, thanks. The hotel is beautiful. We appreciate your setting it up for us.*

Watching the blinking ellipsis, I wait for a response.

And wait.

After a few seconds, my shoulders relax.

I'm about to toss the phone aside and finish getting ready when the blinking begins.

In seconds, I read: *I'm happy for you, Darcy. However, Savoy is indefinitely detained. I'll be your host for the remainder of your stay in Australia.*

# CHAPTER THIRTY-NINE

LISTENING TO A LOCAL CRICKET MATCH, NOAH SITS IN HIS CAR JUST blocks from the hotel, enjoying a black coffee and Chiko roll, when Carter's text arrives: *G'day Noah. Just confirming Detective Norelli and I will need you to get us inside the next half hour. In fact, we'd like to take you to lunch, if that works. Thanks, Carter.*

He responds: *Sounds good. I'll be down front in twenty minutes. Take your time. And thank you for the invitation. Cheers, Noah*

About to call his boss, he hesitates, pondering what the stranger with so many names is up to.

*Finish your breaky first.*

He rolls up the trash and crams it under his seat—bumping a hand against his gun. Looking around, he takes it out, checks the clip, sees one in the pipe, and returns it in the holster and back to its hiding spot. Surveying the lot, he finishes his coffee and dials Tercel.

"Hello, my friend. How are things?"

"I'm about to take them to lunch."

Silence.

"Isn't that cozy. Where are you going?"

"No idea."

"Okay, I'm nearly there. Savoy and I took longer than expected. I had some loose ends to tie up."

Noah doesn't ask any questions.

Tercel begins to say more but stops. "Just text me where you end up."

"Copy that. Don't be surprised if we head to GC shortly."

Smoothing his pristine slacks, Tercel says, "I won't. And I'm certain you will be."

Having spent enough time around criminals during decades of police work, Noah can spot a hustle a mile away. That's when he gets an idea.

NOW PARKED along the limo curb, Noah is finishing a cigarette when he spots Norelli and Carter exit the hotel. Getting out, he grinds out his smoke and circles the car.

"G'day, Officers, I mean, Officer Norelli and Mr. Carter," he says with a broad smile and a touch to his cap's brim.

A bellhop comes up behind them to stand at the trunk. Noah opened my door, looking from the bellhop to me.

"Thank you, Noah. And yes, we decided to keep our bags with us," I say getting in. "Just in case we move around."

"As you wish," he says, closing my door, popping the trunk, and opening Carter's door.

Getting in, Carter has an odd expression.

"What?"

Popping a phony smile, he says, "Nothing. What's for lunch, *honey*?"

Frowning at Carter, I turn to Noah as he gets in. "Noah?"

"Yes, Ma'am?"

"I'm anxious to hear your suggestions for lunch. Perhaps seafood?"

"And near the water," Carter adds.

"Certainly."

"And since we're in no hurry, perhaps we could head on to Gold Coast?"

He nods politely. "I've just the spot."

TWENTY MINUTES INTO THE DRIVE, my phone rings. It's LAPD.

Carter glances over at the screen and cocks an eyebrow.

"Battery's dead," I smirk, disarming the location app before shutting it down.

With the phone buried in my bag, I enjoy the passing Australian countryside.

ANOTHER TWENTY MINUTES and we arrive at Seascape Restaurant in the heart of Surfers Paradise that sits in the center of action and in the shadow of Peppers Soul, a 77-story luxury highrise.

Opening my door, Noah takes my hand. "Thank you. And I can see why it's called Surfers Paradise."

Carter and I admire the long stretch of beach in front of us.

"I could get used to this," Carter sighs.

"Bloody Oath," Noah said. "I mean, *it's true,* Ma'am."

DURING LUNCH, Noah is polite and talkative, telling us about his wife and four children and what it was like growing up in Australia. He asks what it's like living in Hollywood and how many stars we've seen. I share that since I grew up in Beverly Hills, I've seen more than my share of famous people. As expected, he's in awe.

By the end of lunch, we mention a bit more about why we're in town, and I notice how his mood seems to shift when I talk about Tercel. While I keep the strokes broad, there's something odd in his eyes when I refer to the horrors Tercel committed over two decades.

"How did he get away with it for so long?"

"Besides being extremely intelligent, he was remarkably manipulative. To a degree you can't imagine," I say, recalling horrific photos of murder scenes and reliving the rush of fear when I was in his grasp.

Noah asks, "How close did you get? I mean, you said you were the lead on the case."

"Close."

Silence.

"Too close."

Sipping his drink, he only nods.

"My partner and I traveled in his vortex for a fair amount of time before we learned it was him. He was a therapist and I was a patient on his couch."

His eyebrows raise.

"Yeah. Long story, not interesting. Let's just say, it wasn't the best experience."

Noah shakes his head. "I can only imagine."

"But I learned a great deal. About his power of manipulation. About the depth of darkness to which a man can go when he's lost all conscience. And something about my own confidence."

Between broken sleep littered with constant nightmares and the stress of this past year, I feel my sanity getting more tattered by the day. Then, as my mind flashes to Angie on the coroner's table, my anger reignites.

My conversation obviously makes an impact, but the gravity evaporates when Noah claps his hands and says, "Well, let's move away from all that and go find the mongrel!"

As I pay the bill, Noah asks, "Do you have any place specific you'd like to check out? Either in GC or nearby?"

Carter and I look at one another.

"Where he lives would be the best," I say. "That's what we've been looking for all along."

"According to what you've told me, I can offer a guess. And it's close."

"Really?" I suddenly got nervous. "Where?"

A grin forms as he turns and nods toward the window.

"The tower you were looking at on our way in? I'd check the penthouse," he nods. "Well, there are two—which gives us a 50/50 chance —but we can start there."

"Perfect," I say, getting a nod from Carter.

"Excellent. Excuse me just a moment while I hit the *dunny* and we'll head over."

As soon as he's out of sight, I say, "He's turned out to be a welcomed addition, wouldn't you agree?"

Carter gives a polite nod and stares at the ocean.

"What?"

He looks around, leaning forward. "The card? The way he watches and moves? Saying *we* look like cops? Could be nothing, but…"

"*Okaaay.*"

"Usually when I get this itch, something's gonna get scratched."

Turning to look at the ocean, I wonder if I've misread things.

"Another thing," he says, "since when does a limo driver—or *barber*—need to carry a gun?"

# CHAPTER FORTY

As we head out, Carter asks Noah if we can divert our mission for the length of time it takes us to stroll a few blocks to see the Skypoint Observation Deck.

"I was reading about it on the way in and wanted to see the view. You know, since it's such a beautiful day."

Turning a frown into a smile, Noah says, "Sure. It's a stunner."

Four blocks and nearly a thousand feet in the air later, we enjoy a helluva view. At the top waiting to strap us in to walk the sky bridge, Carter spouts off several facts about the building, mentioning it's roughly the same height of the Sidney Tower Eye where we began our trip. When Noah excuses himself to make a call with a standing client he needs to cancel, Carter and I enjoy the view.

"What's up?"

"Not sure." He looks around to see Noah is inside. "But feels like it could be a trap."

"What makes you say that?"

"Well, besides working for the government in my younger years and with criminals over the last several decades, I've observed a lot of patterns—which is pretty much the key to understanding life. Think about it: he's making a call now when he would've already signed off with *standing* clients—especially since we booked him for the rest of our trip. And the other thing."

"The gun," I whisper.

"Right, and while not entirely illegal, their availability isn't the same as in the States. More of an anomaly here."

"Okay, so where's your head?"

"Well, if I'm right, and if Noah *is* in on it, and *if* Tercel is in that tower," he points with his forehead, "we're stepping into something unprepared."

"Uh huh."

"Whereas, if we snag a hotel, dump Noah, then at least we have the element of surprise. On our terms. And it's two against one versus two against two."

I take a moment to temper my urge to barge in guns-a-blazing.

*Life seemed so simple two weeks ago—what the hell happened?*

"He's heading back," Carter whispers.

"Let's go with your plan. I don't *feel* well," I wink.

Noah approaches.

"Okey dokes. All set." Admiring the view, he adds, "Pretty stunning, huh?"

"Certainly is, Noah. Unfortunately, what's not so stunning right now is my girl. I think between the height and, you know, the stress of the past few days, we're going to cut this outing short and just check into a hotel."

Watching his face, I can't decide if Noah's expression is surprise disguised as disappointment or impatience disguised as confusion. Either way, I offer a polite smile and head for the door.

"With a wife and four daughters," Carter says, raising eyebrows, "I'm sure you understand."

"Oh, right, of course. No worries. As you said, we have all the time in the world."

In the elevator, Carter makes small talk with Noah about the surf scene while I search my phone for a hotel.

Back at the restaurant, Carter and I wait at the curb as he gets the car.

"I'm guessing you have a—"

"Sheraton Grand Mirage Resort. I figured since we're officially a couple, might as well enjoy ourselves."

His expression is priceless.

"Besides, what would it look like if we busted our cover?"

# CHAPTER FORTY-ONE

*SYDNEY, AUSTRALIA—*

SAVOY'S GIRLFRIEND WEIJA TONG—A flight attendant with Qantas Airlines—returns home to find Savoy unconscious. Unable to wake her, Weija rushes her to the hospital where they run tests and discover the drug Ketamine in her system.

"Thank God, you got here when you did," Savoy says with a kiss.

"How the hell did this happen…" Weija asks, "and *when* did it happen?"

"I don't know exactly," Savoy frowns. "Last thing I remember, Johnny and I were messing around and…"

Weija tenses.

Savoy slouches.

"Sorry, babe, but you know me," she shrugs. "I've got a wicked soft spot for him."

"And he knows exactly how to work that spot," Weija says, going to the kitchen for a drink.

"Babe, let's not start this, please? And instead, just help me find the fucking prick—and return the favor."

Sitting on the sofa, Weija sips a white wine in silence.

"Okay, I get it—you're mad. And rightly so. But you also knew the rules when we got together," she says, reaching for Weija's hand.

She jerks away. "That was a year ago. I figured we'd gotten to a place—"

"We have. It's just that I like—"

"I know—swinging for *both* fences."

Savoy slides her hand across the couch until it sits atop Weija's hand.

Sipping, Weija takes her hand. "You can't blame me for being jealous," she pouts.

"I don't, and I'm sorry, babe. This is the last time. Promise."

A smile replaces her frown.

"Well, if you're serious and since I have the rest of the week off, yes, I'll help you get that prick—*especially* if it means I can have you all to myself."

"Thank you." Savoy leans in for a kiss. "And I have just the plan."

# CHAPTER FORTY-TWO

*Brisbane, Australia—*

"CARTER, you *do* agree with my staying off the phone and off the radar with the precinct, right?"

Emptying his suitcase and refolding his clothes, he looks over his shoulder. "Does it matter?"

"What?"

"What I think. Does it really matter?" He says putting his clothes into drawers—perfectly spaced.

"Yes, *neatnik*, it does. We're *partners*."

I see him trying to hide a grin and I throw a sweater at him.

Without turning, he catches it midair and slowly walks toward me. Picking me up, he tosses me on the bed, then straddles me, leaning within an inch of my face.

"If it matters to you, it matters to me. Honestly? I'm pretty smitten with you—as I may have intimated before. But I realize, as I've also mentioned, it's prudent for me to be mindful of diving deeper and clouding the water."

He looks at my lips then back to my eyes.

Suddenly, I feel warm and fuzzy in all the right places.

"So, I'd like to suggest, if you're open to it, we enjoy this time we have. And when you come to a place where you feel like you have a better handle on *us*, then I'm all ears," he says, leaning closer to my lips.

Not able to contain myself, I reach up and squeeze his back, pulling him closer until our lips meet.

After a few deep kisses, I pull his shirt up and over his head, whispering, "You better do (kiss) that little thing you did (kiss) the other night (kiss), or I'm gonna (kiss) lose my mind."

"Your wish is my command."

PULLING A U-TURN ON SEAWORLD DRIVE, Noah parks at the curb in front of the hotel, lights a smoke, and dials Tercel. He answers on the second ring.

Sitting on his balcony watching the boats maneuver the Marina, Tercel adjusts his sunglasses and says, "Let me guess; they decided against the tower and checked into a hotel."

"Yep. The Sheraton Grand Mirage."

Tercel feels a twinge of jealousy but quickly dismisses it with a bellowing laugh.

Noah grins on the other end and says nothing.

"That is too damn funny," Tercel says. "If they had any idea just how close they are," he laughs again.

Blowing smoke out the window, Noah says, "No doubt."

"Well, that makes our life all that much easier. Here's what I need you to do…"

AFTER FIFTEEN MINUTES, the two men have a plan. Tercel will take care of the big items while Noah takes care of a few minor ones before meeting up at the cocktail hour—if matters go as planned.

Noah is about to leave when a text arrives. It's Savoy. The minute he sees the name, his crotch awakens.

They had once been an item, helping one another in a variety of ways around the time their mutual friend first landed in Sydney. The slender American needed a driver with an eye for detail and a stomach for pain while two entrepreneurial locals were in the market for anything that paid handsomely and served a perverse addiction. It became an instant alliance, and a year later, the stranger had morphed into someone entirely different, and their lives had taken a dark turn.

The message reads: *Noah, I have a SUPER FAVOR. Do this & we're even. Plus, I'll sweeten the deal with two hot pieces of ass at once. Arriving OOL in one hour. Tell me where to meet. DO NOT mention to Johnny!*

Absently licking his lips, he types: *ALL IN. Anything for you. Let's meet at Fishbowl Bar at the Wharf.*

Tossing the phone on the seat, he checks his watch and pulls from the curb.

*Looks like I'll have my cake and eat them two,* he grins.

# CHAPTER FORTY-THREE

As Carter showers, I grab a robe, and take my phone out to the balcony. Waiting for it to boot up, I consider the risk of HQ tracing me. It's a chance I have to take. Within seconds, my phone chimes like a pinball machine and there are no less than a dozen messages.

*I'll face that heat later.*

About to call Pete, I hear Carter's phone ping. As close as we've become, we aren't close enough to spy on one another's phones, so I disregard it and call Pete.

"Sis, where in the hell—"

"Hang on Pete and, before you start climbing up my ass, please tell me some good news. And I know IA's been burning up my phone."

A long sigh. "You're right. And they've been all up in my shit, trying to see what I knew. We'll get to that in a second. First thing, did I tell you how Dad's gotten Jacobitz to rep you?"

"Yes, that's great news!"

"It is. He believes he has enough to keep you out of harm's way. The *problem* is the evidence they found in your place is pretty undeniable—"

"Except that—"

"Hang on, *except* that your record and reputation take precedence. The sticking point isn't the signed documents—those are easily a forgery—but the drug vial in your freezer is. The syringes in the toilet tank? Well, that's nearly comical, but bottom line, you *have* to come in. It's just going to—"

"Get worse, I know. But I'm about—"

"No, what I was going to say is it's just going to get more *complicated*. Here's why. Are you ready?"

My stomach plummets.

"Yes, give it to me," I say as Carter steps out onto the balcony. "Hold on, Pete, I'm going to put you on speaker."

Back inside, Carter and I sit on the couch. "Okay, shoot."

"Hey, Carter. Having fun yet?"

"Actually, yeah. But something tells me it's about to head south."

"You could say that. Okay Pat, they're going to send an IA agent out to get you."

"WHAT?!"

"Given it's been nearly 24 and you haven't called in, Davenport's going the distance to be sure you're on the upside. He's being a real dick."

"What's new," I snort. "Okay, so who's it gonna be and when's he coming—I'm assuming it's a him."

Pete gets silent long enough I check the phone to see if we're still connected.

"Pete?"

"Yeah, I'm here. The one coming...is Davenport."

After I pick my chin off the floor and Pete listens to some more whining, we decide it's best for me to roll with the punches—figuring things will go better if I do. That decided, I tell him where we'll meet Davenport tomorrow which gives us an extra day.

If things go as hoped, there's a chance we bring Tercel in at the same time Davenport is bringing me in.

*Talk about a perfect storm.*

# CHAPTER FORTY-FOUR

CHECKING HIS WATCH FOR THE UMPTEENTH TIME, NOAH DIALS Norelli's phone. She doesn't answer, so he tries Carter's number.

On the second ring, he says, "Carter."

"Hiya, Carter; it's Noah. I've got some good news."

"Good, let's hear it," he says, waving for me to listen.

"Since you said you two needed some chill time, I took the opportunity to make a quick run from the airport to the Southport Yacht Club which is very close to your hotel. Anyhow, I picked up two executives in town for a meeting, and long story short, I overheard them talking about a man who matches Johnny Grover, I mean your Tercel, perfectly."

"Okay, but what do you mean matching perfectly?"

"There were two of them. One was a doctor—a plastic surgeon from the sounds of it—talking about a client he's been working on for the past year. Oh, and they're both from New York. I could tell by their accents and because the doctor said he's been traveling back and forth to help his client create a new identity."

"Interesting," Carter says. "Who's the second man?"

"I think he's some kind of money manager. Maybe an investor or real estate agent. Something like that. Anyway, he was talking about coming here to wrap some investments that his client was going to roll into a new project. I assumed in New York—not sure."

"That makes sense."

"Sounds like your guy's planning a move. Maybe a big move. And from what I gathered from these two, it's going to happen soon."

"So, where do you suppose Tercel is right now?"

"That's the other thing. They said they were asked to meet him on his yacht where he's been staying for the past couple of weeks. Evidently, he wanted to, as one guy said, 'stay off the radar.'"

"So, I'm guessing they're getting transportation to our guy's yacht."

"That's right. And if this is what I *think* it is, and we're on the same page, I can arrange the same thing for you if you'd like."

"Sounds like a plan. Can you give me fifteen minutes? I'll call you right back and we'll put our plan into motion."

"Sounds good," Noah says, ringing off.

DIALING A NUMBER, Noah lights another smoke. His eyes shift from the rearview to the street in front of him.

"Hello?"

"I think they bought it. I'm waiting to hear back. Should have something inside fifteen minutes."

Inside the silence, Noah waits, taking several long drags.

"Okay, ring me the second you get confirmation."

"Copy that."

Disconnecting, Noah scans the horizon, burning through his cigarette. Grinding it out, he dials a second number.

"Hello?"

"It's me," Noah said. "Looks like we're a go. You ready?"

"Yes."

"Good. Give me ten, maybe fifteen minutes tops. I'll text when we're on the move."

"Got it."

Noah disconnects, takes a long, slow breath, and grins. Cracking his knuckles, he rolls his neck from side to side and wakes his laptop. First, he confirms flight schedules out of both Brisbane and Gold Coast. Next, he opens the yacht club's website and confirms he has the right number programmed into his phone. Last, he checks the weather, tide schedules, and time of sunset.

As he's about to light a third cigarette, his phone rings.

"It's Noah."

"Hi, Noah; it's Carter. Okay, we have an idea, but we need you to do something before you pick us up."

"Okay, shoot."

"Go ahead and book transportation to get us to his yacht. And in order to keep our approach as unassuming as possible, let's connect at sunset, then head out shortly thereafter."

Noah hesitates, not expecting the diversion, but will improvise. "Copy that."

"Good. Then pick us up out front." Carter checks his watch, then the horizon. "Let's call it an hour?"

"Got it. See you in an hour."

"And Noah?"

"Yeah?"

"Pat said to tell you if you help us pull this off, you'll be taking the rest of the year off—on us."

Noah grins wide. "I like the sound of that."

# CHAPTER FORTY-FIVE

CARTER RINGS OFF WITH NOAH AND STARES AT THE FLOOR. As MUCH AS I want to say something, I can see his mind working and leave him alone. I consider that Davenport will be on a plane and here in Australia before we can turn around—and that makes my stomach knot.

Whenever I find my anxiety level getting too high, I take a deep breath and think of Angie. Between avenging her death and saving my own neck, all I have to do is focus my attention on burying Tercel—and that can't come soon enough.

"Sorry," Carter smiles, finally turning his attention from the floor to me. "Just had to work some things out."

"I get it. And no worries. It'll be crunch time soon and the proverbial shit will hit the fan. So, where's your head?"

"About?"

I chuckle. "All of it?"

"Well…" he begins, standing to pace, "as much as I wish my pal from back home was here, that's just not gonna happen."

"Who, Mack?"

He nods. "We've been through literally *everything* together. Good, bad, and everything in between."

The look in his eyes makes me think of how I feel about Stuart. Partners like ours are few and far between.

"What would Mack bring to this situation?"

"First of all, he's an enormous dude," he grins. "His presence alone scares the shit out of most people. Next, he's a former Navy Seal, so his passion for and abilities in the water are equally large. Last, he knows exactly how I think. And me, him. We're wired like one brain. And can get out of pretty much anything. So far, anyway."

I stare at my hands, wondering if I can stand up to pretty much anything.

"Sorry, Patricia," he says, returning to the couch. "I didn't mean that I lacked confidence—"

"Carter, you don't have to explain. I get it. Stuart and I are the same way. It's a bond cemented with time and experience." I attempt a smile. "I just don't want to let you down."

"You won't." He takes my hand. "And I won't let you down."

KNOWING it's going to be a long night, we order room service. Within minutes, I'm spreading out a picnic while Carter cleans and checks our guns. The shredded nerves I was feeling an hour ago seem to have calmed because I'm now focused, centered, and ready for anything.

Looking out at the ocean, I notice the sun beginning its lazy slide into the darkening horizon. I eyeball my phone out of habit, wondering when Pete might check in. There's little he can do now, but I suppose I feel better knowing he's only a phone call away.

"You okay?" Carter asks, startling me.

I spin around and smile. "Yeah, peachy."

"Uh huh."

"I am really. Kinda. *Ish.*"

We laugh.

"Look, all we have to do is go out there. See if he's on the yacht. See if the two men Noah told us about are with him. And, you know, slap some cuffs on him, and cart him back to the States."

"Ohhh, that's all? Goody."

FED AND PREPPED, Carter and I walk through a litany of scenarios. It feels like practicing dance moves before stepping out onto stage—not that I've ever been in that situation before, just more like what I imagine it would be.

Once we're confident we've considered most any situation—short of a tsunami rolling across the ocean and knocking us on our asses or Tercel rigging the yacht with enough plastic explosives to blow us sky high—Carter laughs at my worries, then shoots Noah a text as we head downstairs.

# CHAPTER FORTY-SIX

WE ARRIVE AT THE YACHT CLUB TWO BLOCKS AWAY AND ARE ABOUT TO board a handsome, albeit large, boat called *Alaska*.

"Noah, what are you thinking?"

"What?"

Carter pulls him close. "What is this, a 42, 45-footer?"

"Yeah, 42. Sweet, right?"

"But not very *clandestine*, right?"

His smile disappears. "Um, maybe not. But on such short notice—"

"I get it. But seriously, there's no way we can even *pretend* to sneak up on him. Have any other ideas?"

Noah sighs, looks around, then waves us to follow. "Let me see what I can do. Why don't you two grab a seat at the bar and I'll—"

"No. How about we go find this together," I respond.

I FIND it odd Noah is squirrelly when we downgrade the boats, but I chalk it up to nerves. He excuses himself to the restroom before we board—another thing that gets my attention—but I let it go for the same reason.

In fifteen minutes, we're boarding a much smaller and less noticeable runabout powered by a 200-HP V6, more than enough muscle to get us in and out of trouble.

Maneuvering out of the marina, we merge into the Nerang River before passing Seaworld. As we approach Wave Break Island, we scan the horizon, then slip into the mouth of the Spit Gold Coast and continue in silence.

The night is clear and warm—the ocean spray, cool and refreshing. Looking up, I see a million stars and actually find myself at peace.

In about twenty minutes that peace dissolves as Noah looks over his shoulder, pointing toward Tercel's yacht, less than a mile away. He cuts the engine when we're less than a hundred yards to the yacht. Nervous, I watch Carter place his gun inside a seal-tight bag, then inside his shirt.

"Be careful, Carter," I say. "And if anything goes south—"

"Too late for that," he smiles, giving a thumbs up before lowering himself into the water.

Minutes pass much too slowly as he makes his way toward the yacht. Things seem to be going as planned until bright lights flood the area, making it nearly impossible to see.

"Noah, Detective Norelli, please join us," a voice blares over a loudspeaker.

Frozen, we try to figure out what's happening—and what to do next.

Shielding my eyes, I look at Noah who shrugs.

"Detective Norelli, I'll say it once more," the voice bellows. "Please join us now or your boyfriend gets fed to the sharks!"

It doesn't take long to maneuver our small boat next to the luxury yacht. Tying us off, Noah helps me board, and in short order, we're standing face to face with a man who has been the source of my nightmares for a dozen months. Looking nothing like our former *doctor*, he now resembles the photo I found in Angie's home.

This Tercel is built like a bodybuilder and tan like a surfer. His chin is squared and enhanced with a cleft. His cheeks are dimpled and his cheekbones raised. And his former light blue eyes—once soft and kind —are dark brown; his gaze, penetrating. The long hair, while befitting a bohemian surfer, seems out of place for the man with whom I once shared my deepest secrets.

Carter's gun is in Tercel's hand—pointed at Carter tied to a chair.

"Your expression is priceless, Patricia," Tercel laughs. "Simply priceless. As though you can't decide whether to fear me or crave me," he laughs again.

A rush of adrenaline, combined with the fear of seeing Carter in harm's way, courses through my body at a fever pitch. I feel guilty because Carter is in what appears to be a losing proposition—all because of my crazed obsession.

My heart beats loudly in my temples. My breathing is labored and erratic.

*Stay calm, Norelli.*

"I certainly don't crave you, Tercel. And I'm *not* afraid of you."

His broad white smile slowly dissolves into an emotionless sneer. "We'll see about that."

Reaching to a bank of buttons, he shuts off the bright lights surrounding the yacht. As my eyes adjust, I see two women sitting off to the side.

"How rude of me, Detective Norelli and Carter, uh, whatever your last name is. Allow me to introduce you to, oh wait, you've both met Savoy Hendricks, that's right. In Sydney. But have you met her girl-friend, Weija? Aren't they a lovely, if not terrified, couple?"

While Tercel is distracted, I look to Carter who nods at a harpoon lying on a couch across the boat. I look, then reconnect with Tercel just as he turns back.

"No, I haven't," I say, managing a faux smile to the girls.

"Noah, take this and keep it trained on him," Tercel says, handing him Carter's gun, then approaching me.

*Shit*, I look to Noah, staring long enough for him to get the message. He gives a nonchalant shrug and points the gun at Carter.

I look at Tercel. "Your control of *weak* minds never ceases to amaze me."

As he gets closer, I can see more of the former Tercel—and the fire that burns within.

*Little to lose and much to gain.*

"You really went to great lengths to change, didn't you, Tercel?"

I enjoy watching his frustration at my not being attracted to him.

"Yes, I did, Patricia. Great lengths. But please, call me *Darius*. You know, for old times sake," he grins. "Or even better, call me Johnny Grover, my lovely *Sheila*. Good onya, mate," he says in an Australian accent.

I can't decide whether to be impressed with all the charade or sad at his mania.

"But isn't it funny, or perhaps *sad* in your case, that I was able to track *and* find you halfway around the globe. All that money seems like a loss in my book," I smirk.

His chill veneer is waning, along with my bravado. And each time I poke at his masculine armor, he seems to grimace. I know it's a risk that won't be without consequences.

Pushing a strand of blond behind an ear, he cocks his head.

"Well, you may have a point there. However, let's not forget how I killed your best friend. Even though she was in love with me, she felt such a need to control me and wanted to turn me in for my life of sin," he chuckles. "But pinning it on you? Oh, that was my tour de force," he guffaws. "Bet *that* put a real crimp in your emotional life, didn't it? Yet *another* thing you can't control."

He knows the exact buttons to push and, as hard as I try to hide it, I know my stewing anger will soon show. Gritting my teeth, I attempt his game.

"Yeah, that certainly threw me for a loop," I say, staring at the deck. "But if I had been in your shoes..." I look up, "and stood to lose everything you could have? I'd have done the same thing."

Our stares lock.

"Perhaps you'll feel differently..." he says, taking enough steps to be within a foot of my face, "when I kill your new boyfriend. And then these two lovely gals," he says, tossing his chin in their direction. "All that blood, like all those before, will be on your hands. Sharon, Bobby, Angie. All killed because of *you*," he growls, now inches from my face.

As my heart races, my muscles tighten, and I fight the urge to strangle him with his own hair.

It's my turn to sneer. "Give it your best shot."

For a brief moment, it feels like time stops.

Then, surrendering a sigh, Tercel crosses from starboard to port, removes a syringe from a box, and looks to Noah.

"Give me that."

Noah hands the gun over.

"Now, take this and inject Carter."

Taking the syringe, Noah appears confused, looking from Tercel to Carter to me and back to Tercel.

"Do it, you neanderthal!" He shouts, pointing the gun at me. "What do you think I'm paying you for?"

Carter looks at Noah and shakes his head. "You don't have to do this."

As Tercel starts toward me, Carter looks at me and shoots his eyes back to the harpoon.

To Noah, Carter says, "We both know this guy's a lunatic. Don't do something stupid."

The instant I start toward the harpoon, Tercel swings and slams the butt of the gun into my cheekbone. With stars in my eyes, I crash to the floor, reaching for my bloody face.

He yells, "What are you doing, Norelli?"

I look toward Carter, but Noah blocks my view.

I look up to Tercel, "What's it look like, Tercel? I'm trying to kill you!"

"Get up," he yells, "and sit there," he points, "next to the girls."

Turning to Noah, he yells, "Do it now, Noah. Inject him with the drug or I'll splatter your brains all over this fucking deck!"

Carter stares into Noah's face as he stabs the syringe in his neck.

"You mother-fucker!" I yell, starting to move toward Noah.

Tercel points the Glock in my face. "Stay!"

I look from him to Carter who begins slouching.

Tercel turns to Noah and yells, "Toss him overboard!"

As Noah grabs Carter, it looks like he shoves something in Carter's pocket.

He hoists Carter's slumped body up and over the side of the boat. Silence is met with a loud *SPLASH!*

Terrified, I push Tercel's hand aside and rush to the side of the boat. Carter is nowhere in sight.

I turn to Tercel and growl, "You—fucking—asshole. I'm going to kill you."

Tercel begins a low guttural chuckle that quickly develops into a long and maniacal laugh.

# CHAPTER FORTY-SEVEN

WHEN TERCEL IS FINISHED LAUGHING, HE WIPES HIS EYES WITH THE back of his sleeve, looks at his watch, and points the gun at me.

"Oh, Patricia..." he tries to muffle a lone giggle, "the look on your face, the pain and agony, was worth the price of admission. After all this time, and all the hard work, I thought I might *actually* want to keep you as my own." With a quick sigh, he blurts, "But alas, I don't."

I look from him to Noah and the two women.

"No, you're just like every other woman on earth, moody..." he squints to Savoy, "disloyal..." then turns back to me, "and fucking *unreliable.*"

Both Savoy and Weija—quiet this whole time—stare at Tercel with a look that says: *revenge.*

Tercel turns to Noah. "And speaking of disloyal. Noah, tell me why on earth, after all this time and all I promised to give you, would you betray me?"

I look at Noah. *What?*

"Don't even try," Tercel says, taking a step forward. "They may have bought your barber-driver bullshit, but we both know a washed-up ex-cop who can't even make it as a private dick is nothing but a *loser.*"

"What the hell d'ya mean, *Grover?* I've done everything you've asked."

Tercel turns the gun from me to Noah.

"Except her," Tercel growls, tossing his head toward Savoy. "I told you I was tying up that *loose end* before I bounced from here. But no, you had to be the *hero*," he shakes his head. "Let me guess. They promised you a threesome."

Noah's face goes slack.

"Never gonna happen, *mate*. They were just using you. Like everyone else," he mutters. "Why'd you have to fuck it up? Doesn't loyalty and loads of *cash* mean anything anymore?"

In the instant it takes for Noah's eyes to flick toward the harpoon, Tercel raises the gun.

*BANG! BANG! BANG! BANG!*

With two to the chest and two to the gut, Noah's dead by the time his hulking mass hits the deck.

Air escapes my lungs with a burst and both girls run toward Tercel before the smoke clears.

Savoy lunges for the harpoon gun while Weija jumps on his back. Fortunately, Savoy is able to get up from the deck and get off a shot at Tercel, piercing his thigh with a Hatsan Arrow Launcher.

Making a dramatic spin, she dives off the side of the boat as he fires twice in her direction. Next, he tosses Weija from his back and shoots her in the leg and her stomach.

Somewhere in the gunfire, he sends two errant bullets bouncing off the deck and into the black.

I stand in shock, watching Weija squirm in a pool of blood.

*Eight shots makes two left.*

With ears still ringing, I'm not sure if I can save Weija, but I know I have to do *something*.

In the split second Tercel checks the gun for remaining bullets, I charge toward him, push him to the deck, and take a swan dive off the side of the boat.

Deep into the black, I hear bullets whiz by either side of me. I stay under until I hear the motors of the yacht starting up. Running out of air, I slowly rise to the surface.

Keeping my head low, I watch as he struggles to remove the arrow from his thigh and then pick up Noah and roll him over the side. Next, he cuts the rope attaching our small boat to his yacht.

As he pulls away, panic approaches like a wave.

## CHAPTER FORTY-EIGHT

"Hey, help a guy out, will ya?"

*WHAT?*

Whipping my head in all directions, I can't tell if I'm hearing things, am still in shock, or my monkey mind is playing tricks with me.

"Carter? Is that you?"

"No, it's your shadow. Of course it's me, get over here. You've got a perfectly good boat waiting on you."

I swim the hundred yards between us, then climb aboard, nearly hugging the life from him.

"What the hell? I mean, how'd you even? Wait, you were—"

"Hold on, girl," he laughs, trying to catch his breath. "First thing? That was fast thinking back there. Jumping was the smartest choice. If you'd stayed with him, well, I have a few ideas, but they're not pleasant."

"I saw Savoy do it and thought, what the hell. Wait, where is she?"

Looking around, we don't see or hear anything.

"Shit, do you think…"

"Don't know," he says. "But I do know she was part of Noah's plan."

"Weija was shot twice—in the leg and gut."

"Not good."

"And what do you mean, part of Noah's plan? And what about him? I thought he was helping us, but then…" I take a deep breath. "Sorry, I know I'm babbling, but between the shock of everything and the thought of losing you, not to mention thinking I was going to die out here...." I stop talking in order to give my full attention to shivering.

"Hang on, there's got to be something in here."

He opens a storage container. "It's only a life jacket, but it's something. Now, slow your roll and I'll try to get us back in one piece."

I put on the lifejacket as he takes his shirt off, wringing it tightly.

Within minutes, we're heading toward shore.

"Okay, Noah *was* on our side. He and I made a plan while you were preoccupied. He told me about his alliance with Tercel, but then once he learned who Tercel really was and what he was up to, he no longer wanted any part of it. Wait, let me take some of that back. He was going to be paid rather well for helping Tercel; however, a good many *bad* things had to happen first. I told him if he'd help us out, we'd take even better care of him."

"But what about Savoy?"

"Yeah, looks like Tercel double crossed her—imagine that—by poisoning her. Fortunately, Noah told me that Weija got back into town, found her in time, and saved her life. They started putting the pieces together and figured out Tercel was in the process of tying up loose ends before leaving town. Bottom line: Savoy wanted to get even."

"And?"

"She actually *really* stepped up. I gave Noah a watch with a built-in recording device. It was *supposed* to have the evidence that saves your life. I mean, c'mon," he smacks the wheel. "He confessed everything back there. Shit!"

Suddenly silent, we look out at the dark ocean.

Feeling beaten, I shake my head. "That would've been freaking helpful."

"Yeah."

Taking several long breaths, I try refocusing. "Okay, back to Noah. How did he, I mean, what did he shoot into your neck?"

"Where do I start," he sighs. "That was the one sticking point—pun intended—that we were taking a big risk on. Look, I knew how Tercel had killed many of the others in Hollywood, thanks to your reports. And I knew how he killed Angie, plus how he had worked to take out Savoy, thanks to Noah's intel. And since I've gotten close to you and aware of your nightmares, I had to assume the syringe just became his

M.O. *Sooo*, we packed a syringe, which I always carry in my bag, and hid it with Noah on the off chance what *did* happen would've happened. It was simple saline, by the way."

"And did I see him give you something else?"

"Good eye. Thanks to years of training with my pal, Mack, I know how it's a good idea to keep a couple of cans of pure oxygen with me. They're tiny. And again, something I keep in my bag. This time, in case I would've been frisked—since I was carrying a gun—I gave it to Noah. It was a gamble that—fortunately for me—paid off."

"In case you were drugged and tossed overboard."

"Yes. And again, the *only* reason that doesn't seem too out of the ordinary is because I've been in similar and equally dangerous situations before. This way, I'd have at least five minutes of air—long enough for me to dive deep, stay under long enough for the drama to transpire above water, then tread water by the side of our getaway boat," he says, patting the dash.

I finally allow my shoulders to relax. "And as far as Tercel is concerned?"

"Right. So, let's think about it, from his perspective. I'm dead. Noah's clearly dead. Savoy's potentially dead. Weija is bound to be dead if she doesn't get help. And you're more than likely dead. Well, a pretty good chance, given you dove in the water, and he shot at you several times. Oh, and one more thing: for all he knew, either Noah or I had the key to the boat. I do know we have a pretty good idea—according to Savoy anyway—Tercel has been planning to leave Australia for the past several weeks. But then when you and I showed up, well, it expedited matters. The way I see it? *If* he knows I'm dead, knows the link to Noah is gone, and presumes you're dead…"

"Shit," I mutter, "the only other loose ends are…"

"Yep, Savoy and Weija," he says, looking from me to the lights of the city. "We're getting close. And just to be safe, we'll hang out here on the outer fringe for just a bit longer." He checks the gauges and says, "Well, until we get low on gas. I want to give him enough time to be clearly on his way."

Still overwhelmed, I rub my face the way my brother does when he gets too wound up. "So you feel confident he's done."

"Wait!" Carter shouts so loudly, I jump.

"What?"

There's enough light from the dash I see him squint at something ahead. "Up there—is that..." he cuts the engine back to idle and the waves make us bounce.

As we slowly settle, I see what he's looking at.

"What the hell? Is that? No, it can't be..."

Reaching over, he flips a switch and a spotlight on the bow comes on.

"Savoy!" Carter yells, reaching under the cockpit for a lifejacket.

"Savoy, it's Carter and Norelli!"

"Savoy!" I yell.

She keeps stroking, even and strong, like her life depends on it. As we get closer, she slows, looking over her shoulder. If I'm not mistaken, I can see the fear in her eyes.

Recognizing us, she swims our way.

At the side of the boat, she struggles to catch her breath. "Oh my God," she coughs, "I didn't know if you were *him*."


PULLING INTO THE MARINA, I take care of Savoy's wound while Carter speaks to management. A bullet grazed her leg, but it appears the salt water actually helped keep bleeding at bay. Savoy is bandaged up and we're waiting for a car when Carter joins us.

"Anyone need a drink? I have just the place."


SEATED at the bar and overlooking the ocean we just survived, the three of us stare into the night. A perky bartender approaches, asking if we'd like something to drink.

"What do *you* think," I ask with a smirk.

"Make mine a double," Savoy says. "I think I deserve it."

"No shit, girl." I squeeze her shoulder. "You are one brave woman."

"Don't know about that, but when you're jacked on the amount of adrenaline I had coursing through my body, I guess instincts kick in and anything's possible."

Our drinks arrive and we raise them. Tears form as Savoy whispers: *To Weija.*

"To Weija."

After a long silence, I ask Carter, "There's a *chance* she made it, right?"

Shaking his head, he says, "According to the manager, Tercel arrived alone."

We are quiet again.

"It took some *friendly* persuasion..." Carter winks, "but he told me he was *handsomely* paid to clean the yacht—as this guy said—within an inch of its life."

"Not a surprise," Savoy mutters. "Money buys everything."

"Except a clear conscience," I add.

"Yeah, right," she snorts.

"Evidently, Tercel not only paid for the cleanup but also gave the guy an extra ten-large to keep quiet."

"Okay..." Savoy looks at us and frowns, "but here you are telling us about it, so, how's that work?"

Carter stares at his drink while I say, "Evidently, you haven't seen Carter's methods of persuasion."


A PLATE of grilled tacos and a bucket of beers later, we're feeling better and still have the energy to overanalyze.

"Was it just me or did anyone else notice how Tercel kept watching the time?"

"Yeah," Carter grunts. "Someone had an agenda."

Finishing a drink, Savoy says, "When we were organizing a whacked out idea of mine about how I could get back at the prick, Noah told me about Tercel—I'm still trying to get used to that name—having a private jet on standby. Said he wanted to leave town the minute he wrapped one last piece of business." Looking at me, she quietly says, "I'm guessing that piece of business was *you.*"

A chill shoots down my spine as I consider how close to the end I was.

"And another thing. Tercel and I shared something else besides a bed."

I raise my eyebrows.

"When he first arrived in Sydney, he was a much different man—not just his heart, but his whole appearance."

"Right."

"Duh, I know," she shrugs. "My hotel was among the first he checked into. We got to know one another, and long story short, we started sharing things. One of those was my plastic surgeon."

"Interesting," I smile.

"Right? I was having some touch up work done, and he began asking me who I used. Another long story short, he used my guy, but when it came to more extensive work, he went with someone out of New York. That same guy would come down from time to time. After a while, he made fewer appearances. We'd talk on the phone from time to time, but he said business kept him away for long stretches."

"Okay, I get all that, but what—"

"Sorry, I'm rambling. Here's the point: one night—much later—he shows up very different than before. Anyway, after a great deal of wine, he shares how he had made a lot of connections in New York, and in fact, it was a place he could see himself living one day. Since I thought we might connect—you know on a deeper level and for a longer period of time—I pushed to see what plans he had in mind."

She got quiet, and after a long minute, I push. "And?"

"The next morning—I suppose in the sober light of day—he acted differently. He shut down, saying it was just a daydream. But I knew better. Besides, I would see repeated calls on his cell from a 212 area code. One of them became so frequent, I memorized it."

"*Aaaaand?*"

"It was a realtor in Manhattan."

I look at Carter. "This is *huge*."

"Yep," he smiles.

Exhaling heavily, Savoy says, "Glad I could do something that helps."

"Are you kidding? This is great!"

I wave to the bartender for another round. "Wait a second. Didn't you mention something about a recording?"

"Oh shit," Savoy blurts, wiping the sand and seawater from her watch. "Yeah, Noah was a real surveillance nut. Said he did a lot of that shit back when he was a cop."

Removing the watch, he hands it to Carter. "It's one of his better toys. 64 gigs of ram, a built in camera, and the recorder's really good. It picks up ambient sound, but trust me, unless you're in a windstorm, it should be fine."

Carter grins like a kid at Christmas. "Holy shit."

"Yeah, the only thing I'm not sure about is how much water it can take. I don't know how many miles I swam, but do what you can. It's yours."

"Seriously, Savoy, this is nice work," I give a high five. "And Noah? Even in death he pulls through for us."

Carter mumbles. "Some high tech shit here in the outback," he grins, shaking it next to his ear. "Let's just hope it survived the ocean."

Looking from Carter to Savoy, I say, "Girl, you may have a whole new career."

# CHAPTER FORTY-NINE

IT IS BARELY 7:00 A.M. WHEN THE PHONE ON THE NIGHTSTAND RINGS. It seems so much louder than I recall. Lifting my head from the pillow, I take a couple seconds before I'm fully aware of where I am. Looking over, I see Carter on his back—one arm behind his head, the other across my pillow. He looks peaceful.

By the second ring, he lifts his head. "Huh?"

I grab the phone before it can crush our eardrums a third time. "Norelli."

"Morning, Detective. This is Officer Davenport. Internal Affairs. Perhaps you'll recall—"

"Yeah, yeah, I know who you are. And I know why you're coming here. All I need to know is—"

"No, Detective, not coming. Actually here."

"What?"

"I'm here. In Brisbane. Just landed. Caught the red-eye and ready to take you back home."

Sitting up, I mouth, *Fuck*. Carter frowns.

"Officer Davenport, I've been through hell and back in the last 24 hours and slept a total of two hours last night, so if you'll just be patient with—"

"Detective, I can appreciate all that; however, I have one job and one job only, and given you're a fugitive of—"

I hang up. Then take a deep breath. And wait.

Before Carter can speak, I hold up a finger, then point at the phone, just as it…

*RING!*

I answer with a smile, "Officer, I'm happy to work with you in any way I can; however, you're not getting off on the right foot, so allow me to tell you how this is going to work best—for all of us. Still with me?"

Silence then, "Yes."

"Excellent. And as I said, I'm going to play along. Nicely, even. However, you're going to play along as well. Sound like a plan?"

Silence then, "Okay."

"Good. So you've just landed in Brisbane. If you're renting a car, it'll take you one hour and 15 minutes to get here. If you grab a commuter plane, it'll take about a half-hour, or with a helicopter, maybe fifteen minutes…"

"I work for the government. It'll be the former," he says.

"Understood. And even better. So, how about you and whoever is with you—"

"I'm alone."

I roll my eyes. *Of course you are.*

"Then we'll see you in about 90 minutes. Let's just call it two hours to be on the safe side. My associate and I will meet you in the lobby of the Sheraton. It's easy to find. At that time, the three of us can make our way back to LAX, out of OOL—the airport in Gold Coast—and catch a flight sometime after that. You have my word. Good?"

Sigh then, "Yes."

"And Davenport?"

"Uh huh?"

"All I ask is one thing. And one thing only."

"What's that?"

"No cuffs, okay? I'm happy to be cooperative, but if you intend to—"

"I have to, it's the—"

I hang up and unplug the phone.

With a tiny golf clap, Carter smiles. "Well played, Patricia."

"Thank you."

Next, we take a little time to wake up—*the right way.*

. . .

WE SHARE a cup of coffee with Savoy and tell her to stay at the hotel as long as she likes, saying it's the least we can do given her help with the case is invaluable.

Soon after, Officer Davenport shows up, dressed in a grey suit, grey tie, and grey shirt. I don't recall him looking so pale. With no cuffs in sight, we make little small talk, toss his one bag into our town car, and are on our way. En route, I can't help but feel sad knowing our former driver is likely at the bottom of the ocean.

In short order, tickets are purchased, and we are through security and seated on a Cathay Pacific flight from Gold Coast to Los Angeles, facing a one-hour stopover in Sydney and a two-hour stopover in Hong Kong. Davenport doesn't get approved for First Class, so he gets the last seat in the last row between Business and Economy.

NEARLY TWO-THIRDS of the way to Hong Kong, I awake from a fitful sleep with a spectacularly crazy idea that makes only marginal sense, would once again endanger ourselves, and would definitely break any number of laws. But given I have a piece of evidence that might potentially work in our favor, I'm feeling more than a bit daring.

I give a gentle elbow to my sleeping sidekick and share my idea. He listens with rapt attention. When I finish running all the details, the potential pitfalls, and his involvement for *one more leg of the journey*, he looks at me with a deadpan expression.

"You are certifiably insane."

I hold his stare for an unrealistic length of time. "Right. So, are you in or not?"

As the sides of his mouth slowly curl up, I have my answer.

WITH ONLY AN HOUR and change left before we land in Hong Kong, Carter leaves his seat and puts our plan into motion. Having spent the past few hours sharing pleasant conversation and flirtatious exchanges with our very attractive flight attendant, he doesn't have much trouble gaining her assistance. He begins next steps by taking out his Dopp kit and making a visit to the lavatory. Minutes later, he is sweet talking the waitress before dropping his kit on his seat with a wink to me and heading back to visit our *other* shadow.

.  .  .

THIRTY MINUTES LATER, he returns. Now, his charming smile is replaced with an aggravated snarl as he quietly says, "What a certifiable asshole. I mean, he's just an undeniably *unhappy* person. Talking about miserable. And not a good conversationalist, either. Not to mention, the *worst* breath ever. I mean, my dog Samson, on his worst day, has fresher breath than this dip-shit."

I release a heavy sigh. "Sorry, babe. It was a long shot, and maybe not my smartest idea, but—"

"What?" He looks at me sideways. "No, no, your idea's solid. Hell, I wouldn't have gone along if I didn't see the merit. No, he's just a moron. But yeah, he's out, and I mean out cold!"

Watching his frown morph into a mischievous grin makes my entire week. I can't help but lean over and kiss him.

Suddenly, I withdraw and cover my mouth. "Ooh, speaking of, I bet I've got the same—"

He laughs. "You're fine. But him? That's some real shit soup."


PULLING the steaming towel from my face, I finish a third mint.

"Much better," I say, looking sideways at Carter. "Now, tell me again—just because I'm a brat—exactly how you managed to finesse Officer *Dickensport*."

Overhead, the seatbelt chime sounds and the pilot begins his landing pitch. I lean closer to hear his story—and to smell his cologne.

"Go ahead, Oscar nominee."

Grinning, he says, "It was easy. Just had to find his Achilles heel."

"Which is?"

"Couple things. Come to learn we both served in the Army. Just different divisions. And a half-decade apart. He's older," he winks. "So, there's always that camaraderie. Second, he loves, and I mean *loves,* talking about himself. Get him started and he drones on about how he got into IA, how he was able to climb so fast, and *blah-de-blah.* But dropping the goods in his drink was easy, thanks to a simple distraction. Anyhow, the reason I was there so long, I wanted to be sure he was out. So, given there was an empty seat, I asked if I could just chill out there, given *my old lady is a chatterbox*," he winks.

. . .

As we taxi at Hong Kong International Airport, Carter checks to see that Davenport is still out. So far, so good. As soon as we're able to turn our phones back on, I book two seats on an alternate airline for a flight leaving in 22 minutes for New York.

At the gate, I flash my badge at the attendant, explaining how we absolutely have to appear in Superior Court first thing tomorrow morning and for reasons I'm not at liberty to share. With a concerned expression, she gives a pleasant smile and confirms we have just enough time to board, but our luggage won't likely make it in time. She tells us our emergency shuttle will be outside the door at the bottom of the stairs in about three minutes.

Carter leans forward and flashes a smile.

"Ma'am, we'd be so very grateful, and you'd be doing your country an enormous service, if you could do one more small thing for us."

She nods; he continues.

"There'll be a man exiting the plane and asking for us, perhaps any minute now. However, he's armed and dangerous. And worst of all, he's posing as a federal agent." Showing the attendant his military badge, he says, "But as you can see by Detective Norelli's badge and mine, these are real. However, his is false. Again, armed and dangerous. Oh, and as far as you're concerned," he winks, "We're heading to *Los Angeles,* okay?"

"Copy that, Lieutenant Colonel," she salutes with a smile.

Running down the stairs, I ask, "Lieutenant Colonel?"

"Long story, another time," he says, holding the door for me.

# CHAPTER FIFTY

"YOU WHAT?!"

Pete's voice carries through the phone as though standing beside me. And as much as I know it's coming, I flinch. Carter and I are at the gate about to board our next flight to LaGuardia.

Watching to see if Davenport is tailing us, I say, "Pete, please just let me explain. Three quick things."

Suddenly, I notice several police officers running in our direction.

I tap Carter's shoulder; he looks at me, then in their direction, and approaches the counter where two elderly people directly in front of us are moving slowly.

"Hello?" Pete barks.

"Sorry, we're just, okay, first, I have evidence that will clear me, but—"

"Then you need to present it—"

"Pete, please. I'm crushed for time. Let me finish."

Now, there are four officers getting closer—all of whom were looking from papers in their hands to faces around them.

I turn to Carter who has gone from the counter to help the elderly couple. Approaching the counter, I hand over my papers, smiling.

"Pete, hang with me just ten more seconds, please," I say, not waiting for a response. "Thank you," I say to the attendant and start down the jetway.

"Okay, Pete, second, Davenport's a dirty cop—"

"What? Are you sure? I suppose you have—"

"Yes, I have proof. Actually, Nelson does."

Boarding, I see Carter seating the couple, then arranging our seats.

"Or will," I check my watch. "Nelson will have what he needs inside the next ten minutes."

"Pat, you have to know this is—"

"I know. But Pete, since I saw you last, I've been threatened, shot at, and seen not one, but *two* people…" I lower my voice, "killed right in front of me, so I'm more than a bit wigged out."

"Okay, sorry. And I'll do everything in my power to help. Wait, what is your time?"

Looking at my watch, I do a quick calculation. "Uh, it's 2 a.m. here, so that's what, 6 tomorrow night. Geez, my head's a swirl."

They begin announcing our departure.

"Pete, I'm going to lose you in a minute. We'll land about your dinner time. Can you—"

"I'll have a car for you. No worries. And you can stay with us if you'd like. Wait, there's Carter too…"

"Brother, it's all good. We'll figure it out when we get there. All I need is for you to watch my back."

"Copy that."

"And give me a hug when I see you."

"Done."


I FEEL as though we've been on an airplane for days. My energy is spent, my body is sore, and my hair looks like hell. And I need a drink. Since we have another sixteen hours, I decide it's best to pop a Xanax and break out my sleep mask.

Turning to Carter, I smile. "You are my hero. Seriously, I can't believe how awesome you are. And that you're still hanging in there with me."

"I'm loving every minute of it. And another thing?"

I raise my eyebrows.

"You're mighty fantastic yourself. Now, relax and I'll grab us a little…" he checks his watch, "would you call it a nightcap or a daycap?"

.  .  .

WHEN WE HIT a pocket of turbulence, I slide out from under my mask, feeling marginally better. Carter is reading a book and sipping a coffee.

"Hey," I manage, immediately reaching for bottled water. "How long have I been out?"

"Hey, yourself." He lifts a sleeve. "Nine hours. And you flinched maybe a dozen or so times."

"Really?"

"Maybe two dozen?"

I frown. "So, that makes it what, about 11?"

"Bingo. Can I get you some breakfast?"

"Yes. And start with coffee. Have you been awake long?"

"An hour. I know you've only been up for two minutes, but I overheard you talking to your brother, mentioning something about contacting Nelson. You didn't do that yet, right?"

*Shit.*

Shaking my head, "No, dammit. But I'll do it when we…no, what am I thinking, I can email it. See? Monkey brain meets melatonin shortage. I'm gonna pee, splash my face, then join you for a coffee. How's that sound?"

"In that order? Perfect."


THREE EGGS, two chicken sausages, and a half pot of coffee later, I'm firing on all cylinders and flying through a stack of emails. Carter switched seats with me and is resting his head against the window. Several emails are from Stuart and a couple are from McCloud. I have a draft ready for Nelson and am about to send it when several thoughts come to mind.

Davenport's disloyalty explains how Tercel knew so much ahead of us, how he must've heard Stuart and McCloud's charade in my house, and how he found the evidence so quickly. The only thing I can't figure out is why Davenport arrived on my scene a year ago in the middle of the Johansen murder case and spent so much time snooping around the entire investigation.

*But nothing from him ever materialized.*

*Why not then?*

*Why now?*

Second, feeling something was off between Tercel and Savoy

during one of their last weekends together, I learn how she unlocked Tercel's phone and snapped a photo of a message sent from his phone to Davenport's private email confirming a payment of $2M. While the evidence isn't entirely conclusive, it does present reasonable doubt and a significant link between Tercel and Davenport, so I attach it to my email to Nelson.

*Like so many people before, perhaps Davenport saw the writing on the wall, and since he was being pushed out and/or approaching retirement, decided to take advantage of an opportunity. Like Savoy said, money buys everything.*

The photo was one of Savoy's parting shots, and I can't believe my dumb luck for having received it. Like I told Savoy, if she ever wants to change careers, I'll help her.

I'd like to ask Carter his thoughts, but he's out cold, so I decide to follow my gut. With the email ready, photo attached, and time running out, I push SEND.

# CHAPTER FIFTY-ONE

*New York City—*

At 6:10 p.m. we land at LaGuardia and are taxiing the runway when I turn on my phone and send Stuart, McCloud, and Nelson a text: *Just landed in New York. Will arrange a Zoom call for tomorrow morning (9/E-6/W). Bring your A game. The hunt for Tercel continues.*

I haven't been able to sleep because my mind is spinning, and I know once we land, we will have to hit the ground running.

As we approach baggage, I see Pete standing with a large man I've never seen before.

"Who's that?" I ask out of the side of my mouth.

Grinning wide, Carter shouts, "Mack!"

As we get closer, I realize he's bigger than I imagined. After a round of hugs and high fives, we make our way to the car.

"No luggage?" Pete asks, wrapping an arm around me.

"No. Oh shit, that reminds me—" I turn to Carter.

"I've handled it. We'll get a text the moment it arrives."

Approaching our exit, we're led to the Yukon. I get up front with Pete, and once on our way, I turn in my seat to see both of them.

"So Mack, I've heard a lot about you. And can say you've got an awfully big fan in this guy."

"Yeah? Well, I'm sure at least half is true," he laughs. "And the other, he just makes up to charm the girls."

Grinning like two kids, they fist bump.

"Oh, I've seen that charm at work."

En route to the restaurant, we listen as Mack and Carter get caught up, sharing some of the wacky escapades they'd encountered over the past year. There was plenty of ribbing as to who was the tougher guy, who rescued more damsels in distress, and a bunch of other *guy stuff.* Their animated stories are funny and a nice respite from the chaos of the past 24 hours.

We arrive at our restaurant in good time. *Pepolino* is one of Pete's favorite restaurants in Manhattan. Located on West Broadway between Canal and Lispenard, it serves authentic and homemade Tuscan cuisine. Pete arranged for us to have the large room on the second floor to ourselves. After we place orders and are into our first glass of wine, I lay out a number of items—from a synopsis of the last 24 hours to the email about the warrant for my arrest I'd sent Nelson. Pete confirms he got a copy, then runs down where we are with my legal situation with Andrew Jacobitz, saying dad hadn't missed a beat.

With the new intel about Davenport working with Tercel, Pete feels slightly better about how things will go for me. The biggest challenge he shares is how to make the information stick, especially coming from a civilian who's in bed with—both metaphorically and otherwise—the enemy. Carter and I say we feel McCloud will help in that department.

We're finishing dinner with coffee when the table gets quiet.

"Fellas, words can't express the gratitude I feel having you here with me. Thank you."

As each gives an affirming nod, I try to keep from crying.

"Now, about this asshole we are looking for—I've every intention to put him in the ground, one way or the other."

"Oorah!" They shout in unison.

# CHAPTER FIFTY-TWO

THE NEXT MORNING, CARTER AND I ARE DOWNSTAIRS IN THE LOBBY, sharing a pot of coffee while waiting for Mack to join us. Our temporary home is the Soho Grand, and like much of Manhattan, it is sleek and incredibly hip.

Given Pepolino is only a block away, we were able to walk home last night after turning down a chance to stay with Pete, wife Stephanie, and their twins Jack and Alison. It sounded nice, but after what we had just been through, the thought of waking up to two eight year olds didn't make my list of need-to's.

Pete texts to say he's getting the kids to school and will join our Zoom call shortly. Mid-sip, I look up and see Mack entering the room.

"Jesus, he's big," I mutter through the steam of my coffee.

"And strong as hell," Carter says, grinning at his approaching pal.

"Morning, Detective," Mack growls, tapping the tip of his Angels ball cap.

"Morning, Mack," I smile, offering a fist bump. "*Easy* does it."

His enormous fist barely taps mine and I smirk.

"What?" He looks at me and frowns.

"Just trying to imagine getting hit with that thing."

His funny laugh sounds like a cross between a grunt and someone choking.

"Never happen," his stubbled face spreads a grin."To you, anyway."

Carter pours him a coffee and Mack nods and sips.

"Angels fan?" I ask.

"Yes, Ma'am. I 'specially like their Quality Assurance guy. An old friend we call *Bussy*. Used to be with the Cubs."

"Nice. I always liked the Cubs. Well, until Maddon left," I sip. "Now? Fuck 'em."

Both guys seem to get a kick out of that, so I keep going.

"Now, if you wanna talk *basketball*; let's talk about the Lakers."

Sports talk goes on for a good twenty minutes until breakfast arrives, at which point the chatter turns to weapons. Their excitement over guns and knives is something to behold. They rattle off brands, ammo grain count, and velocity stats until I have to gesture "time out" and excuse myself to the restroom.

When I return to the dining area, our table is empty. I look around thinking I'm in the wrong room until a hostess sees my distress.

"Ms. Norelli?"

"Yes?"

"Let me show you to your friends. Your party enlarged and," she lowers her voice, "required more privacy. We moved you to the Club Room. I think you'll find it to be quite nice."

Entering the heavily draped and super luxe room, I see our group has grown by two. My brother stands and introduces me to our new guest.

"Sis, I mean, *Detective* Norelli, meet Lukas Burton, New York City's Mayor."

Burton is a tall, handsome man with penetrating eyes and a firm handshake. His clothes are tailored, his hair freshly cut, and his cologne expensive.

We manage several minutes of small talk—mostly about our recent travels—before I get to the point.

"Mayor Burton, I'm sure my brother has filled you in; however, I'd like to put things in my own words for matters of clarity as well as shed light on things he may or may not have insight. No disrespect to him; it's just my way of doing things."

"Understood," he smiles. "I'm happy to hear whatever you have to say. Pete's one of our city's finest, and as I'm sure *you* have heard, these two gentlemen have done our city an invaluable service."

"I have and I'm extremely impressed. My singular focus is to locate and arrest Darius Tercel. He's wanted for the murder of...well frankly,

I've lost count. But the most recent are two acquaintances in Australia and one of my closest friends. You may know that at one time he was a practicing therapist in Beverly Hills, a legit doctor who used his thriving business for years as a front. As for when he veered off his professional track and slipped into darkness or lost his way—whatever you choose to call it—he's transformed into a genuine psychopath. He's a pathological liar, a cold-blooded killer, and as we recently witnessed, very much the chameleon—a genuine impostor who'll stop at nothing to get what he wants."

Burton listens intently; his eyes never shift from mine.

"Concerning his appearance," Burton says, "was it a significant change? How long ago was the last time you saw him? And, what do you suppose would keep him from changing his appearance again?"

I let out a deep sigh.

"Yes, it was significant. I mean, he's nearly unrecognizable from a year ago. He put on fifteen, maybe twenty pounds of solid muscle—he's in exceptional shape and he's had a good deal of plastic surgery. I'm happy to share before and after photos with you. Basically, he's gone from looking like a nerdy accountant to a body-building surfer. As for a future change?" I stare at my hands, considering it. "I'm certain he will. And unfortunately, that's what'll make it all the more difficult."

"Especially in a city this size. If he's indeed here."

"Exactly," I say, hoping the blush I'm feeling isn't noticeable. "My gut says he's here. And while I have a few ideas as to his next possible transformation, it's only a guess."

Expressionless, Burton looks from me to Pete and says, "In my book, that sounds like a needle in a haystack."

My stomach drops.

"However, I've seen these two perform miracles most people would have never expected. I mean, Carter's kill shot and accuracy—especially at the distance from his target—are utterly impressive. You add Mack's leadership and strength, well, it makes for a powerful combo. Bottom line? The optimist in me believes in the possibility for miracles."

Burton wraps by explaining how he owes Carter big after what he and his team were able to pull off with his family. He discusses the generous resources he is willing to make available, then excuses himself to attack a very hectic schedule.

# CHAPTER FIFTY-THREE

WITH THAT PART OF OUR MISSION COMPLETE, WE GATHER AROUND MY
laptop back in the suite for our call.

"Man, is it nice to see your mugs," I say. "And I'm sorry it's so
early, but the clock's ticking and we have to get after it."

"Feels like a month since I've seen your face, partner," Stuart says.

"Yeah, and it only feels like I've aged a year. But thanks to this
guy," I toss a thumb at Carter, "I'm still alive. Oh, and meet a new face
on our team. This is Mack McKenzie, Carter's sidekick. Mack, that's
Stuart *my* sidekick, and McCloud our all-around high-tech guru."

"Nice to meet you two."

"By the way, Pat," Stuart leans in, "Nelson couldn't make it this
early. Told me to catch him up later."

"No worries. Same for Pete. Other duties."

Next, I provide a quick synopsis of what had happened since we left
LA. I also share how we lost two people who helped our efforts, but
gained two in Savoy and Mack. I hold up Savoy's watch.

"Speaking of Savoy, McCloud, I've got a recorder that needs your
expertise. It's been run through seawater, but hopefully it'll give us
something. Actually, it *has* to, as it may be the only prime piece of
evidence that'll pin Davenport to the wall. What I'd really like is for
you to fly out here and help us nab this prick. Thoughts?"

"Count me in," he says instantly. "I'm guessing you need me—"

"—as soon as we hang up."

"Copy that."

"Stuart, I'd say the same for you, but—"

"No can do. I'm working a case *and* on baby watch. It's any day now."

I turn to Mack and Carter. "Stuart had a girl about a year ago; in fact, it was about the time we met our demented *Doctor*. Now, they've got a boy on the way."

"And then, we're done," Stuart chuckles.

"Congrats," Carter and Mack say.

"Okay, so to recap: Mayor Burton's giving us wide access and a small battalion to cover Manhattan. McCloud's on the next flight here —bring all your toys. Stuart, you'll let me know the minute Davenport circles back around looking for me, and in the meantime, just say you've lost contact. Oh, and tell Nelson I'll ring him later after he's caught up on his beauty sleep."

Laughing, we wrap up and ring off because it's time to head over to Pete's office to put together our New York team.

STEPPING inside the 1st Precinct on Ericsson Place at Varick Street, I'm nearly overwhelmed with the activity. Serving the southernmost tip of Manhattan, Pete's precinct is home to the World Trade Center, SOHO, Tribeca, and Wall Street. The phrase "nerve center" fits to a tee.

Since Pete took over as Captain, murder, rape, and robbery in his precinct have dropped to less than 10%, a substantial reduction from only years prior. The only crimes that have increased is petty larceny— and in a city this size with their crime history, that's going some.

Pete stands at the front desk talking to two officers nearly the size of Mack when we arrive. Seeing us, he excuses himself and waves us to follow—talking over his shoulder—as we snake through a maze of hallways.

"We'll have coffee in my office," he says, frowning at the smell of burnt coffee coming from a break room we pass. "Shit's not fit to patch the streets."

· · ·

PETE'S SPACE is an older office with high ceilings and outdated overhead lighting. We sit on what looks like a new couch and chairs sitting atop a handsome rug. A wall of awards and photos adorn his office.

"Nice digs, brother," I say, sitting on the couch. Carter joins me and Mack squeezes into a chair opposite us.

Picking up the phone, Pete says, "Nina, would you mind bringing coffee in? And let Jim know our friends are here? Thank you."

Taking a seat, he stops to catch his breath.

"Okay, coffee's coming, as is my team, so in the meantime, what did I miss?"

Carter and Mack look at me and shrug.

"Not much. Except how we have to find a needle in a metropolitan haystack in a limited amount of time and before our monster kills anyone else."

"That all?"

I go over all the details from our call. He nods in all the right places, and when asked if he has any questions, he shakes his head.

"So, with all that in mind, combined with your team and our collective instincts..." I wave a thumb at my sidekicks, "we stand a good chance at finding him."

His grin reminds me of us when we were kids—whenever I got cocky.

"Good for you, Sis. I like your confidence."

*Blow me over with a feather.*

"Thanks," I say quietly.

As I'm about to gush all over myself, the door opens and Pete's secretary escorts a large group of uniformed officers who quietly enter and line the perimeter of the room. After maybe two dozen men and women take their places, one man pulls up the rear.

*Davenport?*

# CHAPTER FIFTY-FOUR

THIS IS THE FIRST TIME I'VE EVER SEEN DAVENPORT SMILE. IN FACT, I would bet my next paycheck he wasn't born with the muscles needed to form a smile. Entering the room with his chest out like a peacock, his expression reads: *Gotchya.*

Mine must read: *What the fuck.*

Pete stands, holding out both arms like a boxing ref.

"Okay, we get it. Take a seat Davenport. Keep yours, Pat. The rest of you, at ease."

The room relaxes and Pete gets to it.

"I want to begin by thanking all of you for volunteering to help me and my sister. We welcome one of her team members, Carter Matheson, whom you may recall from last year's case involving the kidnapping of the Mayor's daughter."

That received plenty of nods.

"He was a great help then, and we're looking forward to having him and his partner Mack McKenzie help us find a Doctor Darius Tercel."

From his desk, he grabs a stack of paper and Nina begins handing them out.

"Nina has a one-pager for each of you. On it, you'll find several photos. The first is a publicity photo of what he used to look like over a year ago. The second several are what he looked like last week—in and around southeastern Australia where he's been holed up for nearly a year. And the third, while only an enhanced sketch, is an idea that we—

or rather my sister—thinks he *may* go for. As I said, it's just an approxi-
mation, but you get the picture."

He takes a sip of coffee and looks at me, raising an eyebrow.

"I'll turn it over to LAPD's Detective Norelli and her team."

Standing, I look at all their faces.

"Thanks, Pete. And thank you all for your support in helping us."
Turning to the group, I add, "As your Captain mentioned, well, he
didn't actually, but I'm sure he *thinks* it—as I'm sure you will—*yes*, it's
a needle in a haystack. But as many of you know, much of our work is
exactly that. However, with the help of Carter and Mack, two guys who
know a lot about finding bad guys whose specialty is not getting found,
I feel confident we'll accomplish our goal. Now, there are several
aspects of this case that need special attention. You'll find a short bio of
our target on the back of your papers."

Everyone in the room turns their papers to follow me.

"In short, he's an incredibly smart guy. Former high-profile Hollywood therapist, an only son of two actor parents who between their
legacy and his thriving practice made him *very* wealthy. He's also
surprisingly accomplished in all manner of murder. In fact, I think
you'll come to find him to be a serial killer of epic proportions. I say
epic because I know of no less than a half-dozen people he murdered
*prior* to my case. Then, he went on to murder three people during my
investigation, a period covering less than a month. Last, he murdered
two people right in front of me just this week—and that doesn't count
his recently murdering my best friend."

Swallowing hard, I look around the room to find sympathetic faces.

"As an odd bonus…" I force an uncomfortable smile, "I was also a
patient of his. And got *much* too close to becoming one of his
victims."

That gets the first audible response from the group.

"So as you can see, this case is personal." I take a breath. "Any
questions?"

One officer raises a hand, then says, "I think I can speak for my co-
workers when I say we've got you. And while it sounds crazy, this is
New York and we're all just a little crazy. Am I right?"

The group laughs.

"And Carter, I was part of the team who helped you sweep Gracie
Mansion back when the Mayor's daughter was kidnapped. I saw how

you and your team worked then, and I wanted to say it's good to see you back."

Carter stands.

"Thank you, Officer. I appreciate the words. And we'll do everything in our power to find this guy—and keep your city safe in the process."

He's about to sit down when he says, "And you know what else? Detective Norelli…" he tosses a thumb at me, "is about as tough as I've seen. Mack and I wouldn't've come aboard if we didn't feel confident we had a chance."

# CHAPTER FIFTY-FIVE

DAVENPORT, REMAINING SILENT THE ENTIRE TIME, STAYS AS THE GROUP leaves. A permanent smirk, however, remains stuck to his face.

*Probably worried I'll lose him again.*

"Very impressive Detective," he says. "For someone who is about to become an example of what a dirty cop looks like."

*I so want to punch that condescending look off his face.*

Flanking either side of me, Carter and Mack stand.

Raising his hands in surrender, Davenport takes a seat. "Just keep your boys on a short leash, Detective."

"Shut your face, Davenport," Pete says as we all take our seats. "This is my city, my rules. And as you can see, my office, so show some fuckin' respect."

"I will. That is, after I cuff her and take her back to LA," he sneers, unwrapping a stick of gum.

"Never happen, Davenport," I say quietly. "Not until after I find the *real* bad guy."

"We'll see," he mumbles.

"Thank God for that," Carter nods toward the gum wrapper.

Davenport looks confused. Carters shakes his head.

"Since we have little time as it is, let's make this quick," Pete says, "And just so you know, Patricia, I actually arranged for Davenport to be here."

"WHAT?!"

I know I'm loud because Carter and Mack jump.

"What the *fuck,* Pete? You don't seriously—"

"Hold on," he says, coming out of his chair. "Listen first. Then, punch my face. Here's the reason," he says, giving me our inside brother-sister look. "I've seen the evidence. Nelson showed me and I have to admit it's convincing. And as hard as this is to hear, I need to understand *his* side. Can we do that? Before we get to work?"

If I were a cartoon right now, there'd be steam coming out both ears. I take a deep breath, wondering if my brother had lost his mind, then finally nod and take a seat.

"Thank you." He cuts me a look I can't read. "Now, Davenport, tell us your side. And as hard as it may be, keep it short and sweet."

"I can," Davenport smirks. "In like in five sentences. She's guilty. I have three pieces of evidence that back me up." He holds up a finger. "An empty vial found in the freezer." He adds a finger, "a syringe in a baggie in her toilet tank." And with a third finger, "and a real estate contract between her and the deceased."

"Bullshit!" I bark, coming out of my seat.

Pete eyeballs me, motions for me to sit, then turns to Davenport. "What else?"

"What?" Davenport whips his head back and forth between us. "I just told you. There are—"

"Yeah, I got that. But what *else* do you have? Fingerprints? On any *one* of the items? Photographs of her in action? Maybe audio or video recordings of *anything* that backs you? How about a second opinion—someone with credentials?"

Quiet, he stares. The truth, he knows.

Pete waits longer than I would've given.

Davenport's frozen expression begins melting.

"That's entirely enough evidence, Captain, and you know it."

Rolling my neck, I pop it several times.

"Okay. Let's say for the sake of argument, you're right about the detective. And for just a moment, let's assume you can take her back, but *only* after we finish this case, would—"

"No freaking way, Captain. I've been pushed around long enough, and it's time for her to pay. And I mean now!"

*And there it is. A man pushed. With little to no power. Who's a greedy liar.*

"Understood, and fortunately for you, I've spoken with Captain Nelson and others on the ninth floor as well as Attorney Jacobitz and the honorable Samuel Norelli. They all say—"

"*Pfft*, nepotism always works," he mumbles.

In a blink, Pete jumps up and gets within inches of his face.

"I've had about enough of you, Davenport. And I'm actually trying to *help* you. But so help me God, if you get in my way, as much as your *division* has its own authority, I will..."

He stops to catch his breath.

"I've got entirely too much shit to handle, so here's what we're going to do. You have my word that I will hand over Detective Norelli *after* our current case is closed. And only after *all three* of us return to Los Angeles and appear before a judge. And I'm *not* talking about my father. Agreed?"

Davenport's jaw twitches, his nostrils flare, and after a long and dramatic sigh, he nods.

"Agreed?"

Standing, he buttons his sportcoat and growls, "Yes." Walking to the door he stops and adds, "However, I'm going to hang around a couple of days. Just to keep an eye on things."

"You do that." Pete follows him to the door. "And have a nice day," he says to his back.

"Pete, what'n the hell—"

He holds up a hand, looking down the hall. "Nina, let me know if he comes back," he says, closing the door and taking a seat with us.

"Such bullshit," I mumble.

Rubbing his face, he says, "Before you start up, just *please* hear me out."

I glance at Carter and Mack. They just stare.

"Here's what's up. I got hold of Nelson and we talked with his boss. This way, they're happy I'm being a team player. I also got Nelson to let Davenport know I called to tell him specifically about your being here. Again, team player, but on Davenport's team. No one but you, me, and dad knows how Nelson's helping us out. Okay, maybe Jacobitz, but trust me it's a win-win. Nelson—about to pull the pin—gets to go out a hero. *But* Davenport has to believe I'm helping him, too, because as far as he and I are concerned, I'm vying for Commissioner and need a win, too. And the *only* reason I didn't tell you all of this before is because…" he takes a deep breath. "Sis, you're a great cop, but a lousy actor. And I needed the reaction that you *just* made in order to sell him."

I squint, "But how'd Davenport believe—"

"I told him you and I were estranged. That you'd become a lone wolf and I didn't see a way I could help—*unless* you came to town where I could keep an eye on you."

"And he bought it," I deadpan.

A nod.

"*Humph.*"

"Since you and I both know Tercel fed him the info—or that's what we hope to confirm shortly—we can keep an eye on him. And flush him out when the time comes."

"Either that…" Carter says, "or he'll trip himself up."

Mack says, "We can only hope."


SOME WOULD SAY our plan is more than a little nuts, but Carter, Mack and I have seen nuttier. There were several things we're counting on and upon which we're basing our strategy with Tercel.

It's time to canvas the city, so we begin by turning 90% of our officers into plainclothes, asking them to wear whatever they'd wear off-duty. Next, we turn a large handful of them into tourists, and for a smaller few who display a dramatic flair, we ask them to "channel their inner movie star." The remaining 5% are just cops.

Carter says, "It's all about averages—average Joes, average cops, and average actors."

Knowing McCloud is on a flight to New York to investigate Savoy's watch, it makes me wonder what Savoy is up to. Having witnessed her bravery in the face of danger, I suddenly have an idea.

After a quick call, another piece of our puzzle falls into place.

# CHAPTER FIFTY-SIX

PETE ARRANGES FOR CARTER, MACK, AND ME TO HAVE AN OFFICE where we work with an oversized map of Manhattan. With the help of Google, we begin targeting a handful of condos, hotels, museums, and art galleries. To cover real estate, we bring in a top realtor to familiarize ourselves with recent home purchases in the most popular neighborhoods. Going on my gut and her instincts, our target becomes exclusively the Upper East Side. We now have a manageable target between 59th Street to the south and 96th Street to the north and between 5th Avenue and the East River.

Savoy will manage covering hotels when she arrives.

For museums and galleries, Carter will lean on the Mayor's wife Claire to share the more prestigious upcoming events. And since Pete's wife is a Family Nurse Practitioner, who also has an undergrad degree in psychiatric care, we'll lean on her to discover therapists who have taken on new patients. Because of privacy issues, it will be the tiniest of haystack needles.

Since landing in New York, my monkey mind continues reminding me how ridiculous of an objective we're facing. However, I push the thought aside, instead choosing to *Hail Mary* my career and fuel my confidence with the knowledge I have Tercel rattled with our near miss in Australia.

.   .   .

McCLOUD ARRIVES AS we finish lunch. I can't decide whether to hug or kiss him, so I do both.

"Damn, it's good to see your face, McCloud."

"You, too," he grins. "Helluva ride so far, huh?"

I hook his arm with mine. "You have no idea. Let me show you around."

He meets the players just as our entire group gathers to hear the *master plan*. Breaking them into categories, we explain how some crews will begin tonight, and by first thing tomorrow morning, a large portion will be dispersed throughout the Upper East Side. By the end of our meeting, everyone knows what time to show up, what areas they'll work, and how to keep their communication systems in check—our Motto: conceal & conspire while we search & secure.


ANSWERING MY PHONE, the voice says, "Know anybody who needs help bringing down a *piker*?"

It's Savoy. From the sounds of it, she's at an airport.

Laughing, I ask, "And by piker, you mean asshole?"

"Where I'm from," she says, "it's a social misfit, but I like *asshole* much better!"

Turning to Carter, I mouth, *Savoy.* "Sounds like you've landed. Good flight?"

"Too right. Just touched down. And yes, long, but good. What'll you have me do, grab a cab?"

"Hell, no. I have a driver waiting for you in baggage claim. Name's Dimitri; he's great fun."

"Thank you."

"We'll meet at our hotel—same place you're staying—in about 30. Then head out for some business mixed with pleasure."

"Good onya, Pat!"

We ring off, and I start to change clothes when I notice Carter staring out the window.

"Where's your head?"

"Couple things. I'm thinking about how big a gamble this is. But then I think it's no bigger a long shot than when Mack and I were here to help Lukas with Donovan Blair."

I step closer.

"They share a lot of similarities."

I watch the way the light flickers in his bright eyes, eyes that are always scanning—a room of people, a large gathering, the horizon— always analyzing threats of danger or points of escape.

"What are they?"

"Both criminals. Both good at what they do. Both are hungry. Both relentless. Both without a conscience."

"And why does that possess you?"

He snorts, "That's funny because it perfectly describes how I feel when I begin to hunt a man. I'm possessed by the way he thinks, the way he hunts. I study his process—be it a manner of escape or method of destruction. All of it tells me a great deal."

Looking at him, I think of how much I admire his instincts and bravery.

"Does any of this scare you?"

He instantly shakes his head, then stops. "Actually, it does. But not like you think. *He* doesn't scare me. What scares me is him hurting *you*."

An overwhelming feeling of protection washes over me and my eyes pool with tears.

"The biggest reality I've had—especially after having seen him face to face and seeing the cavalier way in which he treats those around him —is his obsession is you. It's a real thing. And I'm not sure why. Well, I mean besides the obvious—that you're beautiful and smart and funny and terrifically brave…"

"Stop," I blush.

"Seriously. You're all that. But it's the fact that even after an entire year, working as hard as he has, he still can't have you."

I suddenly realize how I haven't allowed myself to inhabit that reality.

"You're just saying that because—"

"No, and not to interrupt…" he grins, "but to interrupt. Sure it's all that, but do you think for one minute he went to all these lengths and made all these significant changes just because he wanted to *hide* from the law?"

My instinct is to nod, but I don't.

"No," Carter says. "He's done this because he thinks that if *he* changes, then you'll love him."

"What?" I shake my head. "He's a psychopath!"

"Yes. But from the moment I saw his eyes, I considered he may actually be the worst sort. He has all the money and toys he needs, yet he still can't escape us. How that must torture him."

"Right."

"The worst torture is that he can't have *you*—and that brings me full circle."

"Why?"

"Because I'm afraid, as cliche as it may sound, he feels that if he can't have you..."

"Nobody can," I mumble.

He's quiet for a long beat.

"Just remember, he gave you the biggest clue in the love letter he delivered to your hospital room that day—*very close* to death, I might add."

"But didn't," I whisper.

"Right. Perhaps because he figured that he would disappear, take some time to improve himself to whatever version that may be, then find you again—after manufacturing himself to become someone *else*."

I try to let that sink in.

"But then when you came searching for him, you messed with his plan."

We both snap out of our introspective bubble.

I grab his arm. "Carter?"

He steps close. "Yes?"

"Thank you."

"For what?"

"For taking this so seriously—and for watching out for me."

"Of course."

"Also for helping me understand—perhaps in a new way—just how dangerous he is."

His face relaxes into a smile.

"But mostly? For letting me know there are still good men who genuinely care."

He kisses my cheek. "Okay, now you're sounding like a Hallmark card."

I feign hurt, then slowly grin. "A little too heavy?"

He pinches his thumb and index finger together—and I punch his arm.

MACK AND MCCLOUD join Carter and me downstairs at the Grand Bar & Lounge. We're in the process of ordering cocktails when I see a distracted McCloud staring toward the entrance. I'm about to ask what's making him gawk when I look over my shoulder to find Savoy sauntering our way. She's wearing her hair down, her blouse amply open, and a skirt leaving little to the imagination. The tall pumps complete the *fuck me* look.

All heads turn as Mack and McCloud simultaneously mutter, "Wow."

I look at Carter who rolls his eyes. "Put your tongues back in your mouths, boys," he says. "Not polite to drool in public."

Savoy enters with a hearty, "G'day, Mates," and nods to each man as I make introductions.

It's amusing to see her look nearly eye to eye at Mack and to watch McCloud—who offers his seat—to stumble over himself.

Our drinks arrive and we get to business.

"Tonight's important," Carter begins. "Mayor Burton will all but give us the keys to the city. His wife will be instrumental in our access to museums and galleries. And you'll get to see just how efficient this city operates under duress."

Mack adds, "We've been in any number of shit storms, and this city has the ability to pull together like few others."

"Just remember 9-11," Carter adds.

"All that in mind," I say, "I just want us to bring our very best game to the table because our foe is formidable. And as Savoy will share at dinner, he's been planning a lot of this for a very long time."

# CHAPTER FIFTY-SEVEN

"Did I mention how I've only been given four days—including today—to pull this whole thing off?" I say to the group as we finish our drinks.

The entire table looks at me as though I just yelled, *Fire!*

"What?" Savoy says, nearly choking on her Martini. "Today's Tuesday, that means—"

"Yep, Friday. We fly out Saturday, catch our breath Sunday, and then I face the music on Monday."

McCloud eyes bug. "You're shittin' me, right?"

Even Mack shows the first expression I've seen since meeting him.

Carter, on the other hand, doesn't blink.

"Yeah…" I say, "I didn't want to bring that up, you know, while I had all the attention back at the precinct."

Carter and Mack cut a distinctive stare at one another.

Savoy and McCloud look as though they just lost the lottery.

"Yeah, great way to start a week," I frown. "And end a career."

"What's going to happen?" Savoy asks.

"Well, I'll go in front of a judge along with members of the LAPD and Davenport. But according to my brother who should be here any second now, it's all under control."

Emptying my drink, I hand my credit card to the passing waitress.

"But hey, we're here now. We have an enormous crew at our disposal. And Savoy, *you* made a lot of this possible. While you,

McCloud, are about to make me an extremely happy woman. That is, after you tell me the watch she gave us will provide the testimony we so desperately need."

Just then, I see Pete entering the lobby. "Hey guys, excuse me just a second."

AS CARTER FINISHES HIS DRINK, he says, "Thoughts? Questions? Give 'em to me now because as you heard, this train's leaving the station."

"And fast," Mack smirks.

"But you know, mates..." Savoy says, finishing her cocktail, "I'm good with it. Not to be too melodrama for you'uns, but I'm just glad to be *alive*. So, I say we get ripped."

"Cheers," McCloud leans his beer to her glass.

MAYOR BURTON BOOKED our dinner reservations, so we have little to worry about—which is good because the conversations between old and new inebriated friends are loud and animated. We meet the Burtons at the restaurant and are shown to a private room near the back.

By mid meal, our table of nine is engrossed in a conversation about ethics. Lukas, Pete, Carter, and Mack stand firm on the issue of taking someone out if there's even a question of endangerment. I mentally chalk this attitude up to their being in the military. Claire, Stephanie, and I agree how it's not okay to take a life if you aren't sure the person is of a sound mind. Savoy and McCloud remain neutral for differences involving apathy and innocence.

"I've been in this situation—both of us have..." Carter says, tossing a thumb to Mack, "where you literally have a second, maybe two, to make a decision. And let me tell you, when your next heartbeat is in the hands of someone else, you'll do anything in your power to keep that choice in *your* hand."

"What my brother says is true," Mack nods.

"I can appreciate that," Claire says, "especially given what you and Carter did for our daughter. The biggest difference being you knew the guy was a psychopath and had more than ample time to dismantle and destroy him."

"I'm certainly not in y'alls caliber of—whatever you call it—cops and robbers," Savoy says, "but I can tell you this. I stood there facing a man who I wasn't *completely* sure was mad, but was someone I had been having a relationship with, and I *still* had to make a split decision. I'll never forget those few seconds. That's why I jumped—and how I'm sitting here today," she says, taking a hefty swallow of her drink.

The table is quiet until McCloud speaks.

"I'm just too inexperienced to make the call. I mean, I've worked alongside Norelli and her partner Stuart, and they operate in a world I don't feel all that comfortable in. And the saddest part? I'm afraid I'd freeze."

Nodding, Pete says, "It really comes down to timing. That split second when your life's on the line. Thanks to our built-in survival instincts, I think we'd all pull the trigger on them before they had a chance to pull it on us."

Claire claps her hands and says, "And on that note, I say we enjoy a nightcap before going our separate ways. After all, we've got a big day —*several* days—ahead of us."

"Claire, can you share your plans with the group?" I ask.

"Of course. I have the honor of serving on several boards here in the city. We're members of The Metropolitan Museum of Art, MoMa, and The Guggenheim. It just so happens this is Art Week in New York and all the galleries are making public some of the most historic art available. We have a benefit at the Metropolitan tomorrow night, an auction at the Guggenheim on Thursday, and a gala soiree at the MoMa on Friday."

I look from Pete to Carter and back to Claire. "Is everyone thinking the same thing I am?"

All heads do a slow bounce.

Pete says, "Any one of them's a prime target."

"*All* of them," Carter grins.

"Exactly what I'm thinking," I say. "And while he may not make them all, no, screw that, he *will* make them all. It's one of his biggest passions. Tell me Claire, can you share the main draws of each show?"

"Sure. The Met are the classics. We have a Rembrandt show highlighting his entire career. It will benefit children's art programs in all five boroughs. The Guggenheim is auctioning photographs of some never-before-seen work by Robert Mapplethorpe. They'll be among the more controversial."

"Great," I say, grinning at Carter. "Right?"

He nods. "I saw the file on Tercel's home gallery."

"And MoMa?" I ask Claire.

"That show will auction several pieces from Jackson Pollock's retrospective collection."

"Again, perfect."

With that line-up handled, I feel confident we're set and finally let my shoulders relax.

# CHAPTER FIFTY-EIGHT

TERCEL STARES OUT AT THE LIGHTS OF CENTRAL PARK, GLAD TO BE back in the States. He is more than happy to hear a New York accent, especially over the Australian slang he mastered over the past year. While he could easily pass as an Aussie—which he had done many times—he is glad to be done with that part of his facade. That is, unless or until it is needed again. He also looks forward to shifting from a year-long Mediterranean diet—one that kept him trim—to a more carnivorous one which will fit his next identity.

The view from One57 is impressive and, as a haven for the rich and famous on "Billionaires Row," he feels right at home.

Located on 57th between 6th and 7th Avenues, only two blocks from Central Park, he enjoys three exposures, any service money can buy, and a great place to escape. He only has one reservation.

*Is it too obvious of a location?*

Tercel is used to the good life. Hollywood provided all that and more—and he knows it is all about location.

*But would this neighborhood make me a sitting duck?*

Crossing the room to the oversized mirror on the entry wall, he examines the latest version of himself.

*Best I keep this look for a while.*

He rubs his freshly shaved bald head, then strokes the goatee that will take some time getting used to. As soon as it fills in better, he plans to keep it dyed dark.

*I'll miss the dimpled chin.*

He puts on a pair of chunky oversized designer glasses, despite the green contacts, and now has a complete look.

*Nice to see light eyes again.*

Stepping back, he surveys the closet of fine clothing. Even before arriving in New York, he ordered a whole new wardrobe and had it delivered. Trading in whites and tans of linen and silk, he plans to enjoy the new charcoal and navy cotton and wool.

*A new look for a new man.*

Walking to the bar, he pours a short bourbon with hopes of quieting his inner demons.

*Fashion aside, I need to think through the details.*

Leaning on his past profession, he considers how Pat found him.

*Of all the places in the world. Then again, I said exactly where to find me.*

He sips and considers.

*Even after a year, it's more than luck; it's desire.*

His thoughts shift.

*At least I won't have to worry about her no-name sidekick.*

Another sip.

*Poor Noah. Couldn't risk loose ends.*

Turning to the window, he stares at the "ants" scurrying 29 floors below him.

*Savoy shouldn't have brought her girlfriend. Sad she had to die so young.*

He ponders Patricia's diving off the boat and dodging the bullets.

*Even if she wasn't hit, there's no way she could've gotten back to shore.*

Recalling passionate times with Savoy and Patricia, he considers his emotions.

*I'm sure they have all found peace—on the bottom of the ocean.*

He is about to pour another when something pings the back of his mind.

*Wait! In all the mayhem, did I, yes, I cut the boat loose. Right?*

The panic he feels rises—and just as quickly disappears.

*Noah had the key.* He sighs. *I won't give it another thought.*

Ready to leave, he goes to a single keypad and with a quick touch the lights dim, curtains close throughout the handsome space, and soft jazz begins playing.

*Last thing I'll do on my walk to dinner is call Davenport.*

Fetching a walking cane, he puts on a hat and stops at the mirror to admire once again.

"Goodbye, Dr. Darius Tercel. Hello Antiques & Art Dealer, Simon Lockhart."


WALKING along 57th toward Carnegie Hall, "Simon" walks with a slight limp, thanks to a thickened insert in his left shoe. Between the oversized glasses, a handsome fedora angled just so, and a handsome walking cane in his right hand, his ruse is complete.

Taking a left onto 7th Avenue, he enjoys mindless window-shopping while contemplating several dinner options. By the time he hits the 54th Street intersection, he considers Empire Steak House, an exceptional restaurant with a fireplace and impressive wine collection.

*Perhaps a bit stuffy.*

Strolling, his thoughts drift to seafood where he considers Ocean Prime, a sea-lover's paradise. More window-shopping, attractive women passing, and two blocks later, he reaches 52nd Street where a craving for a dry-aged steak and a hefty Cabernet wins the vote.

Decision made, he turns right onto 52nd and crosses Broadway. Steps later, he enters Gallaghers Steakhouse, one of Manhattan's finest steakhouses whose rich history dates back to prohibition where Broadway icons, politicians, and socialites dine.

The restaurant is packed, but he spots an opening seat and tips his hat to the hostess—motioning he'll sit at the bar—before taking the perfect spot for people watching.

# CHAPTER FIFTY-NINE

THERE IS ONLY ONE WAY TO GET THROUGH THE NEXT FOUR DAYS IN ONE piece, physically and mentally: push ahead at 90 miles an hour, spend little time sleeping, and hope that between McCloud securing evidence and my securing Tercel's neck, I'll have all I need to return to a normal life.

*Whatever that is.*

Checking my makeup in the mirror, I imagine a happier time. That's when Angie pops into my mind and I catch myself smiling.

PING goes a phone in the stall behind me, just as Savoy exits the stall adjusting her tight skirt.

"Crikey, had to have a liquid laugh in there. Got any chewie?"

I look at her like she was speaking a foreign language.

"Right. I had to vomit. You have any gum?"

Shaking my head, I reach in my bag and take out a pack of Big Red, handing her that and a tube of lipstick.

She shoves it in her mouth. "And some lippie to boot. Aces!"

I watch her perk herself up and say, "Your country has more slang than any place I've ever heard. I love it."

"Really?"

"Really."

Freshened up, we exit the restroom and return to our table.

Rounding the corner, I see a handsome older couple approaching the bar. As I'm halfway across the room, I spot an equally handsome man sitting at the bar talking to a beautiful woman. Passing him, I catch his eyes, but only for a moment. He has an odd expression, one of near recognition.

*Or could it be my imagination.*

I look back to see him leaning over to whisper in the woman's ear.

TERCEL PICKS up a napkin the woman next to him inadvertently dropped. Handing her a fresh one from the bar, he leans over to whisper something charming as a familiar face passes right by him.

The woman laughs, then returns to her date on the other side of her.

Motionless, Tercel stares at his dinner, suddenly left with no appetite.

*How the hell could that be?*

He pats his damp forehead.

*It's impossible!*

He glances up at the mirror behind the bar, then slowly looks over his shoulder. He sees neither Patricia nor Savoy.

Leaning to one side, he stretches to see into the back room. Nothing.

Turning back to his meal, he takes a long sip of red wine.

Then another.

His mind is spinning as he replays the scene where he saw them last.

*I know I shot them both.*

*Along with their friend and Weija.*

*And Noah.*

His vision narrows at the thought of his "new world" being polluted by his past.

*Dammit!* His mind screams.

Focused on nothing, he stares straight ahead.

"Sir, may I get you something?" A voice asks in the distance.

*What will I do now? And what are the chances—*

"Sir, is everything okay?"

"What?" Tercel says, snapping back. "Oh, yes. Everything's fine. Splendid, in fact," he forces a smile.

The waiter smiles, then moves along.

*Of all the places in the world.*

His mind spins.

*Of course she's here, you idiot. You don't think for a minute that she'll ever stop.*

He looks around again, slowly.

*Wait, she looked right at you and didn't even hesitate. In fact, she smiled right at you.*

Looking across the bar, he sees his reflection in a mirror.

*You crazy bastard.*

He smiles.

*You're not losing your mind. You're gaining a whole new life.*

He takes a deep breath and another sip of wine.

*And she's none the wiser.*

As his appetite returns, he artfully carves the steak in front of him. He methodically devours it, sipping wine between bites.

As the bartender passes, he says, "This wine, this *food*, it's all spectacular," he smiles, energized with confidence. "In fact, this wine? Bring me a bottle of it. Oh, and when I'm done, could you be so kind as to do me a favor?"

"Of course, sir," the bartender smiles. "Anything you need."

"Right. When I'm done, and not a moment before, would you..." standing, he says, "wait *just* a second."

Stepping further into the dining area until he can see into the back room, he searches for familiar faces.

He spots Patricia and Savoy in the back of the room.

*What the fuck?*

Startled, he quickly returns to his seat, trying to remain calm.

*I know Noah injected him, but how—*

"Sir?"

"Oh, right," he says, returning to his seat. "Um, there's a table in the back there, over in the corner?"

The waiter crosses the bar until he can see the back room.

Returning, he smiles, "Ah yes, Mayor Burton and his wife."

*What?!*

"Do you know the Mayor?"

*What would they be...*

"Sir?"

*Stop. Think. Regroup.*

"Yes, of course. The Mayor. Good friend of mine. In fact, that's exactly what I was getting to. When I'm done…" he looks at his nearly empty plate and glass. "In fact, that bottle I mentioned?"

"Yes?"

"Would you be a gem and make that to go?"

"Of course."

"Excellent. As for my table of friends, please send a bottle of your best Veuve Clicquot. Perhaps an older vintage? They're celebrating a special occasion."

"Will you be joining—"

"No, no. It's *their* occasion. Besides, I must run to another event," he says, removing a credit card and handing it to the bartender.

Tercel is finishing his wine when the waiter returns with a wrapped bottle and the bill.

"Here you go, Mr. Lockhart. It's been a pleasure serving you. I'll deliver that as soon as you've departed, just as you asked."

Beginning to leave, he says, "Thank you. Oh, and do me just one more small favor, would you?" He smiles, peeling off a $50 and sliding it across the bar.


"WHAT?" I say, suddenly feeling nauseous. I stare at everyone at the table before looking back to our waiter. "You're *sure* he said *Darius*."

"Absolutely certain," the waiter smiles, filling champagne glasses.

"And where is he sitting now?" I stand to look.

"He isn't Ma'am, but he asked that I deliver it to the Mayor's table, compliments of the good doctor."

I look at Pete. He shakes his head before looking at Carter who says, "And he said, *the good doctor?*"

"Yes. Oh, and lastly, he said to tell you, *happy hunting.*"

"Tell me this, can you describe what he looked like?"

With all eyes on the waiter, he looks down, and as his face goes blank, he says, "You know, with my serving so many people, all the faces run together. Sorry," he says before turning to leave.

I stare at Carter who looks at Mack.

I turn to Pete who frowns at Lukas.

I go around the table until I meet everyone's gaze.

All are expressionless until I say, "Description notwithstanding—no thanks to our waiter—looks like we're in the right place."

# CHAPTER SIXTY

BACK AT OUR HOTEL, MY MIND IS A WHIRLING DERVISH. AT ONE moment, I want to head out and search until I find Tercel; at another, I feel it is smarter to wait until morning. Either way, knowing we are within the same zip code makes the needle in a haystack feel more like a car in a parking lot.

*Don't get too excited, Norelli.*

There's little left to do, except plan for tomorrow, so we return to the bar after our party breaks up.

"Okay, let's assume he was in the restaurant and saw us," I say, kicking into my standard checklists.

"Fair assumption," Pete says, sipping a beer.

"The fact he let us know that he saw us took balls," I say.

"Or it spooked him and he just overcompensated," Carter responds. "Trying to supercharge his ego."

"I'm going with that," Mack says, spinning an oversized cube in his bourbon with a finger. "The dude is spooked."

Scanning the room, Carter frowns, "I know the place is packed, but I gotta believe *one* of us would've seen him."

I look around the room, studying every face, then begin replaying any faces out of the ordinary I might have noticed since arriving, including the couple at the bar.

*But he was bald and fat and had a female companion.*

"Agreed, Carter," Savoy says, dipping an oversized olive in her

Martini. "I don't know, but he was *not* in this restaurant. I promise you that!"

"Well, I know what I'll be spending the rest of the night doing while you guys are sleeping," McCloud says, sipping a black coffee. "Three guesses and the first two don't count."

"Yeah, but who else in the world is as good as you, McCloud?" I say, returning to my inventory.

*I think there were four couples in the perimeter of our room.*

"Gonna be key, bro. I'll help you if I can," Mack says, offering a fist bump to McCloud.

Finishing his beer, Pete says, "Sis, I gotta bounce. Tonight was nice, but I start early and need some sleep. Let's meet at my office at 7, cool?"

"Perfect. I'll bring coffee."

As he stands, everyone follows. Holding up his hands, he says, "Woah, don't bail on my account. I've got kids at home. Enjoy yourself. Just remember—day's gonna start early."

They shrug and sit, while I remain standing and ask, "How about one more?"

BACK IN THE ROOM, I'm brushing my teeth, staring out at the lights of the city while Carter grabs a shower. My mind is racing, wondering where Tercel is right now.

*What's he thinking? What's his plan? Was he there tonight? Passing by? If he was there, could it mean he's staying nearby. A hotel? Does he have an apartment? Did he buy? Is he here short term or on the way to somewhere?*

Returning to the sink, I hear the shower stop.

"Hey, Carter?"

He sticks a wet head out the door. "Yeah?"

"When you were here looking for Donovan Blair in a city this size, how'd you even begin to find him?"

He steps out with a towel around his waist and leans against the door.

"There are a couple things at play. First of all, sometimes in your hunt for someone, instead of you chasing them, you wait for them to come to you. In other words, set a trap with something they want. Trust me, they'll *eventually* come for it."

Brushing my hair, I watch his mind at work. "Okay."

"Second, and in his particular case, the thing was a little girl he kidnapped, but then returned to us—only *after* he had gotten what he wanted, or rather *part* of what he wanted. So then he had to work a second part. A different con."

"I still can't believe he turned their daughter into, what, basically a mule with explosives."

"Yeah," he shook his head. "Certainly one of the sickest fucks I've met. But in that trap—the second time—he had me in a bad place because even though she was in our possession, he still had control over the situation with a remote device. It was easily the worst case scenario."

Nodding, something suddenly occurs to me. "So wait, and let me talk this out to see if I can get a better picture."

He nods.

"Okay, we want him. I go to find him. We nearly have him. He gets away. We go after him again, now in the same relative space. So perhaps—in line with what you're staying—instead of my chasing after him, what could be better is if I were to set a trap *for* him. All I, or *we*, need is something he wants. More than his freedom—at least right now."

Listening intently, a complex expression grows on his face.

"What?"

"You're almost there," he grins.

Silence.

"It has to be...*me*."

We stare.

He nods.

I exhale.

# CHAPTER SIXTY-ONE

BACK IN THE APARTMENT, TERCEL PACES THE WIDE EXPANSE OF HIS living room. In the dark, the lights from the city illuminate him thanks to floor-to-ceiling windows. He can feel his mind beginning to separate as though operating in two different spheres.

*I studied this in school. Complex shit. Doesn't end well.*

He stops pacing to pour a drink.

*I want her. I can't have her.*

*I nearly kill her, then I escape.*

*She comes after me and I run.*

He presses the side of his face against the cool glass.

*FUCK!*

His mind races to a simpler time: his office, a quiet practice, a city of beautiful people as neurotic as he is.

But he is *The Good Doctor.*

The Top Dog.

Therapist to the Stars.

*Why do I want her?*

*What am I afraid of?*

*Because I can't have her, I'll never control her?*

*Suppose she doesn't want me even after all I've done for her?*

He sits, exhausted by the trauma of not knowing.

*And what about the new face? The new body? Does she like it?*

He stands and begins pacing.

*What's wrong with me?*

Looking at his empty glass, he considers something stronger.

*Pills perhaps?*

Crossing the room, he stands close to the mirror and stares.

After a long several minutes, he screams, *WHAT DO YOU WAAAAAAAAANT?*


A RANDOM HORN causes a flinch and a lonely siren blares in the distance. Rolling over, a bloodshot eye blinks open and reads: 4:01.

*Shit!*

Tercel rolls out of bed, walks to the bathroom and cranks the hot water, then goes to the kitchen and drops a pod in the espresso machine.

Waiting for the machine to heat, he gets lost in thought.

*The look on her face when the champagne arrived was worth the price of admission.*

The machine begins making a noise.

*I loved watching them sit in stunned silence.*

The light on the machine turns green.

*Nice thing about being in the city—you can follow people and no one's the wiser.*

He rinses the demitasse cup with hot water, then presses a button.

*I should've anticipated them staying at a hotel so close to her brother's work.*

The rich aroma of espresso fills his nose.

*Does she even realize how much of a trail she leaves?*

Shaking his head, he walks to the window and watches the city sleep, sipping his drink.

*There's only one way this is going to end, isn't it, Patricia?*

# CHAPTER SIXTY-TWO

*WEDNESDAY, 4:50 A.M.—THREE DAYS TO GO*

I AWAKE to the sounds of city traffic, the dull ache of a hangover, and the realization I'm awake before Carter. I watch him sleep before sliding from underneath his warm body. Standing at the full length mirror, I stare at my naked body.

*Not bad for early '40s.*

I suddenly have a flashback of lying naked on Tercel's king bed in his Bel Air home. The rich linens, the blood red velvet drapes hanging at the head of his bed—and the silk kimono sashes binding my ankles and wrists.

*The way he stared at my body.*

In the midst of that fright and the panic of the situation—the dread of not being sure I would live through it—I still felt an odd sense of peace.

*Fuck you, Norelli. That wasn't peace, that was—*

Carter groans. I check to see if I woke him. His breathing returns to the same heavy cadence.

*What a great surprise he's become.*

Looking at the clock on the bedside table, I'm surprised it's before 5 o'clock.

*A run is just what I need to clear my head.*

I peek between the shades and dawn is breaking, so I put on a pair of shorts, shoes, and a t-shirt. Pulling my hair into a ponytail, I grab my cell phone and a room key, snag one of Carter's ball caps, and scribble a note on hotel stationary: *Gone for a quick run. Back shortly. You're handsome when you sleep, XO*

I JOG UP CANAL, cross West Street, and pick up my stride as I hit the Hudson River Greenway. The air is crisp, foot traffic is sparse, and my mind is quiet. Varying my speed from easy run to near sprint, I focus on my breathing to help shake out the cobwebs of last night's booze.

As I approach Rockefeller Park, I slow to a walk, catch my breath, and do a few stretches. Starting to feel normal again, I see One World Trade Center a few blocks away. My quiet mind—one of the best parts of running—pings with an observation.

Like a text message from the grave, I hear Angie's voice say: *That was him sitting at the bar last night.*

Standing alongside the Hudson, I look across to Jersey City, trying to retrace my steps from last night.

*We left the hotel. Drove uptown to the steakhouse. Went straight to our table. I sat facing the front window with my back to the restaurant.*

I run down every detail I can recall: what we ate, what our waiter looked like, the conversations we were having. Since we had cocktails at the hotel before we left and I was a couple of glasses of red wine into the meal, my memory is a little foggy.

*Halfway through dinner, Savoy and I went to the restroom because she wasn't feeling great. And when we came out I saw an elderly couple at the end of the bar—I recall because they reminded me of a couple who sat near us when we were in Melbourne.*

*But there was another couple—in the middle of the bar.*

*The man at the bar looked straight at me. He was with a woman.*

*Wait, were they a couple or was he flirting with her?*

*Men always notice me, but his expression was specific—or was it?*

*Was it a surprise? Recognition?*

I badger my detective mind, *Focus, Norelli.*

*What was he wearing? Anything unusual? What about his date?*

*She was striking—hair done up into a twist—dress, backless.*

*Glasses—I recall large, funky glasses. And he was bald. His eyes were light and his goatee, dark.*

Staring into the water, I search for more, but that's all I can recall.

Leaving Rockefeller Park, I make my way down Vesey Street until I hit West where I stare up at One World Trade. There's a thin fog halo around the top.

Suddenly, a chill runs down my spine as my mind flashes to the images of planes crashing into the towers. I keep walking until I reach the 9/11 Memorial. Taking in the moment, I put my thoughts of last night on pause, staring at the hundreds of names on the walls.

*PING!*

I take out my cell phone. It's from Carter: *Morning beautiful. You good?*

I text: *Morning. I'm good. At 1WTC. Running back now.*

A second later: *See you soon.*

Checking the time, I realize we've got to be at Pete's office in less than an hour, so I kiss my fingertips and place my hand on the wall before retracing my path back to the hotel.

STANDING at a window counter inside Everyman Espresso across the street, Tercel hides behind oversized glasses and *The New York Times* as Patricia comes running up the street.

He slides back a crisp French cuff where his Jaeger-LeCoultre reads: 5:58 a.m..

Watching her lean against the building to stretch, he admires her form.

*Best watch your back, Detective. You never know who's watching.*

CARTER, MACK, McCLOUD, SAVOY and I are at Pete's office within minutes of 7 a.m., another good reason to stay in a hotel so close to his work. Over coffee, we discuss our plan for the day, and within an hour, have a strategy laid out.

I'm about to call Claire to confirm our meeting for tonight's event at the Met when a thought crosses my mind—something Carter said about hunting and setting a trap. It's another ridiculous long shot, but given the last two weeks, I'm not worried about appearing ridiculous.

*My new mantra: Anything goes.*

I check the time and call Claire's number. She answers before the second ring.

"Hello, this is Claire."

"Hi, Claire. It's Pat. Hope this isn't too early."

"Are you kidding? With a husband who never sleeps and a daughter who can't wait to get to school, my day starts early."

*I can see Carter's attraction; she's kind, attentive, and emotionally transparent.*

I cut to the chase. Aware of the vast array of beautiful models and actresses who live in New York, I ask for Claire's help. She shares how she's worked with several agencies, and given the shortage of time but the wealth of access, we set up appointments to meet with one of the larger agencies and agree to meet in SoHo, just a few blocks from our hotel.

AN HOUR LATER, Claire and I, plus Carter, Mack, and Savoy, meet at New York Models. Having already searched their website, I have two dozen women close to fitting my requirements. We pass our candidates on the way in and are seated in an elegant room.

Leaning over, Mack whispers, "I like this kind of undercover work."

Grinning at him, I look down the row to Savoy and say, "Keep him restrained, will you?"

When he and Carter bump fists, I eyeball Carter. "You too, Sparky."

Opening a folder with photos, he says, "Hey, I'm here to work."

AFTER THIRTY-FIVE MINUTES, I find exactly what I'm looking for and am astonished at the similarity. Turning to my crew, I get affirming eyebrow raises from each of them. The model-actress named Elizabeth takes the photo I'm holding and smiles.

"Can you believe it?" I ask.

"It is uncanny. Paint a tiny mole on my cheek and we could be twins."

*That's exactly what I'm going to do.*

Mack is still shaking his head, comparing the model in front of us with the photo. "That shit's crazy."

We spend the next few minutes signing contracts with her team. Exiting the office, we head to where Dimitri is waiting to drive us to our next stop.

"That's about the *second* craziest thing I've seen in a while," Carter says.

I whip my head toward Carter. "What's the first?"

"You going to Australia," he grins, putting on sunglasses, "on a wing and a prayer."

Even though my plan is off the beaten path, will cost me dearly, and could end up being nothing but a diversion—*plus* has zero guarantee of working—it's worth it just to *feel* like I have another piece of the puzzle in place.

# CHAPTER SIXTY-THREE

Back at our "home away from home," I am anxious to see how McCloud is coming with the audio recording. Pulling to the curb, I see him out front, leaning against the wall and smoking a cigarette with a female police officer. I tell Dimitri to keep his phone and vehicle close because I'm not sure when we'll be taking off. Getting out, I shake my head and cut a sideways glance to McCloud as we approach the front door. Grinding out the smoke, he says goodbye to his friend and joins us as we enter.

"Thought you were gonna quit," I smirk, barreling ahead without waiting for an answer.

"I am," he says. "Soon."

Weaving through the hallways, we arrive at our office and plop in chairs.

"Please, oh pretty please, with a pack of smokes on top..." I grin, "tell me you have good news."

His expression isn't hopeful. I can't tell if he's constipated or ready to belch.

"What?" I nearly cry.

After a heavy sigh, he mutters, "Well, as the old saying goes—"

"And please, for the love of Jesus, Mary, and Joseph, don't say there's good news and bad news."

He shrugs, then heads to a chair.

"Wait!" I shout, startling him and everyone else in the room. "Just give it to me," I grumble—my stomach now sinking to a new low.

"Well, I tried everything, Norelli," he says to me. "And I can't even imagine what you went through," he says, looking at Savoy. "But geez, Pat, she musta been in the saltwater for what, an hour?"

Savoy nods, looking at me with a crushed expression.

"Shit," I say, looking at Carter who looks as though he's about to grin. "Wait," I blurt, whipping my head back to McCloud. "What?"

He breaks into a wide grin and says, "Well, that's the *good* news. Yeah, I got it. It's fucking perfect."

"AHHHHH!" I scream, running over to squeeze him so tightly he starts coughing.

"Sorry, McCloud, but this is fuckin' great, and see? I told you to stop smoking. Shit'll kill you!"

We are all high-fiving when Pete enters.

"What the fuck's going on in here?"

I explain what just happened and his frown morphs into a grin.

"Oh, do *not* tell me you already knew," I punch his arm.

"Ow!"

Turning to Carter, "And you," I walk over to punch his arm. "When did you know?"

Rubbing his arm, he feigns pain and says, "I got a text as we were leaving the agency."

We're all laughing by now, and I'm so ecstatic I can barely contain myself.

"And I knew about an hour ago," Pete chuckles. "Just after he cracked it open."

"Here's the thing, Norelli," McCloud says, grinning. "I so seldom get to punk anyone. Besides, I remember a day when you used to do it all the time. It was so worth it to see that expression just now."

Between the grinning and the excitement, I go back over and kiss him on the mouth.

"Thank you. Seriously. You have no idea."

Nodding, he says, "Well, I kinda do. But again, hella props to Savoy. If she hadn't, you know, uh, or if Tercel had, you know, then, shit, well, it'd be a whole other—hell, you know what I'm saying."

Laughing, we actually do.

# CHAPTER SIXTY-FOUR

IT TAKES THREE MINUTES FOR ME TO GET ON THE HORN WITH CAPTAIN Nelson, and we spend all of five minutes getting caught up on the past several days. I share how McCloud will send a copy of the recording with the transcript by end of business day. To say he's excited would be an understatement.

"Patricia, I don't have to remind you just how important it is that you *not*—under any circumstances whatsoever—let Davenport get wind of this. You have to keep your crew under complete lockdown. You follow?"

"Yes, sir. And you can—"

"Seriously, Patricia, not a word. You, me, Pete, and your team. No one else. In fact, if you're shipping that via Fedex, do it from the hotel. I can't be more serious. You understand?"

"Yes, sir. I do. A hundred percent. After all, we didn't think that one of—"

"—our own, exactly. And my point precisely. Any leak, and between the two nut jobs you're dealing with..."

"And I'm not sure which is worse, Captain," I chuckle nervously.

"I get it," Nelson laughs. "And as much as I think you're *kinda* kidding, I know you're not. Anyhow, you don't need me to tell you your job. Hell, look at you, you followed your instincts, traveled halfway around the world to find this fuckin' killer, and now you've got evidence that proves you didn't kill your friend—which, by the way, is the most ridiculous notion ever. These guys really worked the system."

"Yes, sir, they did. And they are. Nut jobs. But…"

"What is it, Norelli?"

"Just going to say two things."

"What are they?"

"The first is I've still got to appear in court on Monday, right?"

"Of course, it's protocol. But yeah, we'll have the evidence, hear your side, and then be done with it. I'm 99.9% certain. So, yes, an even bigger emphasis on keeping this quiet."

"Understood."

"And what's the other thing?"

"Sir, I still have yet to hook the big fish. And I'd be lying if I said I wasn't the tiniest bit scared."

He sighs. "Patricia, don't you worry about *the how*. Just worry about *the what*. And *the what* is to catch this guy and bring him in. *The how*? It'll take care of itself. You know that. You've trained for this. You've done it your way. And your instincts are right on point."

*Knock me over with a feather.*


WHILE MCCLOUD IS DUPLICATING his recording onto a flash drive— simultaneously running it through a secure online transcription service —I share the Nelson conversation with Savoy and him, confirming that no eyes or ears must see or hear any bit of the evidence. Furthermore, I instruct him to FedEx it overnight to Nelson with a return address of Carter Matheson. Handing him Carter's card, I half expect a response, but he simply looks at me, says nothing, and returns to his duties.

My next conversation is with Pete.

He, Carter, Mack, and I cover notes of where and how our canvassing of the area has gone. To put it simply, it hasn't.

"Okay, there's a *little* good news; not much, but it's something— well, besides your windfall of good news," he says, reaching across the desk for a fist bump. I oblige.

"We have the Upper East Side saturated as you'll see on the map," he says, referring to a map that mirrors the one in our office.

"We have that super realtor Claire recommended along with a small team who are checking all new rentals and new purchases inside that area. The less than good news is that privacy issues being what they are, most can't reveal sources. However," he leans in and lowers his voice, "with the help of his picture, some people have been okay with sharing a nod or a frown *if* someone even close to matching his description showed up."

Pete flips through a short stack of papers. "Elsewhere, we have—thanks to Lukas—an APB on him along with a dozen pairs of extra eyes at Command Central where all the "big brother cameras" are; we'll be able to see all coming and going as best we can."

I lean back in my chair, trying to force my shoulders to relax.

"Well, that's something. And with our three events tonight, tomorrow night, and Friday night, we'll have our chance."

"Slim as it may be," he mumbles.

I stare at him.

"Hey, don't listen to me. I'm a born cynic," he smiles.

*Ah, brotherly love.*

"Okay, elsewhere. We've come up goose-eggs on therapists as you can imagine. It's been equally difficult with plastic surgeons. Again, easy to understand. And I'll tell you, I was hoping someone somewhere would ask Tercel for permission to use him as a "before and after" patient. Just think of the business they'd be able to bring in after showing that piece of work."

"No shit," I mutter, having a hard time not feeling more enthusiastic.

"What is it?" Carter asks.

"Oh, just that if the cameras don't see him, if the undercovers don't spot him, if we can't get any help from doctors, surgeons, therapists, or realtors, then it's just…" I toss my head back and close my eyes.

"You're right. Impossible odds," Carter says. "But we have your plan in place to be used these three nights. And who knows, he could be following you—or *us*, for that matter. And *that* opens a door we don't know. Yet."

"Geez, bro, you're so comforting," Mack says, frowning at Carter, then winking at me.

"Thanks, Mack. And you're right, Carter. Let's just not forget there are plenty of people back home who said I'd never find him."

. . .

WE RUN DOWN EVERYTHING we possibly can and are ordering coffee when Carter—tossing a golf ball he's taken from Pete's desk—brings up an idea. Turning to Mack, he says, "Hey buddy, remember last year, when we were here for the—"

He nods.

"And the video Donovan made of Abigail's kidnapping and the—"

"Uh yeah," he says, sitting up. "Only burned into my brain, never to leave my dreams, thank you very much, Donovan Ballsack."

"What if we did something similar? Times Square. Using reverse psychology, so to speak."

Everyone sits up straight.

"Dish," I say.

"Okay, imagine we whip together a video. Call it a montage or an *ad* of some sort. I don't know exactly, but we could..." he stands and begins pacing. "We could create a piece of propaganda. Terrorist style, for lack of a better word. I'm just spitballing here, but let's—"

"I'm following," Pete says. "Like a sophisticated milk carton ad," he chuckles.

"Yeah, exactly, but not at all," Carter laughs. "But maybe *something* like that?"

I'm chewing the inside of my lip, trying to picture where he's going when something pops. Going to my bag for my phone, I hold up a finger. "Hold that thought."

I text McCloud: *When you're done, come to Pete's office. Stat!*

Before I can sit back down, he comes barging through the door.

"What?"

"Were you hanging outside the door?"

"No," he frowns, obviously taking me seriously. "I was just finishing and..." he says, looking around the room at all the eyes focused on him. "What're you all looking at?"

Grinning at one another, we turn back to look at McCloud.

I GET SAVOY on the phone with the sales departments of both television stations and the company who handles the billboards. She works her accent handsomely as we work on getting an ad placement. A call from the Mayor helps grease the wheels.

While McCloud deploys his magic on the video we discussed, I finagle my own magic by contacting our model and arranging a meeting with Savoy at a production studio.

I have 24 hours to accomplish what I hope will make for some high-concept art. Before leaving, I ask Carter and Mack to join Claire at all three art galleries in order to put eyes on the set-ups.

On the way to the studio, I call Claire and ask if she has a list of art dealers in the area we're targeting. I share how I think Tercel might be setting up a new business and art would be a logical assumption. I suggest that if there are any new shops open or if there is a way she can learn of any recent takeovers, it would help thin the herd.

She mentions having just the right person to help and should have something by the time we connect at tonight's benefit at the Met.

# CHAPTER SIXTY-FIVE

TWO HOURS LATER WE WRAP AT THE STUDIO, PLEASED WITH OUR creation and anxious to see what McCloud has come up with. We're also hungry, so I call Pepolino and have them make a small buffet for my crew and deliver it, so we can save time and keep working.

The Metropolitan benefit begins in less than three hours.

As Dimitri drops us at the station, I share our schedule for the remaining 48-plus hours. I suggest grabbing rest when he can because we'll be burning the candle at both ends right up until we leave town.

Inside, we find McCloud with his feet on the desk, watching his laptop.

"Tell me something good, *wah wah...*" I sing, entering the office.

"Hey, I didn't know you couldn't sing," he smirks.

"You just don't appreciate Stevie Wonder—as performed by Rufus and Chaka Khan. *Chaka Khan.*"

Rolling his eyes like he thought I was insane, he waves me over while tapping the keyboard. "Here's what I have so far."

He returns the cursor to the beginning and clicks play.

We watch as Tercel's face slowly changes.

McCloud explains how he took Tercel's original press photographs, used some animation techniques, and made them morph into several incarnations of what Tercel could look like.

By the end of the video, the final image looks like the Tercel we saw in Brisbane.

"Awesome," I say, "and curious to hear what Carter thinks."

"About what?" Carter says, entering the room with Mack.

Turning, I look and smile. He gets the message.

"Check out McCloud's magic."

After we watch it twice, Savoy brings us up to speed with the ad schedule she arranged for the billboards and local TV stations.

"A very late lunch is on the way, and—"

"Wait a second," Carter interrupts, still staring at the screen. "Nice work, McCloud, but I have an idea." Looking at me, he squints. "Remember at the restaurant when you said you saw a man who looked at you funny?"

"Yeah."

"And how you thought that if there was *any* way it was him—"

"I see where you're going," I say, turning back to the screen. "McCloud, take that last photo—the one with him standing next to Angie…"

"Copy that."

"Now, remove his hair."

"Make him bald as a cueball," Carter says.

"Right," he says, opening the photo in another program.

Doing something I don't understand, he moves the cursor to outline his head and removes the long blond hair. Then with another move that completely perplexes me, he makes the top of his head match the color of his face.

"Wow. Okay, now paint a dark goatee on him. While you're doing that, I'll find you some glasses," I say, opening my phone's browser to google eyeglass stores.

"Hey, McCloud, any way you can…" Carter hesitates, looks at me, then continues, "cut Angie out of the frame and single him out?"

"Duh," McCloud mumbles.

By the time McCloud has the bald head, dark goatee, and added weight perfected, I have some oversized, artsy frames from designer Tom Ford.

"I'm airdropping you a link to a site for eyeglasses."

His phone pings; he connects, points to the frames, looks at me for a nod, then clicks, copies, pastes, edits, and done.

"Holy shit," I mumble. "Our guy from last night. Close, anyway."

Staring at each other, Carter and I simultaneously say, "*Boom.*"

# CHAPTER SIXTY-SIX

Traffic from SoHo to the Upper East Side is painfully slow. The distance is only eight miles, but it takes us nearly an hour to get there. McCloud spends most of the time on his phone and Savoy's head is on a sightseeing swivel while Carter and Mack talk sports with our driver. We are nearly at the Museum when I break the silence.

"Is it me or could anyone else use a drink?"

Carter, Mack, Savoy, and McCloud instantly raise their hands.

Dimitri follows.

Laughing, I say, "Well, the minute this is over, the first drink's on me. Until then, we gotta be sharp."

Carter says, "Seeing the layout and talking to security was a big help today."

"And I'm guessing with a classy gig like this," Mack says, "there won't be half the chaos we ran into last time, right, bro?"

"That was a nightmare," Carter says. "One psychopath, several lunatics, and a literal ticking bomb. But this one? Just one lunatic psychopath who's—"

"A ticking bomb," Mack snorts.

The Metropolitan Museum of Art is on 5th Avenue at 82nd Street. At four blocks wide and nearly two blocks deep, it is impressive. Even though I've seen it in movies before, this will be the first time I've ever been inside. Entering, we're immediately directed to Claire who is playing hostess to a tight gaggle of wealthy socialites. She looks right at home.

Carter and Mack work with Pete in order to cloak the event with nearly four dozen plainclothes cops. Their jobs range from coat checkers to cocktail waiters and from art critics to art investors. Only a small handful are dressed and acting as actual security.

The updated photograph McCloud created only hours earlier is circulated to everyone's phone. McCloud takes his position behind the main stage where he can control electronics as well as see the audience facing front. Savoy and Mack, dressed as Hollywood starlet and bodyguard, take their positions of hobnobbing with the other socialites. Carter will change positions throughout the evening, moving between being my date-bodyguard and hanging with the head of security behind a two-way mirror overlooking the main floor.

*BRRR-BRRR* goes my phone. Our team is on a text chain.

McCloud: *I'm in place.*

Savoy: *Mack and I are at the auction table.*

When Pete and Stephanie arrive, they're joined by Lukas at the door and then head our way. Seeing the program is about to begin, Carter says hello, then excuses himself to head to the security desk.

---

TERCEL DECIDED that if his new life in his new city was going to revolve around a new career of arts and antiques, he must become both acclimated to and immersed in the culture by meeting the Who's Who of the New York City arts and social scene.

Nearly forty minutes into the event, he arrives to a packed house.

Making his way in, he skips coat check, deciding at the last minute to keep his hat on. The crowds are impressive, the people beautiful, and the art and location magnificent.

Standing at the door, he notices a couple in front of him who are both on their phones.

*Who does that when there's so much beauty in front of you?*

As he's about to push through the crowd, he glances over the man's shoulder to his phone. What he sees stops him in his tracks—and nearly stops his heart.

On the screen is a picture of Tercel as Simon Lockhart.

With the exception of the glasses looking sillier than he feels they are and the goatee looking more fake than he hoped, the retouched photograph holds a remarkable resemblance to him.

*Shit!*

He feels sweat instantly form under his cap which he pulls forward slightly. Dipping his chin, he takes a step backwards, bumping into someone. Turning around, he politely excuses himself and moves swiftly toward the door.

*BRRR-BRRR* GOES MY PHONE.

It's McCloud: *Norelli, I think I just spotted Tercel near the entrance where we have a team stationed.*

I look up but see nothing familiar.

Back to my screen: *He's wearing all black, a hat and glasses. He's leaving.*

I look back just in time to see the back of a man fitting McCloud's description.

I text Carter: *Entrance! About to exit. Wearing all black, a hat, glasses. Go!*

Pete looks at me, sees my expression, and we both move quickly toward the exit.

WITHOUT TAKING the time to look over his shoulder, Tercel bypasses his faux limp and walks briskly toward his waiting car at the curb across the street. The one-way traffic—heading south—has the green, so he has to wait.

Fighting the urge to look back, he works to stay calm.

Pulling out his phone, he texts his driver: *Open the door. I'm across the street.*

Looking up, he sees the driver get out of the car and open the back door.

The light turns red; he crosses and barks, "Get in and drive! Now!"

Because of congestion, the car isn't able to merge into traffic.

. . .

CARTER JOINS PETE and me in the lobby.

McCloud pulls up the rear as we head toward the door.

"C'mon, he couldn't have gone far," I shout.

Exiting, we look in both directions. Because of the nice evening and several events taking place at the museum, the crowds are thick. I quickly scan for his face, thinking he might be on foot.

Running toward 5th Avenue, I push through a throng of people and arrive at the curb. As the light turns green, cabs, limos, buses, and cars pour through the 82nd Street intersection.

"Shit!" I yell, searching every car for a familiar face.

THE LIGHT CHANGES and Tercel's driver catches a break when a pedestrian drops something in the middle of the crosswalk.

"Go!" Tercel barks, and the driver shoots through the intersection just before the person stands back up.

Looking through the darkened glass, Tercel sees Norelli and several people running to the curb just as the light changes. Knowing the back glass isn't dark, he faces front.

Leaning back into his seat, fully aware of just how close he'd come to getting caught, he releases a heavy breath and says, "Circle the block."

The driver hesitates. "Sir?"

"Circle the block! Right back to where we were," he stares out the window. "Just approach slowly."

LOOKING AT CARTER, I snap, "We were *this close*, dammit!"

Pete, Mack, Savoy, and McCloud quickly approach, stopping at the curb to catch their breath.

"I couldn't have gotten a license plate if I wanted because I never saw the car. Did anyone?" Carter asks.

They all shake their heads.

"Perhaps it's my being hopeful, but I could've sworn he jumped into a limo or town car across the street. But honestly, I can't be sure," I say, looking up and down the street.

"Don't sweat it," Pete says. "*If* that was him, he knows we've got his number."

"And what he looks like," Mack adds.

"Exactly," Carter says. "But you know what? There's a part of me that thinks somehow he likes that fact."

McCloud says, "What?"

"And likes that we're chasing him."

I look from the street to Carter. "I wondered the same thing about the time we hit Brisbane. And you want to know one of the things Tercel said to me when I was his patient and we were discussing Bobby Shapiro—one of the suspects in my last case? He said: *Criminals experience something called super-optimism. It's where the more they get away with their crimes, the more they become emboldened while developing a sense of invulnerability.* I thought that was interesting then and even more so now."

Carter looks at each of us. "Think about it, he's in the limelight his entire career. Therapist to the stars and all that bullshit. I recall reading: *The man who can greenlight any struggling actor.* But then, the gig is up. He's caught, escapes, and completely reinvents himself. *And*, he does so with no friends or associates. Then, a whole year goes by and bang—he's got the biggest city in the free world looking for him. And he's being chased by…*the one who got away.*"

I nod, recognizing the line from Tercel's letter to me.

"I agree, Carter. And see that?" Pete says, tossing a chin toward 5th Avenue heading south.

We all follow his gaze toward an ocean of black town cars and yellow cabs.

"Yet another haystack."

# CHAPTER SIXTY-SEVEN

*THURSDAY, 5:00 A.M. — TWO DAYS TO GO*

THE NEXT MORNING I awake before the alarm clock.

*He knows I'm in town. That I'm looking for him. Didn't he think I'd show up there?*

Lying here, I realize this time tomorrow, I'll only have one day to make this all work. And two days from now, we'll be jumping on a plane home. Three days, I'll be preparing for court. And day four is judgement day.

*And I'll return to work without catching the person responsible for killing my best friend.*

Tears begin to well in my eyes. Holding my breath, I wish them away. Turning toward Carter, I consider how he'll be waking up shortly and the day will roll on without a pause.

*And what will I do? What will we do when this job is over? Will we see one another? He won't move to LA. I certainly won't move to Carolina. And long distance is bullshit.*

My mind returns to Angie and I feel the heat start deep in my belly. It bubbles up like acid in my throat, and I realize how ridiculous it is that the very *doctor* I used to help me figure my shit out is the same person who killed her.

*I want him dead so badly—even more than justice.*

I know even if we are able to capture Tercel and take him back to LA that, what, he'll go to trial? And be found guilty? But what then? Go to jail? Big deal.

*Not just any jail. San Quentin. Death row. Forever.*

*Which is worse?*

*Death now? Or death by old age.*

Carter begins rustling and I catch myself holding my breath, wishing for an answer from Angie on the other side or from myself, right here and now.

*PING!*

Startled, I get up and grab it before it pings again.

I check the screen: *You awake?*

Not recognizing the number, I stop in my tracks.

*Is it him?*

I swallow hard and text back: *No. Can't sleep.*

Three blinking dots, then: *Me either. Haven't slept soundly for nearly a year.*

I text: *Welcome to my world.*

I hang on, waiting for the pulsating dots to give me something.

Then: *You can, you know.*

Frowning, I type: *What, sleep? No, I can't. Not as long as you're free.*

A surge of adrenaline shoots through my body as I wonder if that was the right thing to do. And I stare.

Nothing.

No blinking dots.

No comeback message.

*Shit!*

I wait.

Carter starts to wake.

I continue to stare, holding my breath.

As I'm about to give up, the pulsating ellipsis reignites.

"Morning, beautiful," Carter says in his groggy morning voice.

I continue staring at the blinking dots.

"Morning," I say, looking up to see him smile. "Sleep well?"

"Like a bag of rocks. You?"

"Not bad," I smile, looking back at the screen.

*Shit, it stopped!*

"You got action?"

"Just checking messages."

About to turn it off, a new message appears: *You had your chance. Twice. Last night, you had another. They say that third time's a charm, but in your case, we both know it's more like three strikes and you're out.*

My heart races as a drum bangs inside my head.

My palms sweat as I await a return message.

Then: *And Patricia, I'm sorry Davenport ratted you out. But not to worry—I cleaned up that mess for you, too. Stand by for one last gift.*

Wanting to scream, I stare at Carter as he gets out of bed and kneels at my feet. "What's he saying?"

Tears bubble up again and I feel the phone vibrate.

Looking down, the dots blink, then a photo appears.

It's Davenport, sitting at a desk with a gun in his left hand, a bullet in his temple, and his face laying in a pool of blood.

"What the fuck?"

The next photo is of a handwritten letter laying on the table next to him.

It reads: *Captain Nelson, I'm sorry for the confusion, but I had to tell you that Norelli didn't kill Angie, Tercel did. Then he paid me to plant the evidence. But between cancer slowly eating me alive and retirement too far away, I couldn't live with the guilt. Seeing the writing on the wall, I decided to pull the permanent pin. -Jonathan Davenport*

# CHAPTER SIXTY-EIGHT

WITH THAT ALARM WAKING MY EVERY SENSE, I GRAB A QUICK SHOWER before we head downstairs to meet up with everyone. Within minutes, we're next door, grabbing cartons of Dunkin' coffee and donuts.

On the way to the precinct, Carter and I discuss keeping the texts quiet until we can fully digest them all. We'll share with Pete when we start our day in a caffeine-fueled think tank before moving to Phase 2: *Leave no psychopath unturned.*

THE ENTIRE GROUP has multiple stimulants going when Pete arrives.

"Morning *Team Norelli*," he says in an unusually bright mood.

He's met with a variety of greetings.

"Let's discuss a couple of things—" he says, eyeballing the sugar buffet, "starting with the billboard and TV ads. But first coffee," he says, reaching for a cup.

We begin with an update of all locales our teams searched. Nearly every report returns roughly the same results:

No sightings of that face.

No recent rentals or purchases by that name.

No appointments and/or procedures involving a similar person.

. . .

AFTER MINDLESS MORNING CHATTER, Pete calls us to order, and McCloud stands and presents our plan for the print and video ads he created that will launch at noon. We have a quarter-page ad scheduled to run in *The New York Times* and a half-page ad in *The Post*. Both run through Saturday and the TV ads will run on the local CBS affiliate through midnight tomorrow.

Savoy commands the room next with a presentation on the Times Square billboards. Fortunately, Mayor Burton has someone from his office helping her, thus saving us a great deal of time and money.

"Our first choice is a real beauty they call the ABC Supersign," she says. "It's the 4,000 square foot icon known for its wavy LED. Even I, in little old Sydney, recognize it as the backdrop on *Good Morning America*. And with about 1.5 million tourists and residents passing through *TSQ* every day, we'll get a bangin' audience."

I give Pete a thumb's up and he winks.

"The next sign has full-motion video and social media feeds. If you've seen the NASDAQ feed, this is that. It's *hella* tall at seven stories, oh, and Patty? Crikey, it's pricey."

I wave for her to continue.

"Right, and last, is a *ginormous* display in the middle of TSQ above the new Pedestrian Plaza which means between people and cars, freakin' *scads* of mates will see it."

They clap and she takes a bow.

"Great work, Savoy," I say, giving a high-five as she takes a seat. "An amazing job in a short time. And while it'll nearly destroy my retirement plans, it'll do *wonders* to flush this fucker out!"

As they finish clapping, I nod to McCloud.

"Guess the last thing to do is watch the ad that our own Boy Wonder created while you slept last night."

McCloud points to Pete, "Can you get the lights?"

Pete hits the switch. McCloud hits play.

The video begins like a movie trailer—complete with throbbing bass—showing flashes of a skinny young Beverly Hills doctor. First, he's sitting behind his desk, talking with a patient; a wall of degrees decorate the wall behind him. Cut to: Tercel receiving an award at a glossy Hollywood show. Next, he's surrounded by beautiful women at a variety of events.

This morphs into crime scene photos of murder after murder after murder—all of which he's been connected to. They appear as tabloid magazine covers. This cuts to a headshot of him morphing from an old press photo into a recent photo—this, after many plastic surgeries. And that morphs into what he looks like today, or as close as we could get using what we saw last night. The video ends with his mugshot along with details of a $500,000 cash offer for information leading to his whereabouts.

At the end, Pete turns on the lights, revealing a stunned group. As we clap, Pete gives him a fist bump.

"That's freakin' fantastic, McCloud. If *that* and the matching newspaper and billboard ads don't get people's attention, I don't know what will."

In short order, we wrap up and move out, making our way to TSQ to see McCloud's work launch in person.

ARRIVING in time to grab lunch, we snag seats in the middle of the square to watch. Seeing the ad in brilliant color and on multiple enormous screens is stunning.

I can't help checking my phone throughout the day, thinking Tercel will reach out again. It isn't that I'm naive thinking he'll drop a clue or tell me where he's going next, but more a way of toying with me as he has before.

But he does neither.

# CHAPTER SIXTY-NINE

THURSDAY MORNING AND AFTERNOON PASS WITHOUT A SIGHTING, without any fanfare, and without any hope of my catching Tercel. It does, however, nearly blow up the phone systems where we route the calls for the $500,000 dollar reward. It takes an entire battalion of phones to answer them all.

One particular message isn't voiced by Tercel—it's a woman; however, the message is clearly from him.

I play it over the speaker for all to hear.

*Hello, Darcy. My name is Lucy. I have information about your good doctor. He wants me to tell you that a shot to the head is better than an arrow through the heart, and that you'll need a crystal ball to find him because you can't see the forest from whence the Ticonderogas come; however, it's right in front of you in black and white. If you want to catch him, he says you better pray you can connect the dots.*

"What the fuck?" Mack barks, scratching his big head. "Sounds like a demented puzzle."

"Or a puzzle from a demented fuck," I grin at him, considering what move Tercel might play next.

"Explain the significance," Carter smiles, "for our unenlightened friends."

"Yeah, these *Sheilas* need some help," Savoy winks.

"Okay..." I sigh. "It begins with my given name, followed by my dog's name who passed away two summers ago—both of which few would know about. Next, certain phrases. *Shot to the head* references the original suicide that began his obsession with the same and eventually became his murder signature. Follow with *arrow through the heart* referencing the last murder he committed during our investigation— one Bobby Shapiro. Next, *crystal* references a tool by which he hypnotized Angie and myself—perhaps many others, for that matter—in order to drop his patients into a trance. And *Ticonderoga* references the pencils he used in his practice and *chewed* on a daily basis. The last part? I have no fucking clue."

"Sounds pretty benign," Pete mutters. "Maybe *cliche* is a better word."

Carter slaps his hands together. "Wait! Black and white, as in the—"

"*Photographs!*" we blurt simultaneously.

"Of course. The Mapplethorpe exhibit at the Guggenheim!"

Pete stands, checks his watch, then says, "Nice pull. And since we're about 90 minutes away from showtime, what do you say we move out?"


THE GUGGENHEIM MUSEUM sits across the street from the Jackie O Reservoir at the corner of 89th Street and 5th Avenue. Architecturally, it's a marvel. Artistically, it's inspiring. And tonight, I know the show will be captivating. As an art lover, Tercel is bound to show up. His obsession with dark materials makes him a perfect candidate for this particular show. And given his collection of rarities—many of which were confiscated from his home before he escaped—I feel certain this show will add to his priceless collection.

*I'm betting on it, anyway.*

"One down, two to go," Carter whispers over my shoulder as we step from the SUV at the front of the museum.

"Don't you know it?" I force a smile. "Tonight should be a layup, given his macabre sensibilities."

"Dang girl, you talk nerdy," Mack laughs, giving me a playful punch.

"And don't you know he will love the...*avant-garde work of Mapplethorpe,*" I drag out the words, speaking like a melodramatic aristocrat.

McCloud laughs behind me. Spinning around, I catch him about to light up.

"All right, already," he frowns, returning the pack to his pocket.

ARRIVING WITH THREE VERY TALL, striking women and two equally fetching men, Tercel enters the event and takes a place among the large gathering of art lovers. Tercel along with one of the men and two of the women are wearing masks. Some masks are sexier while others are more avante-garde.

Given a sizable group of attendees wearing outfits more akin to what a dominatrix would wear, they all appear to feel at home—while masking their true identity.

THE SHOW IS WELL on its way and multiple dozens of pieces are being sold at astronomical prices. Tercel and his entourage make their way to the front to avail themselves of prime auctioning. Tercel manages to outbid and secure two rare pieces: *Lady Liza Lyoness,* a body-builder with perfect proportions, and an enormous, perverse piece called *Mr. Stephenson's 11-inch*—both of which get wide stares from many audience members.

He and his friends are well into several bottles of champagne, awaiting the unveiling of what is being called a "never-before-seen masterpiece."

As the organizers are preparing to reveal a piece created by a local artist who was a one-time intern of the master photographer, the emcee calls for the lights to dim.

"OKAY, people, give me a short confirm you're all alert," I say into my sleeve.

"Copy that," McCloud says.

"On point," Mack growls.

"Ready, ready," Savoy giggles.

"Pete and company of twenty-four are a go," Pete adds.

"Excellent," I say. "Lights are dimming; showtime's close."

"Let's stay frosty, folks," Carter finishes.

Shaking my head, I look at him and mouth, *Very funny.*

THE LIGHTS DIM halfway and a curtain falls from the ceiling revealing what appears to be ten-foot tall by twenty-foot wide canvas. However, at one moment the canvas appears flat while in another, 3-dimensional.

Tercel stares at the image and his jaw slowly goes slack.

His eyes widen as his heart races.

In a moment of near panic, the image brings a deep pain rushing back. Somewhere in the depths of his being, he feels a little boy beginning to cry as he sees his mother lying on a bed—half-naked and apparently incoherent. He absently shakes his head, trying to focus his loopy mind.

Looking around, he stares at real faces in an attempt to ground himself—but he can't stop staring.

*Mum?*

Slowly rising from the bed, the woman pushes aside empty bottles of booze from the bed as a sheet falls from her naked body, her white breasts sagging as she stands. She reaches to the bedside table and slowly swipes at a dozen pill bottles. Turning to the audience, she opens her mouth as if to scream—but only silence.

The crowd is mesmerized, frozen in the moment.

A sudden shrill scream makes everyone jum as she yells, *WHY DARIUS, WHY?*

Suddenly in a full-blown panic, Tercel, unable to catch his breath, can't stand the sight or stop the pain in his chest.

When Tercel is about to break into hysterical tears, he looks over his shoulder and finds Norelli looking in his direction with one hand to her ear while searching the room.

He quickly scans the crowd and, seeing an opportunity, grabs his friends and starts toward the restrooms.

"LOOK ALIVE, PEOPLE," I bark into the mic. "Eyes on the front row."

Mack and McCloud reply: "Copy that."

Pete breaks in with light static, "Pats, Alpha Team and I are moving to the front. Beta Team, cover the rear."

Several chirps confirm.

. . .

AT THE RESTROOMS, Tercel hands his female partners each an envelope.

"Thanks for the party, but I have to run." To one, he says, "Please be a love and see that my art is delivered to my place. Everything you need is in there."

To another, he hands an auction paddle and says, "And as soon as my boys and I get to that door," he points, "do your thing."

They both nod and go their separate ways.

As Tercel and his two enormous escorts make their way to the front door, he looks over his shoulder. He sees Norelli and team scatter in chaos as he watches the curtain drop on the exhibit *Mother In Suicide* —then he steps outside as a fire alarm sounds.

# CHAPTER SEVENTY

*Friday, 6:49 a.m.*

THE NEXT MORNING, a ringing phone wakes us up. Neither of us wants to get it, but it's so loud, I grab it.

"Norelli," I groan—my voice, raspy and tired.

"Hello, it's your favorite chain-smoking, smart-ass babbling, high-tech guru Boy Wonder...wondering where the hell y'all be!"

If it wasn't for the fact I like him so much, I'd hang up on McCloud.

Suddenly, I realized I hadn't heard the alarm. Pushing a pillow aside, I stretch and find the clock silenced. It's 6:49.

"Shit!" I bark, waking Carter.

"What?"

"Thanks, McCloud, but do me a solid, will ya? Go next door, repeat yesterday's order, and head to the office. We'll be there in—"

"Twenty," Carter whispers, climbing out of bed and starting toward the shower.

"Twenty. Twenty five, tops," I say, sitting up. "And tell Pete that... never mind. Just be sure the donuts are fresh and the coffee's hot'n he'll be fine."

Hanging up, I sprint to the shower, pushing Carter aside.

. . .

AT 7:15 WE ENTER THE OFFICE—hair still damp, clothes less than pressed—only to find the gang munching and slurping, but no Pete.

"Where's Pete?"

Mack looks up from *The Post* and says through the steam of his cup, "Upstairs. Talking to the heat."

McCloud shrugs, shoving an oversized glazed into his mouth. "Pmon bamds gnt fmid."

"Really?"

Swallowing, he says, "Phone banks got fried."

"Ooookay," I say, grabbing a coffee and sitting next to Savoy. "Any new leads?"

Bright-eyed, she smiles and tosses a chin toward the corner of the room where several stacks of boxes—filled with pink phone message slips—sit, one atop another. I do a quick count.

"I counted like ten boxes, I'm guessing—"

"Thirteen. And yes, all leads that have *yet* to be confirmed." Savoy rolls her eyes.

IT'S NEARLY four o'clock when Team Norelli and a couple dozen of our field ops finish reading and following up the messages we feel have any significant merit. Very few amounted to much. Big surprise. However, because I've committed to the process, I'm determined to give it my best shot.

As we all take a break, I step outside for some fresh air. The boys join me. Crossing the street to a spot of grass that can barely be called a park—although it is Albert Capsouto Park to be exact—I breathe deeply, happy to be out of the office confinement.

McCloud lights up a smoke, Carter stretches like a sunning cat, and Mack drops to the ground and bangs out a hundred pushups in the time it would take me to dial Tercel and tell him to kiss my pretty pink ass.

Looking at Carter but tossing a chin toward Mack, I say, "Boy's got too much pent up energy."

Carter glances over, then back to me. "Said it was the quietest mission he'd ever done. Had to do *something* to stay awake."

I shrug, see McCloud light a second smoke to the end of the first one, and mutter, "Talking about both ends of the spectrum."

Carter snorts and Savoy snaps pics for her Instagram account.

"Well gang, the way I see it is...we only got one shot. This opportunity comes once in a lifetime, you better..." I stop. "What? Nobody knows—"

"Yeah," McCloud says, looking surprised. "Just didn't know—"

"Hey, I know music." I shake my head, exasperated. "C'mon, might as well go through the motions of our last gig before we hop a flight tomorrow. Then it's...*back to reality*."


LATER THAT EVENING, we arrive at the Jackson Pollock retrospective at the Museum of Modern Art, take our places, and conduct a repeat performance of last night at the Guggenheim. Only this time, we've doubled our crew. And as disenchanted, disappointed, or disillusioned as I may feel, I press on.

Minutes into the show, a pale and freckled Catholic priest wearing tiny wire-framed glasses and a black cassock surveys the crowd. With a mop of silver hair and a matching thick beard, he looks more like a sloppy Santa than a serial killer.

Smiling continuously, he leans against a cane, watching the auctioneer secure hundreds of thousands of dollars for school and church art programs all around New York. A brilliant artist's work will soon hang on the wall of one art-loving supporter who has an impressive collection to rebuild—thanks to a detective who made sure his collection, worth millions, was seized.

Tercel shifts his focus from his program to the little girl standing next to him.

*What a brilliant last minute addition to my masquerade.*

The girl looks up at the helpful Father O'Halloran who volunteered to watch her while her mother assists onstage. He smiles in return, but his mind is on the "surrogate buyer" standing next to him.

After a meeting in a SoHo office yesterday, the man in the four-thousand dollar suit was hired to make the purchase for Tercel. Aside from the purchase price, a handsome retainer was paid in advance in exchange for complete anonymity.

*He's not even aware his buyer is standing next to him.*

His collaborator is ready to bid on a particularly impressive Pollock work, *The Blue Unconscious*, which Tercel has admired for years but never had the opportunity to own. It's from 1946, just ten years before

Pollock died in a car accident, and is an oil on canvas representing a different abstract period prior to the "drip paintings" for which he became famous.

Tercel hears a familiar accent behind him. Turning just enough, he peeks past the people behind him.

His heart nearly stops when he sees her.

*Of course, you've come to help Norelli find me, Savoy.*

Careful to remain calm, he notices Norelli and her sidekick scanning the crowds.

*Not very clandestine.*

With a deep breath, the heat inside his fat suit increases and he starts to worry.

*Wonder how many there are.*

Still smiling, he hopes unnecessary attention doesn't follow him.

The auctioneer introduces the piece, stating it's easily worth $1 million.

Someone across the room makes a motion and the price instantly jumps to $1.25 million.

*There'll never be another chance like this.*

The auctioneer asks for a new bid of $1.5 million and the man next to him raises a paddle. It climbs to $1.5.

A hushed breath shoots through the crowd and three other buyers enter the bid within minutes.

The price goes from $1.5 to $1.75. More quickly than he expected, he hears the number climb to $2 million. The auctioneer rapidly prattles on until it becomes $2.25 million.

His contact accidentally bumps Tercel's elbow, turns to apologize, then returns to lift his paddle. The price instantly shoots to $2.5 million.

*What?*

Tercel knows the history of the piece and the fact the acquisition fee was around $1 million. He figures it could be worth up to two, but his limit is $3 million.

The auctioneer goads the clients and a bid from across the room raises to $2.75, then instantly jumps again—thanks to his contact who raises it to $3 million.

As much as Tercel wants to elbow him and say *back off*, he doesn't. Nervous they will surpass his limit and equally anxious he can't cover it—thanks to lavish overspending and unexpected costs in Australia— he begins sweating.

The crowd becomes energized by the bouncing bids.

The bidders appear increasingly excited.

And his buyer appears calm, yet cocky.

The auctioneer appears to think they're reaching the top and begins to wind it down when a bid from across the room jumps it to $3.5 million.

His contact hesitates and Tercel holds his breath. The auctioneer pushes it an extra notch, his contact raises the paddle, and it climbs to $4 million.

Now, in over his head by a million, and beginning to sweat profusely, the little girl next to him suddenly screams. Startled, he looks down and realizes he's squeezing her hand too tightly.

Trying to console her, he flinches when several in the crowd turn to see the commotion.

The auctioneer doesn't hear the scream and pushes the bid.

From across the room a paddle is raised, the crowd cheers, and it jumps to $4.5 million.

Tercel tries again to quiet the little girl, but she releases his hand, and he bumps into the man next to him who pushes forward.

The auctioneer shouts, "And we have a new bid at $5 million to the man to my left."

The crowd cheers. Tercel wipes his eyes—inadvertently smearing makeup away—and a woman in front of him notices and tries to help. He pushes her away—much too brusquely—and she stumbles, accidentally falling into the arms of her date.

Taking a quick look over his shoulder, Tercel sees Savoy's date grab a wire in his ear and turn toward the exit.

The man to his left asks, "Are you all right?"

Ignoring him, Tercel sees the woman's date in front of him coming toward him just as the little girl runs to the stage.

The auctioneer calls out, "The bid is $5 million dollars and is going *once*…"

A hand from behind Tercel grabs his arm.

"Going *twice*…"

He turns and comes face to face with Savoy.

"Going *three* times…"

At this close distance, she sees the dissolving makeup and recognizes his face.

"And it's *SOLD* to the man to my left."

In the time it takes to register for Savoy, Tercel removes the handle of his cane and aims for center mass. Anxious to run, but slightly off balance, he thrusts toward her.

She doesn't feel the razor sharpness of the knife at first, but as blood rushes from her body, the realization hits. Turning to Mack with a look of shock, Savoy falls forward. Mack grabs her, and in a fraction of a second he connects with Tercel's eyes.

Tercel hesitates, looks to Savoy, then turns and sprints toward the exit, pushing through the crowds.

Because of the pandemonium, the frightened little girl, the bleeding woman, the hulking man, and the hysterical crowds choke the exits, Tercel has enough time to find a gap in the mass and slip out a hidden door.

"Scatter, people! Check all exits!" I yell into my mic.

The crowd disperses in a chaotic jumble.

"I repeat. Check all exits. Tercel's on the run!"

# CHAPTER SEVENTY-ONE

OUTSIDE ONE OF THE SIX EXITS, A FRANTIC PRIEST RUNS DIRECTLY INTO the path of Carter and a batch of police officers. The man is grabbed and spun around; two officers wrap zip cuffs on his wrists, yanking him toward the main entrance.

At a different exit, another priest pushes a heavy door and trips over the threshold, falling into the hands of another group of officers.

In the back of the building, yet another priest slams an exit door against a wall and sprints down the sidewalk until three officers knock him to the ground.

OUT FRONT ON 53RD STREET, our team has not one or two, nor three or four, but six different Catholic priests zip-cuffed and in a line on the street. A long row of police vehicles surround the building.

"What in the hell!" I shout before turning to Pete. "Can you believe this shit?"

Pete glares at six of his officers, each standing behind the perps.

Shaking his head, he says, "Un-fucking-believable."

"Is there any limit to what this guy will do?" Carter frowns, handing off one of the priests who is still trying to catch his breath.

"And this one's *actually* fat. No makeup required," he snorts, looking at two perps whose robes have fallen open to reveal fat-suits beneath.

Mack towers over one of them. "They're fuckin' identical until you get close," he growls. "Then they're just fuckin' ugly."

"Wait!" I shout. "Where's Savoy?"

Mack says, "I got her in an ambulance and told McCloud not to leave her side. They're in the ER at Mount Sinai Morningside. I'll head there now."

"Thanks, Mack," I say, turning to Pete. "What do you think?"

"I say we take these clowns in and see what we can learn."

"Reading my mind, bro."

AT THE STATION, one of the six "Tercels" sits chained to a table in an interrogation room while Pete, Carter, and I wait in the room next door, watching through a two-way mirror.

I'm disconnecting from a call with McCloud when Carter asks, "How is she?"

"She's gonna pull through. But an inch further and he would've pierced her heart," I say. "Damn, she's a tough gal."

"I'd call it lucky as hell."

"You'd know something about that," Mack grins.

ENTERING THE INTERROGATION ROOM, I stand in the corner. One of our six suspects sits staring at the wall, motionless. He still has remnants of makeup, and the fat suit he wore under his cassock is missing, but he looks nearly *identical* to Tercel.

Carter and Mack stand in opposite corners as Pete takes a chair opposite our guy. Opening a thick folder, he dramatically flips it open, leafing through the pages.

I can't stand it any longer and cross the room, leaning on the table.

"What's going on? And who the *fuck* are you?"

The man laughs for a minute until Pete slams his fists on the table. "STOP!"

"Who are you and where is Tercel," I bark, leaning to within inches of the man's face.

Grinning, he says, "Just wish Tercel could be here to enjoy it."

"You best speak up, or we'll find out pretty quickly how much you'll be enjoying this," Carter scowls.

I watch as the two men stare at one another. Carter doesn't budge.

"Okay, I'll tell you," the perp says, "because you've got *nothing* on me. I have no record. I've done *nothing* wrong—besides making a spectacle of things—but really *nada*."

*I want to smack the smirk off this prick's face.*

"I've been told to tell you, in case I was caught—which we planned —that Tercel wants to remind you, Detective, that he got inside your head a long time ago. And he knows you're wondering where he is right now. Well, he's still in Manhattan where he plans to stay because he's set up a new business here. The only thing is, he wants you to know he's going to have to disappear for a bit—you know, to reinvent himself *again*." He laughs.

"You give us something now," Pete says, "and there's a 99% chance you walk out of here. You don't, and obstruction of justice will be only the beginning of the terror I will rain down on your pathetic, arrogant head. Feel me?"

As his false bravado begins to vanish, the man swallows hard, looks at us, then sits up straight, and lets out a long sigh.

"Okay. Understood. My name's Daniel Whitney. Friends call me Danny. I'm just an ordinary guy. Well, I've done some acting in the past, but long story short, Tercel approached my agent looking for someone who looks a lot like him. Build wise, anyway. He offers to pay me *$1 million dollars* to have my face reconstructed to look like his. Since I'd never be a model and acting gigs are hit 'n miss, I thought, what the hell. His photos looked good. I have or *had* a fairly ordinary face, so I went for it."

I look at Pete and Carter.

"This is fucking crazy," Pete says, rubbing his face.

"Yeah, I've seen some whacked out shit before," Carter snorts, "but this takes it."

"But look at it from where I'm sitting," Whitney says. "Yeah, the operations required some downtime and took a month or so, but c'mon, a million bucks to look *really* handsome? Hell, it was a no brainer."

Clearly at a dead end with little hope of finding Tercel, we realize we've done all we can at this point. And while we could continue scouring the city, we feel convinced it would be a wash.

Given the small fortune I've spent and the fact we have to leave tomorrow, we reluctantly pack it in.

# CHAPTER SEVENTY-TWO

LATE THAT NIGHT, I AWAKE FROM A TERRIBLE NIGHTMARE, NOT MUCH different than those tormenting me for nearly a year.

I check the time: 1:45 a.m.

I lie still—not wanting to disturb Carter—staring at the ceiling and considering what a colossal mockery this has become. In order to regain some peace, I allow my mind to drift to thoughts of Angie. After some tears, but mostly happy memories, I'm almost asleep when I hear my phone vibrate.

Easing out of bed, I get my phone from the table. A text reads: *One57 on 57th Street. Unit 29-C.*

I run a quick trace: it's a burner phone.

Intrigued and confident it's something substantial, I wake Carter. We then call Mack. And within minutes, the three of us are armed in a car, heading uptown to that address.

En route, I propose an idea. Both men look at me like I'm insane.

They shake their heads and simultaneously say, "Why not?"


INSIDE THE LOBBY OF ONE57, I flash my badge, Carter and Mack show theirs, but because of a questionable story and heightened security, they refuse to let us upstairs. We understand their thinking, but we have an insane desire to persuade them otherwise. No go.

However, five minutes and a phone call from our friendly Mayor—

explaining how we'll be granted carte blanche access within the bounds of normal—we're allowed upstairs.

We first take several moments studying the glass model of the building in the center of the lobby. Carter comments how the building is shaped like an L. I'm about to ask why that's important and I notice Mack grinning like he ate the canary. Carter asks the manager if we can see a schematic of the building and inquires as to how many of the units are filled. More importantly, we learn which ones are vacant.

Now that we have two significant answers, Mack returns to the car for some backup.

As Carter and I wait for the elevator, Mack returns with a large case in one hand, a smaller but similar case in his other hand, and a backpack over his shoulder.

With several keys, we head upstairs.

Finding what Carter calls "a near perfect location," we set up in one leg of the L. Even though dark in our unit, there's enough reflecting light from the city to see him smiling as he stares through a pair of tiny binoculars.

"And bingo."

I ask, "What?"

He holds up a finger—*wait*—hands the binoculars off to Mack who takes a look, then grins like his partner, and mutters, "Sweet, bro."

Carter then hands them to me and takes my shoulders to position me in the direction they're looking. "See the floor that's even with ours, but there at the far corner—the one with the best view of the park?"

"Uh…"

"See the enormous lamp by the window and the grand piano in the corner?"

"Got it," I whisper. "Oh, hell yeah. He's in the living room pouring a drink."

"Right. Now…" Carter says in my ear, "look to the left. Master bedroom. There's an amber-colored lamp in the corner…"

I hear Mack unsnapping the case behind me.

"Yeah. Oh, I see suitcases."

"Right," Carter says, taking pieces of a rifle from Mack and assembling them. "Here's our variation on your plan. You with me?"

"Yes."

"Okay, now you're going back downstairs. So that you're properly announced. Be sure the doorman introduces you via the phone. Meaning, he announces you, but you ask for Tercel to hear your voice. He may not fully understand what's happening, but he won't be able to turn you down once he hears you."

"Copy."

"Now, give me your gun," he says, putting it in the small of his back. "You know he'll want to frisk you, so let him. Hell, play with him. *Some.* But give him the story we rehearsed on the way here, okay?"

"Okay."

"And then we'll do our thing. Cool?"

Suddenly, my heart begins racing, my mouth goes dry, and I hesitate.

"Patricia?" Carter says, handing his now assembled rifle to Mack. Taking my shoulders, he quietly says, "You know what to do. BUT if you don't want to go through with it, no harm, no foul. Okay? Seriously, there's a big risk in—"

"NO! I'm doing this. He won't hurt me."

Taking a breath, he calmly says, "Play it just the way we said. Trust me, we've got your back."

I nod.

"Just two things—both are *extremely* important."

I nod again, trying to work up enough spit to swallow.

"One. Get him to the window. He has to be close to the window. If not—"

"The shot could go through the glass and into another building," I say, suddenly petrified.

"Right. But I've had much longer distances and worse weather conditions. And while this angle's a bit of a challenge, it's *going* to work, okay?"

Squinting, I nod.

"All you have to do is exactly as we discussed. If you have him in place, for even two-seconds, we'll be good."

I swallow hard.

"Second. IF at any time, and I mean, *any* time, you get spooked, scared, have second thoughts, whatever, just get to the window, without undue attention, and—facing out toward the park—cross your arms like this," he says, crossing his arms to fashion an X. Got it?"

"Got it."

"Good," he smiles, looking at Mack who gives a thumbs-up.

"I've seen you in action, Norelli. You're *hella* fierce," Mack growls. "Now, go—get—that—fucker."

He holds his meaty fist out. I bump it.

"Okay," Carter says, "Deep breath. Think of Angie. Know we're literally *inches* from you. And as much as I hate to say it," he says through a deep breath, "smear it on thick."

# CHAPTER SEVENTY-THREE

AFTER RETURNING DOWNSTAIRS AND BEING ANNOUNCED, I THANK THE concierge and proceed. As the elevator rises, so does my anxiety. I rise the two dozen floors and several long, deep breaths later, I reach his floor. Fluffing my hair and unbuttoning my top button, I dial in my energy and step onto his floor.

Seconds later, his door opens and he appears like the chill running down my spine.

"Patricia, how incredibly nice, yet...terribly surprising to see you," he smiles through a confused squint. "Please, come in."

When I step in, he leans out cautiously, inching his head around the corner to look down the hall. Convinced no one is with me, he locks the doors behind me and waves for me to enter.

"I know this is crazy and the hour's late, but truthfully, I had to see you."

Before I can go any further than the foyer, he takes my shoulder and firmly places me against the wall.

"Forgive me, but I must do this."

"Of course. And Darius, trust me, I'm not armed. I'm here on my own accord."

He pats me down slowly and methodically, not missing a single inch. I shiver when his hands remain too long on my crotch.

"Sorry, Patricia," he smirks, "but that would be such a likely place to hide a tiny weapon."

"Are you done?" I snap.

Surprised, but satisfied, he waves me into his lavish home.

"This is handsome," I say, walking toward the window with the piano. "And talking about a view."

As I turn back, he's staring at me with a frown.

"Patricia, trust when I say I'm thrilled to see you. However, given our past—*especially* in light of these past few days and *this* hour—this feels *highly* circumspect."

"I know. And completely understand. But here's the skinny. And please, open your mind to what I'm about to say."

He stares, unflinching. I continue, unrelenting.

"Look, I've traveled halfway around the world for you. And yes, I was on a mission to take you in. But honestly—" I slowly bring on the tears.

He stares.

"I give up. Truly, Darius, I just flat out give up. I can't control the situation any longer. Hell, I can barely control my own life." More tears. "And ever since, maybe the beginning, I can't get you out of my mind."

He continues staring.

Walking closer, I say, "Honestly, I suppose I feel as though, somehow, and in some way..." stepping closer, "we're *meant* to be together."

Gently taking both sides of his face, I pull him close and kiss him softly at first; then, I engage his tongue. In seconds, our temperatures rise.

Reaching down, he unbuttons my blouse. His eyes don't leave mine.

"Why, Patricia..." he whispers, "after all this time, why do you finally want to give yourself to me?"

I hold open my blouse and whisper, "I'll tell you. All of it. But after all that's happened, I could really use a drink," I say, wiping away my tears.

He leans over and kisses my neck. "Of course. Where are my manners?"

At the bar, he looks over his shoulder and says, "Bourbon, I seem to recall."

"Yes, perfect."

When he turns to pour, I look toward the window.

As I turn back, he stares at me with a frown.

"What are you looking at, Patricia?"

"What?" I reach for the drink and chuckle, "The park of course, Darius. It's so *romantic*."

We look out at the city lights and sip.

He begins doing something I would watch him do when I was a patient: chew the inside of his bottom lip when a pencil wasn't nearby.

"What is it, Darius? You look…perplexed."

He takes another sip and turns to face me directly. "What are you doing here? I mean, really?"

"I told you, I was—"

"Bullshit aside, Patricia. I mean, c'mon…" he snorts, turning back to the window, "All this time, I'm longing for you but can't have you. Then suddenly, you appear out of nowhere, ready to shoot me in the face or take me in. And what? I'm supposed to believe this—" he says, waving the air between us, "this charade of yours isn't a trap? It isn't your way of luring me into a place of vulnerabi—"

He stops and looks around—in the windows of a building to our right, then to our left, and finally across the way. Cupping his hands to the glass, he begins looking at the other part of his own building—the long part of the L.

I realize I'm holding my breath and release it.

"Darius," I say, taking him firmly by his arm.

He whips his head toward me, looks at my hand, looks back outside, then finally says, "What? And be honest, Patricia. You owe me that. Don't you?"

I bite my tongue—literally, so the pain makes my eyes fill with tears.

"Yes," I whisper. "A thousand times, yes." I look down at my hands. "I'm so sorry, Darius," I cry. "I feel I've completely blown this."

Staring outside, I can see from the corner of my eye that he's holding his distance. Not sure what to do next, I set down my drink and begin to button my blouse.

"I know it was a crazy move," I whimper. "My partners have called me crazy ever since…"

"What?" He takes my hands. "What have they said?" he asks, wiping away a tear.

"I'm so embarrassed. They want to discharge me. I couldn't bring you in...and my work has suffered terribly...plus I can't sleep...and I'm drinking too much...I mi—"

"What?"

Looking into his eyes, I whisper, "I *miss* you. And I *want* you, terribly. I can't be...more...serious."

After a long moment, he leans forward and ever so gently kisses my lips, then my cheeks, and then my forehead. Smiling, he reaches down and slowly unbuttons one last button until my blouse is open. He softly rubs the sides of my breasts and I moan quietly.

We kiss more passionately.

Playfully pushing him back, I make a show of ever-so-slowly sliding my skirt down my hips, revealing tiny pink panties.

"Remember back in Bel Air? You saw this but never took it."

He nods.

"If I recall, the last words you whispered were: *Another time.* Do you recall?"

His intense gaze becomes a smile. "You heard that? I thought you were passed out by then," he says, gently pushing a strand of hair behind one ear. "It thrills me to know you heard me say that. And yes, I've longed for you every single day since."

His breathing increases as his eyes shift from my eyes to my body.

"Darius," I whisper, "I know I've been terrible. Deplorable even. But trust me when I say I'm done with all that. My team has left, I'm quitting my job as soon as I return, and, well, the life I once knew...is over."

"And?"

"And if you would still have me—I'm yours."

I sense that as much as he wants me, he's still trying to figure out my motives. After another long hesitation, he begins unbuckling his pants, but stops and looks around, studying the nearby buildings again.

"That sounds delicious," he says, squinting in the direction of Carter and Mack.

"But first..." he says, reaching for a remote, "let's make one adjustment..."

# CHAPTER SEVENTY-FOUR

"Shit!" Carter barks, removing the scope from his eye.

Mack's head pops up. "What?"

"He just turned off the lights!"

"Okay," Mack mutters as he finishes cutting a circle in the glass. "I'll be done in two seconds. Would've been nice if all this glass had windows that opened."

"Insurance," Carter mumbles, squinting through the binoculars. "Okay, good news and bad."

Pulling the suction, Mack grabs the circle of glass as it pops and an instant breeze enters the room.

"Never fun when you give me choices," Mack grunts. "What's the good?"

"As far as ease and distance: no brainer. *If* she gets him into position."

"Oh, she'll do that," Mack chuckles. "But seriously, what's the bad?"

Carter sighs, "With the reflection of those two buildings..." he points, "without the contrast of interior light, it's gonna be tricky."

"Yeah, but that's what we do best, *brah*," Mack grins.


"But the lights, Darius. You know I like to watch. Besides, I *have* to see this new and rather *magnificent* specimen of a body," I say, rubbing my hands across his chest, down his abs, and on his crotch.

"Spent a lot of time—crafting this perfection," he smiles. "Just for you."

"Remember that video you showed me at your house that night. When you had me tied to the bed?"

He nods.

"I was *so* wet for you. Didn't you see that?"

"Maybe," he grins, setting down the remote as he returns to kissing my neck. "Patricia, what's the *real* reason you're here?" He says through kisses.

"I told you," I moan.

"Sure you aren't here to kill me?"

I softly push him away and say, "What? I told you. I want—"

"Right, but forgive me if I don't buy it, it's just—"

Reaching for the remote, I say, "Okay! I want you to see my eyes when I tell you this…"


"Ow!" Carter says, pulling the scope from his eyes. "And they're back on."

"Sorry, boss," Mack sits back, "Know how that feels."

Carter covers his eyes, trying to clear them. After a long beat, he slowly opens them.

"S'all good. Let's just get this done. I'm tired of this *dipstick*."

Mack adjusts the platform for the rifle.

"Nice work, Mack," Carter says, sliding the barrel through the hole. With the rifle planted, Carter takes a last look.

"We are cleared for takeoff."


"OKAY, ARE YOU HAPPY NOW?" Darius asks, laying aside the remote.

There was a part of me, somewhere, that was enjoying this masquerade—perhaps because he had tormented me for so long.

"No need to get *aggro*, Darius," I say with both hands on my hips. "I'm only trying to be honest with you. I know you don't want to believe me. But I came here for you," I pout, reaching for my skirt.

"Okay, woah," he says, waving for me to continue, then taking a sip of his drink.

"I can't explain it any other way, but I'm…" I look away.

"You're what?"

Looking away—my voice turning sultry—I say, "There's no other way to say it, except…I'm in love with you."

His shocked expression is highlighted by a loud laugh that bounces off the high ceilings. When he's finished, he steps closer. "Patricia, please don't play me. You know better than that."

"Darius, I'm not. Look, Meredith fell for you. Sharon fell for you. Hell, I think in some sick or *twisted* sort of way, Bobby fell for you. My point is that they were your *patients*. What makes you think I wouldn't or *couldn't* have fallen for you—especially after all this time? And all this *effort!*"

He appears perplexed.

"Besides, you know what *really* did it?"

Now, he looks engaged. "What?"

"You've always been attractive. Everyone knows that. But when I saw you for the first time, after all you did to, well, *enhance* yourself. I'm serious, you are *so* incredibly handsome. And *very* sexy."

He is clearly aroused. Stepping closer, he reaches for the remote.

"No, Darius! I said leave the lights on. Here's what *I* want for a change. I want you to toy with me—really get me all lathered up while I stare out at the park—and our *new life together.* I know it sounds silly, but that's what I want. Then, just before you're about to burst, I want you to take me in your room and make love to me. All. Night. Long."

His eyes open wider, his breathing increases, and he growls, "Yes, Ma'am."

I get fully naked, then turn facing the window, spreading my arms wide against the glass. Spreading my feet wide, I look over my shoulder and whisper, "Like what you see?"

Nodding, he slides off his pants and approaches, putting both of his hands on either of my hips.

My head is clear. I take a quiet but deep breath.

And as I feel his body get close…

CARTER, ignoring what he sees, focuses intently. Slowly releasing his breath, he shifts his finger from the side of the trigger guard to the trigger. At the end of the breath, he squeezes.

## CHAPTER SEVENTY-FIVE

WHAT COMES NEXT ISN'T AS DARIUS EXPECTED.
Suspended between anticipation and ecstasy...
Lost in a fraction of a second...
As his hips thrusts...
And his body tenses...
His chest heaves—then explodes.

A PIERCING CRACKLE is followed by a wall of glass showering like a waterfall around me.
As the last fragments hit the ground, I feel cool air filling the room.
Tercel's body drops against me before toppling to the floor with a thud.
Taking a deep breath, I smell a burst of wet copper.
I remain crouched on the floor for what seems like an eternity.
Trembling with fear, yet energized with adrenaline, I open my eyes and stand.
Without looking behind, I run to the door and wait.
After I hear a tap-tap, I open it.

THE ROOM IS ABUZZ WITH PEOPLE. Pete manages a small crew of three officers, two forensic technicians, a coroner, a photographer, and a medic. The photographer captures every angle of the room, the coroner and forensics team thoroughly dissect the scene, and the medic gives me first aid.

Pete and Mack tower over Tercel's body while someone from management attends to the shattered window. Carter stands next to me. I'm wrapped in a blanket as the medic finishes bandaging my face and hand.

The coroner steps aside as I cross the room.

Tercel is lying on his back in a pool of crimson, the cavity of his chest wide open. I catch myself staring at a face that has morphed many times—thankful he will never terrorize another person or invade my dreams ever again.

SINCE OUR FLIGHT IS DELAYED, we drive the few blocks to the hospital to check on Savoy, only to learn she passed away in the night.

An attendant gives me her belongings: a purse, jewelry, a burner phone, and a note.

While Carter and Mack attend to paperwork, I find a quiet spot to read her note:

*Dear Patricia,*

*They tell me I've been in and out of consciousness, and that my condition is worse than they thought. So while I'm awake, I'm having a nurse write this letter because I'm not sure I'm going to make it. If you get this, I didn't.*

*What I failed to tell you was how I kept in touch with Tercel. I know, stupid. But he's been like a drug I couldn't shake. I'm sure you think I'm crazy, and honestly, I'm embarrassed. I'm also very sorry to say I've kept him in the loop with some of our progress along the way—not all of it, but some. That's how he knew so much. I know; I'm an asshole.*

*He began to think I would turn on him, and you see what he did. So, here in the quiet of the morning, I have to tell you where he is. I'm texting you the address of his new home. Again, I'm sorry I didn't tell you earlier. I truly was going to. Patty, he's a powerful man. An angel and demon. But also a seducer and a thief. If I don't make it, please promise me you'll take him out for good. Do this for me and Weija. And for YOU.*

*Love, Savoy*

When I join Carter and Mack outside her room, they both look at me. Without saying anything, I hand Carter the note. After he finishes reading, his expression mirrors my thoughts.

*Holy shit.*

For whatever reason, all I can do is stand there, shaking my head. I watch him stare off into the distance for a long beat before he says, "I didn't see that coming."

"Me either. I knew she was...*conflicted*, but I didn't think she had it *that* bad."

Carter looks at the note again and frowns.

"What?"

He looks up. "Guy had a mighty strong control over people."

"You mean like me."

"Well, yeah. But also Angie and Savoy. And as we retrace his steps, it reaches back to Bobby, Sharon, and Meredith." Returning the note, he whispers, "And no telling how many more."

"Yeah," I whisper. "But never again."

AFTER WRAPPING MATTERS AT THE STATION, Carter, Mack, McCloud, and I enjoy a quiet brunch with Pete and his family at their home in Greenwich Village.

As we leave, I promise Pete's family I'll make an effort to see them more often.

Before leaving for the airport, Carter, Mack, and McCloud wait in the car while Pete and I stand outside his brownstone to grab a few minutes together.

"Sis, I gotta tell you..." his voice breaks, "you've turned out to be one helluva cop. And I've never been more proud of you than right now."

With a hug, I whisper in his ear, "Just following in your footsteps."

# CHAPTER SEVENTY-SIX

*MANHATTAN BEACH, CALIFORNIA—*

AFTER A SHORT RUN SATURDAY MORNING, I make a smoothie while waiting for the coffee to brew.

Stretching out on a chaise lounge on the deck, I skim the *LA Times* headlines. I'm flipping pages when I land on an article that captures my attention.

Sure, it's cool to see my name in print, but even better? Making a checkmark in one *very* important column called: *Case Closed*.

All the way through the newspaper and a pot of coffee, I am blissfully enjoying the sun and warm breeze of my little spot of paradise when my thoughts turn to Angie.

For the first time since her passing, I can finally rest easy, knowing we can both be at peace now.

About the time my thoughts drift to another certain someone, my phone rings.

Looking at the screen, I enjoy a familiar tingle as a smile spreads across my face.

"Hey, I was *just* thinking about you…"

Thank you for reading *The Impostor*.

If you enjoyed it as much I hope you did, would you please take a
moment and leave a review? You can do so at your favorite bookstore
or reading spot. Also, take a quick minute and stop by my website;
there you can join my newsletter, receive alerts about future books, and
get free ones! Drop me a note, I'd love for us to keep in touch!
Thanks again.

DavidTempleBooks.com

# ABOUT THE AUTHOR

**David Temple** is an emerging thriller writer. With seven novels under his belt, *The Impostor* marks his eighth, and is the second book in the Detective Pat Norelli Series—which began with *The Poser*.

Others include the stand-alone psychological thriller, *Devour*; the Carter Matheson Series: *Knuckle Down, Behind The 8 Ball,* & *Lucky Strikes*; and the family drama, *Chasing Grace*, a novel-turned-film that David wrote, produced, directed & starred in. It can be seen on Netflix, AmazonPrime, and in over 100 countries.

His prolific career includes: Morning Radio host in New York, LA, Chicago, Detroit, Philadelphia & Charlotte, and on Westwood One & Armed Forces Radio Networks; as an actor in TV & Film, and as a nationally-recognized VoiceOver artist.

David will inject that vast experience into a brand new thriller, ***Dark Underbelly***, in 2022. He and wife Tammy live in San Diego.

# ACKNOWLEDGMENTS

It's funny how my first career of hosting morning radio shows, and then working as an actor on television & film sets, both involve working with large teams of people. So, when it came time to craft my "third chapter" and work in solitude as a writer, the shift was profound. The good news? Quiet sparks creative thought. The bad? I really enjoy being around people and working with teams.

Speaking of—it takes a small team of dedicated friends and allies to make a book come to life. With that said, I would like to thank the following people.

First, my wife Tammy; if it were not for her unbridled encouragement, I doubt I'd be following my dream today. Second, thanks to my sister, Barbara Ann, whose commitment to editing and cheerleading has kept my pilot light going. Thanks to Rafael Andres for his powerful vision for my book cover. Thanks to Kimberly "KJ" Howe whose profound inspiration is helping launch my next chapter. Lastly, thanks to Don Winslow, whose friendship and mantra of "Never Give Up" has kept me banging the keys into the wee hours; your epic talent and sincere support means more than you can imagine.

And a hearty *Thank You*—dear reader—for taking a chance on me; I hope to bring you hours of enjoyment and for many years to come.

*—David*

Lightning Source UK Ltd.
Milton Keynes UK
UKHW011038151221
395639UK00002B/148